HOMESICK

The so-called orange juice smelled right and tasted right and even looked right, but it just wouldn't *sit* right. Instead, the stuff tried to pull away from the drinking vessel's plastic walls, straining toward its own middle so that it bulged up from its edges. Subtract five-sixths of Earth-normal gravity, and surface tension could accomplish a lot more, Morrison realized glumly. He added the datum to his personal, private list of reminders, confirming yet again the unpleasant truth.

He was on the Moon.

HUMAN
RESOURCE

PIERCE ASKEGREN

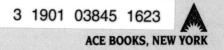

ACE BOOKS, NEW YORK

THE BERKLEY PUBLISHING GROUP
Published by the Penguin Group
Penguin Group (USA) Inc.
375 Hudson Street, New York, New York 10014, USA
Penguin Group (Canada), 10 Alcorn Avenue, Toronto, Ontario M4V 3B2, Canada
(a division of Pearson Penguin Canada Inc.)
Penguin Books Ltd., 80 Strand, London WC2R 0RL, England
Penguin Group Ireland, 25 St. Stephen's Green, Dublin 2, Ireland (a division of Penguin Books Ltd.)
Penguin Group (Australia), 250 Camberwell Road, Camberwell, Victoria 3124, Australia
(a division of Pearson Australia Group Pty. Ltd.)
Penguin Books India Pvt. Ltd., 11 Community Centre, Panchsheel Park, New Delhi—110 017, India
Penguin Group (NZ), Cnr. Airborne and Rosedale Roads, Albany, Auckland 1310, New Zealand
(a division of Pearson New Zealand Ltd.)
Penguin Books (South Africa) (Pty.) Ltd., 24 Sturdee Avenue, Rosebank, Johannesburg 2196, South
Africa

Penguin Books Ltd., Registered Offices: 80 Strand, London WC2R 0RL, England

This is a work of fiction. Names, characters, places, and incidents either are the product of the author's imagination or are used fictitiously, and any resemblance to actual persons, living or dead, business establishments, events, or locales is entirely coincidental.

HUMAN RESOURCE

An Ace Book / published by arrangement with the author

PRINTING HISTORY
Ace mass market edition / February 2005

Copyright © 2005 by Pierce Askegren.
Cover art by Larry Rostant.
Cover design by Annette Fiore.
Interior text design by Kristin del Rosario.

ISBN: 0-441-01079-2

ACE
Ace Books are published by The Berkley Publishing Group,
a division of Penguin Group (USA) Inc.,
375 Hudson Street, New York, New York 10014.
ACE and the "A" design
are trademarks belonging to Penguin Group (USA) Inc.

PRINTED IN THE UNITED STATES OF AMERICA

10 9 8 7 6 5 4 3 2 1

For Andy Greenfield, who is a longtime friend of the Askegren family and who, one snow-swept night long ago, saved at least one finger on my writin' hand.

Special thanks to Jennifer Jackson, Keith R. A. DeCandido, and especially Ginjer Buchanan, for the absurd patience shown in their respective roles.

CHAPTER 1

THE so-called orange juice smelled right and tasted right and even looked right, but it just wouldn't *sit* right. Instead, the stuff tried to pull away from the drinking vessel's plastic walls, straining toward its own middle so that it bulged up from its edges. Subtract five-sixths of Earth-normal gravity, and surface tension could accomplish a lot more, Erik Morrison realized glumly. He added the datum to his personal, private list of reminders, confirming yet again the unpleasant truth.

He was on the Moon.

Whoever had designed the lounge had worked very hard to hide that truth by making the place look as Earthlike as possible. It was all permanently shined plastic with metal trim, furnished with padded stools and dark-topped tables. Even the walls were set to familiar images, urban vistas that reassured with familiarity and anonymity. At casual glance, he could have been in San Francisco or Toronto or even New Sacramento, instead of in a sparsely populated nook just off Chrisium Port's third level.

Perhaps a dozen other patrons, men and women alike, sat at tables or in shadowed booths, but Erik was alone at the bar. Glasses hung from overhead racks. Shelves that looked more substantial than they probably were held bottles of different shapes. They held different levels of variously colored liquids, all presenting the same troubling curvature. Looking at the bottles and what they held made Erik's stomach twist, but seeing the ersatz cityscape behind them made him homesick and sad.

Erik was big, built wide but not especially tall. Never much of an athlete, he had earned his muscles the hard way, with weekend hobbies that included hiking and landscaping. That kind of activity gave him ready, constant awareness of his body's relationship to its surroundings. He knew without thinking what he weighed, knew how his elbows should rest on a surface like the bar's, knew how a bar stool should feel as his fundament dug into it.

What he felt now was terribly wrong. Wrong like the orange juice in his glass.

"Anything else?" the bartender asked, as he drifted closer. The man was tall, with a build that had willowy arms and legs sprouting from a pudgy trunk. His face was smooth and unlined, and he moved with a slow grace that bordered on stately as he gestured at the bar top for the menu. "Something to eat?" he asked. "Just bar food, but it's not bad."

A dozen high-resolution images appeared near where Erik's hands rested. He saw tacos and borscht-pops and egg rolls. He shuddered.

The bartender made a toothy grin. "It'll come back," he said.

"Yeah. It would."

The bartender grinned again. "No," he said. "I didn't mean the food. Your appetite." He reached beneath the counter, did something, then set another glass next to Erik's first. The colorless liquid inside behaved no better than the juice, but transparency made its antics less obvious. "Drink up," the bartender said.

Erik drank. Something cool and minty filled his mouth, then his throat. The knots in his stomach seemed to loosen, and the ringing in his ears subsided.

But just a bit.

"It'll take a week," the bartender said. "Maybe more. You were just getting used to zero, and now you're back at a sixth. Your stomach's confused. But it'll learn."

Erik shuddered again. He was going to feel like this for a week? Aloud, he said, "Is it that obvious?" The point concerned him. He didn't want to look like a rube.

The bartender laughed, nodded. "It couldn't be more. The orange juice was a tip-off. And a mistake—too much acid."

"I wanted to order something I was sure I could get. I figured the orange juice was a safe bet, even on Luna."

Too late, Erik realized that the bartender was probably a native, or at a least long-term resident. The other man's expression became a fraction less agreeable, and his voice became cooler. *"Even?"* he asked.

Erik shrugged, mildly embarrassed but at a loss for words.

"Villanueva is first class all the way," the bartender said. "There's not much you can't find here, if you've got the credit."

"I know, I know," Erik said. "It's just—"

"It's just, you're a quarter-million miles from home,

and you haven't gotten used to the idea yet," someone else said. "You never will. Or your body won't. Not completely."

Erik glanced to his left. Someone had settled onto the neighboring stool. He was short, with dark eyes, narrow features, and close-cropped russet hair. He sported bushy sideburns that had been all the rage two years before. He had a slight paunch, and the skin on his bare arms hung in loose folds, but his arms and legs seemed to be of appropriate length.

"Doug Stewart," the man said, extending his hand. He spoke like a salesman.

"Erik Morrison," Erik replied, and hooked thumbs with him. "You talk like a man who knows."

Stewart nodded. "Three years out," he said. "Of four. On contract with Snackles."

"I don't know the name."

Stewart nodded again, drank the last of his glass's contents. He had big hands, too, with worn and calloused skin. "Not a surprise," he said. "No glamour. But you know the product, I'll bet—Crackly Crawlers."

"I know them," Erik said, his stomach churning at the thought of the ubiquitous sesame-chili spirals. "Nasty little things."

"They're ours," Stewart said, grinning. He gestured to the bartender, who set a fresh drink in front of him before drifting away. "Them, and half the stuff they serve here."

Erik grunted. Stewart's words had shaken something loose from the undigested jumble of facts that filled his head, debris from the dozens of files he had reviewed over the preceding days. Chrisium Port, like the rest of Villanueva Base, was owned and operated by the five companies of the Allied Lunar Combine. Each of those five companies, however, had a myriad of subsidiaries and subcontractors, all scrambling for a place. "Snackles," he said. "Zonix contractor, right? Sales or production?"

Stewart spoke as if by rote. "I do some sales, but I'm primarily here as a production consultant." He looked pleased with himself, and slightly embarrassed at being pleased.

That was a surprise. Erik's briefing had been reasonably thorough, but fast. He hadn't realized the extent of on-site manufacture. A moment's thought told him that Stewart's words made sense. Snack foods were fragile, tough to ship, and demanded a low price-point for effective sales. But if you knew how to make them, all you really had to import was the method and the trademark.

"Costs too much to import," Stewart continued. "Even if they do travel better than most foods."

That made sense; Zonix had been moving into new business areas for years, augmenting its core entertainment concerns with leisure foods and restaurant services. Chances were that Zonix owned the lounge, too, or at least its service contracts.

"That's because they're hardly food at all," Erik said.

"Maybe not, but they keep my plate full," Stewart said affably. "And my glass." He was already halfway through his second drink, something pale blue that had a strong astringent smell. A single piece of ice floated in its center, cast in the shape of the Zonix Infotainment logo. "Profitable, relatively speaking. Zonix thinks so, anyway."

"Three years?" Erik asked. He couldn't imagine being on the Moon for three years.

"One to go." Stewart sipped again. "By then, the system

should be at full capacity. Quality control will be licked, too. They won't need me anymore. They'll buy us out, and I'll go home then."

Erik wished that he could say the same. Instead, he said, "No chance of staying on with Zonix?" The conglomerate was the second largest of the five ALC companies and the biggest single local employer, providing goods and services to all lunar residents. Stewart had customers here, but Erik's were back home.

EnTek's prime markets were all on Earth. Hell, *all* the prime markets were on Earth.

Stewart shook his head. "They can find someone cheaper," he said. "Someone who likes it here."

The bartender approached again, bearing another glass of blue stuff. He coughed softly and glanced in Stewart's direction.

"That means someone who was born here," Stewart continued. He nodded at the bartender, then drained his old drink and gently released the glass. It drifted slowly to the bar's surface in a way that made Erik look hastily in another direction.

"Native?" Erik asked the bartender.

He nodded in response and said, "Second generation." He cupped his hand beneath the lazily descending glass and caught it, then ambled toward the other end of the bar.

"Should have noticed before," Stewart said. "Big in the belly, long in the bones. I'm pretty good on picking up on stuff like that, and I didn't." He sipped.

Erik was ready for a drink, too, but he knew that his stomach wasn't. Instead of ordering, he said, "He didn't seem to take offense." Usually, he wasn't much for idle chatter, but this conversation, at least, had a diverting effect. Besides, he had spent many hours sitting in bars and listening to salesmen. There was comfort to be found in habit.

"Don't care whether he was offended or not. I'm just annoyed I didn't notice." Stewart set his glass down again. "Anyone with that little muscle was born here. I should have seen it." He spoke with the abrupt peevishness of a practiced drunk.

"They get therapy. Gene patches."

Stewart nodded. "That's in the terms of employment. That guy can go back too—he can go to Earth if he wants, maybe even walk around some, after a few months in a wheelchair." He took a long drink before continuing. "He won't, though. Most don't. Most stay here, and the ones who leave the Moon take their world with them. Same for me, and for you. Nothing's ever going to change that."

Peevishness had become something stronger, maybe bitterness. Erik wondered what the other man was drinking and wondered what a hangover would be like in low gravity. He supposed Stewart already knew.

"What about you?" Stewart asked.

"What about me?"

"Tourist? Contract job? Medical?" Stewart was passing his glass from hand to hand now, fidgeting, as if he wanted to take a sip but didn't think it would be a good idea. "No one takes a half-million-mile ride without a reason."

"Quarter-million," Erik corrected. The number had mystique all its own and made expressing the distance in miles almost automatic in common parlance.

"Half," Stewart said. He gestured with his busy hand, and the mounded blue fluid nearly slopped over the brim of his glass. "You count the round trip. No one comes here planning to stay. Anyone who does, changes his mind. Two years from now, you'll be glad the Mesh has your return fare sitting in escrow. God knows I am. Sometimes I pull my account just to look at the number and have something to smile about."

There was some truth to his words. The few of Erik's acquaintances who had relocated to the Moon had all claimed the move was temporary, all pledged to return. Not all of them had, bound to their new world by health or new families, but all had promised to return, and most had at least tried.

Erik planned to try very hard.

"What about you?" Stewart repeated.

"Work," Erik said briefly. "I'm with EnTek."

"For how long?"

"Not term," Erik said. There wasn't much he felt proud about these days, but he still took pleasure in saying what came next. "Core-corporate. Career management."

The last two words held a hidden irony, at least to Erik's ears, but Stewart didn't seem to notice. "Company bones. That's a surprise," he said. "Mostly, we get termers here. You must pull a lot of weight, or carry some real baggage." His words were almost a question.

"It was a promotion," Erik said, but he went no further. There was no need to satisfy Stewart's curiosity, however understandable. Bad enough that the Moon had been his only option—talking about his career path could only make things worse.

He wasn't about to tell anyone about Alaska.

"Look," Stewart said lightly. "Magic." Yet another drink had appeared before him, as automatically as if issued by machine. "Here's to promotions," he said, and made the beverage disappear. "I've had promotions like that."

Erik shrugged. It was time to change the subject. "What about you?" he asked.

"Me? Snackles, remember? 'Nasty little things.' "

Erik shook his head. "I remember. Snackles, four years, one to go before *you* go. That's not what I meant. Why are you sitting in a spaceport bar? There must be cheaper places to drink."

Stewart laughed. "Not by much, and not that it makes much difference," he said. "I was seeing off a friend. She's taking the *Buzz Aldrin* back to China. They've got her strapped in by now."

From Earth orbit to the Moon took two standard days, which was entirely too long to sit in one place, but not quite long enough to justify making staterooms available. A very long time to be nauseated. Drugs helped, but not enough, at least not for Erik.

He had learned that the hard way.

"And now, I'm just spending time. Time and money," Stewart said. "What about you? Can't handle the tubes yet?"

Subsurface tunnels, tracks, and trains tied the spaceport to Villanueva and to the half-dozen other facilities hidden beneath Mare Chrisium, the ancient plain of congealed lava that sprawled just north of Luna's equator. Originally, Villanueva had been served by a spaceport at its center, but as years passed and the installation expanded, residents had become increasingly skeptical about the wisdom of launching and receiving superorbital flights in the settlement's heart. Thus, Chrisium Port, and thus, the tubes.

"I'm waiting for someone," Erik said. "She's late."

A movement to his right caught his attention, and he turned just in time to see a black man with neatly styled cheek curls settle onto the empty stool there. The newcomer had bypassed a dozen empty seats to make himself Erik's neighbor, but didn't introduce himself. Instead, he gestured for the bartender. As Erik turned to face left again, Stewart said to him, "Place is filling up."

It wasn't, really. There were still plenty of empty booths and stools. Maybe Stewart had a low tolerance for crowds.

"Do you need someone to show you around?" Stewart asked. "I remember my first day here. It can get pretty confusing."

"I'll be fine." Erik's orientation had included a list of contact codes and some bare-minimum guidance on the local transit system. If he got tired enough of waiting, he could probably find his way around.

"It's no trouble. Like I said, I'm just spending time. I'm off duty today." After serving the black man to Erik's right, the bartender had given Stewart yet another glass. He raised it now to his lips. He grimaced at what he tasted.

"This isn't what I'm drinking," Stewart said.

"Yes, it is," the bartender said, before moving on to another patron. "Now."

"Huh." Stewart scowled and stared at his drink. "It looks like it's about time for me to leave," he said. "Join me?"

"No," Erik said. He was in no rush to board more transit, especially not with someone as intrusive and annoying and borderline drunk as Stewart seemed. "Thanks. I'll wait."

"It's no problem," Stewart said. "At least let me give you directions." He reached into his pocket, pulled out a computer. The transparent sheet of layered polymers rustled as he unfolded the device and thumbed it on. For a split second, the bar's pseudo-wood surface remained visible through the computer, and then a familiar logo intruded. Stewart grinned and glanced at Erik. "See?" he said, and pointed. "It's an EnTek."

That was no surprise; Erik's employers had a lock on the lunar market. "Consumer gear's not my priority," he said.

Stewart thumbed a translucent icon, and a spiderweb diagram resolved itself on the computer's surface, pale blue lines defining enclosed spaces and greenish ones indicating connectors. "It's preloaded," he said.

One display faded and another took its place, then another, as Stewart paged through the diagram's various levels. "They update the Mesh map masters once a week. This one's a month old, but there isn't any current construction in the core neighborhoods. Give me your assigned address and we can—"

"That won't be necessary," Erik said, slightly irritated now. He repeated himself. "I'll wait. My escort will be here soon." Company procedure said that his chief of staff would meet him.

Stewart snorted. "Ah, come on. A stockholder? Waiting for staff?" he said. "Now, what's your address?"

"I don't—"

"Don't know your address?" Stewart laughed. "That fits. Look, I'll just—"

"I know my address," Erik said, irritation giving way to anger, just strong enough to make him lie. "I'd just prefer to—"

The black man to Erik's right spoke, his voice polite but powerful. "Why don't you give the man your address? He's trying to do you a favor."

Erik turned, irritated at the interruption. "Look, I can handle this. If you'll just—"

The black man smiled. He had big teeth, strong and white against his dark skin, and the left incisor bore the image of a man Erik vaguely recognized as Vladimir Lenin. The image gave Erik pause.

Yesterday's fads lived on, it seemed, at least on the Moon.

"He's just trying to help," the black man said.

"Here it is!" Stewart said. He had accessed some directory. "Level Three, Red Sector, just off the Tesla Conduit." He tried to whistle. "Nice neighborhood they've put you in. Recent construction."

"Thanks, I—"

"Hey!" the black man said. "I'm going that way myself. That's my sector."

Erik could feel control of the conversation slipping away from him.

"Good," Stewart said, standing. "You can come with us, then. We can share a compartment." He extended one hand, touched his thumb to the black man's. "Doug Stewart, Snackles."

"Horace Peabody, Dynamo. Good to know you."

Stewart nodded. "Maybe we can stop somewhere and get a real drink," he said. His mood and tone had changed again, from peevishness to bonhomie.

"Sounds good," the black man said. He stood, too, and extended his hand in Erik's direction. "Horace Peabody," he repeated. His voice was a rumble that came from somewhere deep in his chest. "And you're—?"

"Not going anywhere," Erik said flatly, ignoring the proffered hand. "I'll wait for my escort, thanks."

Stewart and Peabody stared at him, and Erik suddenly realized that he had spoken much more loudly than he had intended. He hooked thumbs with Peabody and forced himself to smile. "Look," he said without rising, "I appreciate the offer, but I'd rather wait."

"You came in on the *Eugene Cerman,* right?" Stewart asked. When Erik nodded, he continued, "Then she's almost three hours late."

"You don't want to spend your first day on Luna in the port," Peabody said. He spoke as if he were saying the most obvious thing in the world.

"I'm not going to," Erik said. "My escort will—"

"Come on, Erik," Stewart said. "It'll be easier if you—"

"Mr. Morrison?" A blonde woman with blue eyes and high cheekbones had approached them. Even in the Moon's lesser gravity, which eased the load on muscles and tended to smooth the face, her features were lean and angular, and her skin looked like it had been drawn tight against the bones of her face. She wore a picto-tooth, too, and the face of some forgotten celebrity looked out at Erik from her mouth as she spoke. "Erik Morrison?"

"That's me," he said.

"Oh, good. I've been looking everywhere. I'm Juanita Garcia," the blonde woman said. "I'm so sorry I'm late, but the brainware burped again. We lost a day's scheduling, and then there was a datastorm, and the Mesh almost went down." She paused and took a deep breath. "It's a real mess."

Erik heard her excuses and committed them to memory for later consideration. Datastorms weren't common Earthside, but not unheard-of, either. They happened when the semiorganic processors that were central to most Mesh subsystems proved unequal to their jobs, were overwhelmed by data and commands, and failed. EnTek's Villanueva facilities served in part as a test bed for experimental systems and prototypes, and Erik supposed that failures might be more frequent here.

"You're from the office, then?" He had never seen her before, not even over the phone or in a file image. His orientation and departure had been too rushed for such niceties.

She nodded. "I'm terribly sorry. I'm Juanita Garcia," she said for the second time. "I'm here to show you around."

"Okay." Erik nodded, which didn't do much for his nausea. "Glad you're here. I won't need to impose on these gentlemen, then." He turned make the good-byes that manners required and then paused in mild surprise.

Stewart and Peabody were gone, as if they'd never been.

Before he could say anything, Juanita spoke again. "Do you want to get a pair of smartshoes?" she asked. "This is your first visit, isn't it? They might help."

"Smartshoes?" he asked. He had heard the term before, but he wasn't sure where.

"They help with the gravity," the bartender said. "There's a kiosk around the corner." Again, he made a faint smile. "Very popular with the tourists," he said.

Erik shook his head. "No smartshoes," he told Garcia. "I'll manage."

Like it or not, he was on the Moon, and he was going to be there for a while. That meant taking the place on its own terms.

TWENTY minutes later they had boarded a tram and were on their way to his quarters. The rest of his personal cargo would follow.

"I think you'll like the apartment," Garcia said. Her cheerfulness sounded forced. "We usually use it for company guests, but no one's scheduled for at least six months, and housing isn't exactly at a premium. But you don't like it, we can arrange new quarters . . ."

Her words trailed off into silence, and now that she wasn't speaking, Erik could hear the hum of their tram's motors. Low and steady, the sound filtered through the walls of their private compartment. The accommodations were nice enough, he supposed. Everything looked and smelled so new that they could have been the vehicle's inaugural passengers.

She had given him a portfolio before boarding. He opened it now. Lightweight and supple, the case felt like leather, but he knew that couldn't be. Inside was a newer version of Stewart's computer. He unfolded it, thumbed it on to confirm the charge. A generic welcome display condensed into view. He looked at Garcia but didn't say anything.

"It's not loaded yet," she said. Her voice had a slight quaver. "It's got basic software, but not your personal files. They should download tonight, at midnight."

Erik nodded, in acknowledgment but not approval. He rolled up the computer and tucked it into a pocket. A small zipped case was next, and he started to open it, then paused. "How about the phone?"

"The account's not active," Juanita said. "It was, but the datastorm wiped it." She paused. "You won't get as much use out of that here, anyway. The merchants don't like them."

Erik grunted and left the phone in its case, in the portfolio. He didn't have anyone to call, anyway. "Doesn't say much for the service," he said. "Any of our products at fault?"

Juanita nodded. "Probably," she said. "There would almost have to be."

ALC members gave their partner companies buying preference. Even if they hadn't, EnTek would be the vendor of choice. It was an industry leader for artificial intelligence and data processing systems, and held an effective monopoly in Villanueva.

"I want to know what's wrong. Find out." Saying that made him feel better. Giving orders was something he knew how to do.

"They don't know. It's happened before, never for more than a few hours," Juanita said. "It's an in-house problem. There's a bug in the brainware."

"Find out," Erik repeated. "I want a report by the end of the week. If we don't know the solution, I want to know what we're doing to find one."

Erik reached into the portfolio again, pulled out a hard-copy document. It was midway between a brochure and a hard book, with the ALC's distinctive seal adorning its cover. Erik glanced at the image, five corporate logos set against a field of stars. He knew them well. Zonix Infotainment, EnTek, Biome, Applied System Dynamics, and Duckworth Foundries were the five companies that had taken a world and remade at least part of it in their image.

"Souvenir history," Juanita said. "Mostly for tourists, but there's some good information in it. I thought you might like a copy."

Erik shook his head and tucked the document back into the portfolio. "I know as much about the history of the Combine as I need to," he said. "The real history."

"Oh."

Erik settled back, trying to sink into the padded seat,

but failing. He felt better now, though. Whatever the bartender had fed him was doing its work. Or maybe taking
up his practiced role of authority had calmed his nerves.
Either way, the nausea had faded and the motor hum had
taken on a soothing quality. He wanted very much to
sleep.

Instead, he said, "Give me a download. How many are
on my staff?"

"Eight, under direct supervision. Me, and seven others. The division heads report to you, too, but only for
purposes of coordination. Activity reports route through
your office before going Earthside."

That fit; for now, at least, his title was Site Coordinator. "Review authority?"

"Only on the eight, but you have input down to depart-
ment head level," she said. "Really, we can go over this
when you're—"

"We can do it now," Erik said.

"Semiannual reviews on line staff, like me," Juanita
continued. "Quarterly assessments of division heads, in
advisory capacity to the board back on Earth."

"Which means, if they meet or exceed their quotas,
nothing I say makes any difference."

Juanita didn't respond.

"Or nothing's supposed to," Erik said, more softly
this time. He spoke more to himself than her, but he
watched the attractive woman carefully. "Earthside sets
the quotas, right?"

She looked even more nervous, but said nothing.

"I want to talk to them," Erik said. "Net up a conference for first thing."

"There's already an in-person meeting planned for
tomorrow afternoon," she said. "At headquarters. To

introduce you. Most of the division heads are big believers in face-to-face."

Erik decided not to press the issue just yet. "Face-to-face, then," he said. "Tomorrow afternoon. In person, but don't get used to it. What about my liaison duties?"

"You've got equivalents at each of the other four ALC components. Their positions are pretty much the same as yours, but their duties and authorities vary slightly. Your Mesh account has background files, on them and our people, along with welcomes."

"Extend them my greetings, set up meet-and-greets for next week. Anyone else?" Erik asked. The question was mostly a formality; the ALC owned more than 90 percent of the Lunar infrastructure. What it didn't own wasn't much.

Garcia surprised him. "There's Project Halo, over at Armstrong Base," she said.

"I thought they'd shut that down," Erik said. Echo was a federal project, a facility that, to his way of thinking, represented a waste of time and taxpayer money—especially corporate taxpayer money.

Juanita shook her head. "They found a congressional sponsor at the last minute. Twelve-percent funding cuts, but they're still going. We have a liaison there—Wendy Scheer. You'll like her; everyone does. You're scheduled for a tour and reception next week."

"Find an excuse."

"It's just a courtesy call, but it's an important one," Juanita said slowly. "Halo—"

"Find an excuse," Erik repeated. He wasn't interested in meeting with the Feds, and there was no reason that he had to.

Juanita nodded. "Will there be anything else?"

"No," Erik said slowly. The relaxant was definitely do-ing its work, and the fatigue that washed over him had reached near-tidal proportions. He didn't feel like speak-ing anymore.

The distance passed in near silence.

CHAPTER 2

WENDY Scheer rode alone from Armstrong to Villanueva's north perimeter nexus, where short- and long-range arteries came together in a tangle and then moved apart again. There, she left her private, government-issue transport and drifted through increasingly crowded passageways toward the public platform before boarding the trans-Carnegie run.

This was the only segment of her jaunt that required public transportation, and the difference was obvious. Even in the best of times, the Carnegie was crowded. Today, the cars were packed as tightly as cargo pods in an ore convoy, because it was Founder's Day.

Wendy knew that, but CenTrans's scheduling Gummi had slipped a calendar field or two and forgotten. Thus, no extra cars on the trains, and thus, the cargo pod effect.

Founder's was, in effect, an antiholiday. If you worked

Duckworth, you worked Founder's Day. It commemorated the birth of Milton Duckworth, Jr., founder of one of many competing concerns that had merged and become the company that bore his name. Duckworth's family line had died out in the Bad Times, but his name lived on as an appropriately neutral trademark. It had come back into prominent use just before the foundry conglomerate joined the Allied Lunar Combine.

Missing Founder's was a bad idea for Duckworth associates. Taking leave, sick or personal, meant that line supervisors and teammates alike would decline to max the "company spirit" score on your screen, and you'd end up working New Christmas, all eight days. Accordingly, even when CenTrans did its job properly, an open seat on the trans-Carnegie was a rarity on Founder's Day.

Not for Wendy. Neatly attired in red and tan, the trim young woman sat comfortably in an enhanced double seat, at home in the marginally more luxurious accommodations intended for special needs passengers. Its previous occupants had eagerly volunteered full use of the seat, so Wendy's handbag and work shoes had a place to rest, too.

Surrounding her, seated and standing, were rank and file members of Villanueva's workforce. They shuffled and murmured and waited for their stops. Everyone kept a courteous distance, even though it meant jamming elbows into bellies and inhaling twice-breathed air. A few bystanders, the closest, stared attentively in Wendy's direction; more used phone feeds or file updates to pass the time. All wore patient expressions.

In that, at least, Wendy Scheer was little different from her fellow passengers. Her face was a mask of detached serenity as she went about her work. Disdaining the seat's public terminal, she unrolled her personal computer and began reviewing one screen after another. Though seemingly unmindful of her surroundings, she actually took some care to display no feeds inappropriate for over-the-shoulder viewing. Instead, she chose more prosaic outputs, the stuff of business and commerce, mining them for nuggets of information and deeper meaning. Wendy was ten paragraphs into a statistical analysis of the tourist trade that compared who had come to the Moon with how much money they had left behind when she looked up at the sound of a stranger's voice.

"Are you sure you don't need more room?" asked a man seated opposite her. He was stocky and pale, and his lips had a bluish tinge under the artificial light. He looked to be a cardiac patient, in Villanueva to take advantage of Luna's lower gravity until appropriate therapies took effect.

"Mmmm?" Wendy asked, mildly surprised at the query. She was an attractive woman, but not a beautiful one, with strong features and deep-set eyes. Her hair was auburn this month and she wore it long, styled like a waterfall.

"I mean, you can have my seat, too, if you want," the heart patient said. He started to stand. "It's no trouble. Really, if you'd like to spread out or put your feet up—"

She shook her head. "No, no," she said, "that's very kind, but I'm fine. Thank you so much."

Wendy smiled.

The man smiled, too, in instant response. His color improved, if only slightly, losing some of its pastiness, and his breathing eased. Wendy guessed that his blood pressure had dropped at least ten points, and she was sure that his heart was beating more regularly.

The man sighed. Several other passengers, lucky

enough to be looking in Wendy's direction, sighed, too.

She nodded, polite but uncaring, and turned her attention again to her computer's display. The shuttle wasn't just crowded but slow, and she had plenty to review before her briefing.

According to a live CenTrans release, shuttles were twelve minutes behind schedule; as Wendy read, the quantity blurred and changed from twelve to twenty-three. Sources within EnTek had reported that the brainware glitches were getting worse, not better. Management was looking for heads to roll.

Glancing at the clock view, Wendy saw that it was nine and seventeen. Her briefing was at nine and a half, but she knew that she was going to be late. She allowed herself the luxury of smiling without premeditation and didn't bother to note its effect on the herd surrounding her. She preferred being on time, but personal tardiness had never been a problem, either.

Wendy had not met very many people who objected to anything that she did, ever.

She continued reviewing what Mesh editors liked to think was hard news. Duckworth Construction had begun a major new build-out a full week ahead of schedule. Zonix employee account dividends had matched projection. EnTek management anticipated resolving brainware production issues promptly. The entries blurred one into another, but Wendy at least skimmed them all and paid reasonable attention to detail.

Most of what she read was lies, or at least hopelessly inaccurate, filtered and censored and massaged by corporate management until its content was all but nonexistent, but she read it anyway. Sometimes the façade was too obvious to mask the truth that lay behind it, and Wendy had always found it good to know what input others used for their decisions.

It was very helpful to know what others knew, and what they did not.

One of the Earth-news entries caught her attention. It was the usual stuff, about a paracholera outbreak in Alaska, but it spurred a memory. After a brief glance to confirm that her neighbors were watching her and not what she watched, she opened a link to Armstrong and accessed a camouflaged report. Written in turgid bureaucratese, a memo that seemed to announce new requisitioning procedures told her something very different.

EnTek's new man, Morrison, had arrived on schedule and would be settling into his apartment about now. No direct contact yet, but his profile said that he liked German food and drank old-fashioned alcohol. He could find both in Villanueva, albeit at a healthy premium, and she was sure that he would, too. According to Morrison's compensation schedule, the man could afford to eat and drink as he liked.

A status report said that Morrison had scheduled a download of his own, a meet-and-greet that should take most of the later day. Tomorrow would probably be taken up by a preliminary tour. Chances were that Morrison was going to hear a lot of stalling and excuses about EnTek's recent spate of missed production quotas and release dates. Days would pass before his subordinates trusted him with anything substantive.

Wendy figured she had at least a standard week.

She closed that link and opened one to the Mesh. The public library held one hundred forty-seven major files and a thousand minor references on German cuisine, focusing on theory, practice, and anthropology. She selected one, accessed it, and began to read.

Fourteen minutes later, she was still reading, when the plodding train finally braked to a halt at Bessemer Place, nearly thirty-six minutes past schedule. Almost as one, the commuters swarmed toward the doors. They jostled and crowded for the exits, impatient to be first at their workstations, eager to offset the impact of Founder's Day tardiness on their personnel records.

Wendy didn't concern herself with the crush. She rolled up her computer, shouldered her bag, picked up her shoes, and stepped in the general direction of the nearest exit. A path opened for her in the crush, as fellow passengers shouldered one another aside to let her pass.

She scarcely noticed; long experience had made her blasé about others' courtesies.

DUCKWORTH'S reception area was bigger than big, a vaulted chamber that peaked some ten meters above a lushly carpeted floor. It was entirely real space, too. Instead of trompe l'oeil image screens, heavy silicate slabs bounded the space, held by metal beams. Glossy in diffuse light, the exposed support members demonstrated Duckworth's primary stock in trade, heavy metal fabrication. The hard steel bones that made up so much of Villanueva were all of them Duckworth's work.

At the center of the domed chamber, inside a ring-shaped desk that was also made of stone and steel, sat a woman who wore a dress and had hair that were both the color of iron. She was pretty, in a circumspect way, and looked as much a part of the place as the walls or thick carpeting.

"Good morning," she said. "Happy Founder's." Her voice, professional, cool and reserved, echoed as she spoke. The acoustics were an affectation of the place's designers, and one of the reasons Wendy disliked the Duckworth facility. She valued clarity.

Wendy had been here before, though not often and not recently. The place embodied a philosophy of design that had enjoyed a brief vogue some forty years before, when energy had officially become cheap and made enclosed space cheap, too. Shareholders and contractors alike, anxious to prove their success and to demonstrate that they were on the Moon to stay, had spent millions creating environments that worked as hard to impress as they did to shelter. Too many were only slightly less chilly and foreboding than the dead world's surface.

The style suited Duckworth, though—big and heavy and functional, the style of factories and foundries. This place had been built for machines.

"Valerie Harrada," Wendy identified herself. "I have a nine and thirty." Ten had come and gone already.

"Of course," the seated woman said. She didn't ask for any identification, and her reserved tones became warm with immediate trust. "The project review is in the main conference room. They're waiting for you."

Wendy nodded.

"Do you know where that is, Ms. Harrada?" the greeter asked, eager to please.

Wendy shook her head. Her hair rippled and flowed. "I'm sure I can find my way," she said. "I made it here from the mines."

The receptionist flushed, embarrassed.

Wendy continued, "I hope I haven't kept them too long. There was a problem with the shuttle."

"I'm sure Mr. Shadrach will understand," the greeter said. "There've been so many glitches. There was even a datastorm yesterday. Those slackers at EnTek—"

Wendy couldn't resist. "We're all on the same team here," she said. "We all work for the ALC, don't we?"

"Of course we are," the woman said. She executed the conversational turnaround with professional grace. "I didn't mean—"

"I'm sure you didn't," Wendy said. Her lips pulled back and formed a gentle curve. "Don't worry about it. Let them know I'm coming, will you? I need to stop in the fresher."

The greeter nodded eagerly. Wendy thought briefly of her childhood on Earth, and of the dog she had owned then.

TEN minutes later, with fresh shoes and fresh makeup, with all mail checked and all messages reviewed, Wendy glided into the main conference room. She moved as fluidly as water on rocks through the open metal doors and heard them whisper shut behind her. This space was of the same vintage as the reception area, but slightly smaller and more intimate; the architect's intent here had been less to impress than to ensure privacy. No one spoke as she took the only seat remaining open.

"Sorry to keep you all waiting," she said, from the head of the table. That was for manners' sake. None of the nine seated men and women was likely to mind her tardiness.

"No problem at all."

"None, no, of course not, Ms. Harrada."

"I was late myself."

"Darned brainware."

The conciliatory comments would have continued for

much longer if permitted. Wendy interrupted them with a brisk, "Good. Then to business, shall we? Who's first?"

"That would be me," said a tall man with white hair and a bearing that was just short of regal. It fit him like a second skin. Conrad Shadrach's title put him much higher in the Duckworth hierarchy than Valerie Harrada. "Let me just run the data—"

The conference table was steel and stone, too, like the receptionist's desk, but its expansive surface included recessed, beveled spaces so that each meeting participant could view a personal screen with reasonable privacy. Wendy's nook was bigger than the others and more private, oriented so that only she could see what it presented. Beside it was a plate that bore something that looked sweet and gooey, and a mug of new-coffee. The pastry called to her, but she ignored it and drank instead. As if in response, her screen's blanking fields faded and gave way to elaborate graphs and legends, flanked by columns of numbers. All input came from secured files; there was no Mesh connectivity here.

"Biome production of precursors and media is up 4 percent," Shadrach said. "And Sales has been put on alert. That's probably a feint. The best information we have is that their new product, the respirant, has unexpected attributes—something to do with repairing arterial plaques. That wasn't what they were looking for, so they've taken a step back to examine their options—what to call it, how to market it, how to use it. In the meantime, they need additional revenue and a place to hide the expense. I'll give you the details off-line."

"Why didn't we know about this earlier?" Wendy wanted to know.

"Communication restrictions," Shadrach said. "It's a

new development—very new—and getting reliable data wasn't easy. I only found out the details yesterday, I knew you were coming and wanted to wait until we were on a completely secure system."

Wendy nodded. "Good thinking, Con," she said.

Shadrach beamed like a schoolboy and continued his report.

One after another, the others took their turns. Ralph LaCombe explained that Zonix's profits were off, despite the company's absolute lock on Villanueva programming, both import and export. It sounded to Wendy like another Earthside fad was coming to an end. Millions of home viewers were finally tiring of the Moon shows.

Oscar Janes reported that CenTrans was reviewing bids for new shuttle engines and passenger cars and was looking to import talent to build them.

Lucille Cunnard wasn't sure why, but Applied System Dynamics—Dynamo—planned an upgrade to the brainware that ran its proprietary cold fusion systems, scheduled sometime the following year.

"Better hope EnTek is back on track by then," Wendy said, and was rewarded with laughter that was heartfelt but nervous.

Villanueva was the only commercial installation on Luna, but it hadn't been the first. That honor belonged to EnerCorp Site, named for one of the ten companies that had become Dynamo. All that remained now of the EnerCorp facility was several hundred cubic kilometers of fused rock in Mare Tranquilliatus. That, and a retired trademark that had become an impolite word to use in mixed company.

Some glitches were worse than others.

"They plan extensive testing," Cunnard said.

"I should hope so," Shadrach said. "I just hope we're not sleeping in the test bed."

No one laughed, perhaps because Wendy chose not to; she was rapidly getting bored. Six times in most years she called in-person meetings like this, assembling groups rather than conducting personal interviews. Six times a year was as frequent as she could manage without drawing excessive attention to herself or to the others.

Like Wendy, many at her table spoke under assumed names. All gave reports demonstrating that they knew more than they should, given their titles and roles within the five ALC companies. Most thought that they reported, under the guise of a project review, to a committee within Duckworth devoted to what was discreetly termed *competitive information* on the other ALC companies. Several thought precisely the reverse, that they were intercepting data gathered by their fellows for later report to their true employers.

All were right, but all were wrong.

The meetings were essential but typically boring, serving as much to build team spirit and bond as to exchange information. Most attendees believed that Valerie Harrada was, in fact, an obscure functionary within the Duckworth management structure, someone whose title as a selenological engineer hid greater expertise in corporate espionage.

After nearly an hour of sequential reportage, a pudgy man with a spindly neck concluded with the datum that Duckworth's prospectors had found another bed of rare earths some two hundred kilometers south, and trace moisture thirty beyond that.

"I'm aware of both finds," Wendy said. "My team made them."

"Of course, Ms. Harrada," the man said. "But—"

Wendy leaned back in her chair and made a gesture of dismissal. She took a sip of new-coffee as the man fell silent. "Now," she said. "Is there any word on Ramirez?"

This time, no laughter came, no eager comments—only silence, awkward and strained. Wendy knew what it meant. They wanted to please her and tell her what she wanted to hear, but they couldn't.

"Con?" she prompted.

"Nothing," the man said. His air of dignity had suddenly fallen aside, giving way to a more crestfallen quality. "It's as if he vanished." He had scarcely finished the last word before the others joined in, each shaking his or her head, each muttering explanations or apologies.

"I do *not* believe this," Wendy said. Her words, even spoken softly, made many of the others flinch. "We live in a *closed environment.* People can't just vanish here! This is the *Moon,* for God's sake!"

"It's a closed system," LaCombe said slowly, filling the sudden, awkward silence. He nodded. "But a loose one. There are cracks, crannies . . ."

Wendy turned her steady gaze in his direction.

"He—he could have gone dingo," LaCombe continued edgily.

"Dingo?" Wendy didn't know the word.

"He means, 'rat,'" Lucille Cunnard said. She glanced spitefully at LaCombe, clearly annoyed at the attention the man was receiving. "We don't have *dingoes* here, Ralph. Not much use for the word, either."

Wendy nodded. "Rat" was different, a word that had come up many times in meetings like this, both face-to-face and Meshed sessions.

To rat was to go native.

Not just by taking a job at the colony and living there. To rat, whether on the Earth or the Moon, was to opt out of the system as completely as possible. In Villanueva, that meant joining the underclass that was emerging, in fits and starts, from the colony's rich social mulch. It took money to get to the Moon, whether travelers' money or employers', but it didn't cost much to live there. Residents paid their way, more or less, by consumption taxes, but other than that, they were free to move credit around among themselves as best they could. That was one thing that was consistent about people in Wendy's experience— no matter where they lived, they spent and they consumed. The nature of currency might change, but the transaction itself did not. Rats tended to be more discreet about the process, but most of them weren't in hiding.

Those that were, didn't stay hidden very long from the resources at Wendy's disposal. Not typically.

"You're just restating the problem," she said, mildly annoyed. "Of course he's gone rat. That's why we're looking for him."

LaCombe shook his head. He was big, with more muscle than most of the others and the nasal twang of his voice still held a hint of his birthplace's dialect. "I said 'dingo,' and I meant 'dingo,'" he said. "We had that in Australia, during the Insurrection. Refugees headed for the Outback, tried to live off the land."

Wendy almost laughed. "You think he's on the surface?" she asked. "That's one place we know he's not. I spend some time on the surface, remember? There's nothing there. Nothing." Casually, without trying to hide her inattention, she opened another view in her display and began accessing files. As far as she was concerned, the topic was closed.

"Caves," LaCombe continued. "Natural or man-made. That's all this place is, a big artificial cave with furniture. Ramirez is a capable man, and he was a prospector, once upon a time. He wouldn't need much to get started—power cells, a cutting torch, sealant, recyclers—he could get it all in a single tractor hold."

It was a thought. Wendy considered it for a moment, then rejected it. "Not Ramirez," Wendy said. "Someone else, maybe, but not him. I've read his profile, and several of you have met him." She had met him as well, but that had been nearly a year before and under her own name. There was no need for the others to know that. "He likes crowds. He's just not that self-sufficient."

"Or that capable," Lucille Cunnard said darkly.

"Or that capable," Wendy agreed. She paused. "Lucky, though. And able to surprise."

LaCombe proved himself able to surprise, too. He actually managed to shake his head slightly, in disagreement with her words. That put him close to showing disrespect. Wendy was surprised and vaguely pleased. LaCombe's willingness to disagree, and his tenacity in doing so in public demonstrated strength of will and self-assertiveness. That could make him useful.

Wendy composed her features and spoke with careful neutrality. "Do you have any views on that, Ralph?" she asked.

The big man spoke slowly. "I think you're—we're underestimating him," he said carefully. "I've never met the gent. All I've seen are the feeds about him, but he strikes me as a sharper tool than most. He'd have to be, to hide this well."

Wendy tried to quell sudden irritation. She remembered all too well her mixed emotions upon learning of the discovery Ramirez claimed to have made. She had no room in her life at the moment for that kind of turmoil, or for the sloppy kind of thinking that was its companion.

That Ramirez, of all people, had found *what* he had found. That the man had possessed the presence of mind to act on his discovery as he had—

Wendy pushed the thought from her mind. "The specialists disagree," she said. "I disagree."

"Maybe he's dead," Lucille said.

Wendy shook her head. "He's not dead," she said. "And if he is, we need to know. Alive or dead, he has to be found."

"Three months is a long time," Lucille said. "With the tourist boom and the construction—"

"He has to be found," Wendy repeated. "And we have to find him before the others do."

"I don't think he's dead," LaCombe said, in belated agreement. "My guess is, he's scared."

"He should be," Oscar Janes said. "He's got three Combine members looking for him."

"Five," Wendy said softly.

They all looked in her direction.

"Five?" LaCombe asked. "Biome wants him now, too?"

Wendy felt irritation at the slip, but did not voice it. What was done, was done.

She nodded. "Biome has formed a search committee," she said. "Never mind how I know. Zonix is about to."

"Maybe he approached us—them, too," LaCombe said. His cover identity worked for Zonix.

"Never mind how I know," Wendy repeated. This time, the words were a command.

LaCombe shook his head. "I'm not wondering that," he said. "I'm wondering why Zonix is looking for him."

"Why do they even care?" Lucille asked. "Or do they just want him because we want him, too?"

"The thrill of the chase, maybe," Janes said. Like La-Combe, his cover was with Zonix. His office, in the passive displays division, was low priority by the entertainment conglomerate's standards, but a good place to get information. Earlier, off-line, he had told Wendy of the Zonix committee's impending formation. Now, he said, "The 'hardy pioneer' feeds are losing points in under-twelves, but—"

Wendy realized with faint surprise that she had come close to losing control of the conversation. "That's enough," she said. Her tone was soft, but her words carried well.

The others fell silent.

"You had the lead, Ralph," Wendy continued. "But we need to close. It's Founder's Day, after all."

LaCombe nodded. "I still think there's more to Ramirez. I'd like to do some backtracking, find if there's anything we missed."

"At this point, that might raise more questions than it answers," Wendy said. "Are you looking for anything in particular?"

The sandy-haired man paused. "Look, I know each of us has some assignments and initiatives the others don't know about," he said. "But I have to ask—has anyone looked into Hello?"

"Project Halo is off-limits," Wendy said, stressing the project's proper name. She ignored the whispered comments suddenly being exchanged by other attendees and raised her assessment of LaCombe. "I've made this point before, more than once," she told him. "Halo is still in the dark. Even if they aren't, we can't risk letting them know of our interests. Can you imagine their reaction?"

"That's not going to be an easy secret to keep,"

LaCombe said. "If all of the five know and have programs—"

"The ALC is a closed shop," Wendy said. "Hello—
Halo—isn't part of it. It's one thing to compete with partners, but I'm not going to let the government profit from
our research. We'll do nothing to arouse their interest."

"They're already aroused," LaCombe said doggedly.
"They have to be. It's in their charter. And we're supposed to cooperate. That's in ours."

"You know what I mean."

"What if Ramirez went to them?" LaCombe continued
stubbornly. "What if he's in Armstrong?"

"You don't think we'd know?" Wendy asked, almost
amused.

"I don't."

"I do," Janes interrupted. "I checked the logs for the
Villanueva–Armstrong run."

"And none of his other runs intersected Armstrong territory," Wendy said. "I checked that. I appreciate your dili-
gence, Ralph, but you need to look in another direction."

"There are ways around that, and Project Halo—"

"Another direction, Ralph," Wendy said. Her gaze
found his and locked on it.

LaCombe nodded.

Could she trust him to obey? That wasn't a question she
had to ask herself often, but for the moment, she decided
that she could. At any rate, an overachiever was the least of
her problems right now. She smiled at him and at the others. "New business, then. What's the situation at EnTek?"

The woman from EnTek cleared her throat. "Morrison
arrived yesterday," she said. "There was a delay getting
him to his quarters . . ."

Her words trailed off into silence, a silence that Ralph

LaCombe filled eagerly. "Zonix did a search, and our—their—media resources are the best. Most of what we found was obvious enough. That business in Alaska, but they clamped down on the specifics pretty fast there. Earthside archives turned up some old canned publicity and bid résumés, though, and we have some other mass media materials. Morrison was quite the promising young up and comer, once upon a time. I'll give you copies of what we've got."

"Good. Anything else?" Wendy asked.

"I'd like to know why he's here," Conrad Shadrach said.

"To replace Caspian," Lucille Cunnard said.

"That's not what I mean," the older man replied. He was holding a mug of tea, and his pale hands shook slightly as they passed it back and forth. "Someone had to replace Caspian, but I can't imagine why they would have chosen Morrison to do it. He barely qualifies for the position, and he's got a history. If he'd been Duckworth, he'd be retired now—whether he wanted or not. Some companies, he'd be worse off than that."

"Instead, they moved him up," Wendy said, "Literally." The joke was weak, but she knew that it would bring a response and waited until she got it before continuing. "That costs. Is there any chance he's more than he seems?"

"Before he had the history, he had a reputation. It's not in his résumé, but you can see it between the words. He was a troubleshooter," Shadrach said.

"EnTek has troubles?" Wendy asked idly. "Ones we don't know about, I mean."

No one wanted to respond. Even Shadrach merely shrugged.

"The coordinator's office doesn't really have much

power," Wendy mused. "At least, he's not supposed to." She had already thought the matter through fairly thoroughly, but wanted to see if any of the others had something to add. "Maybe his superiors just wanted him out of the way, or maybe they wanted a representative on the Moon with some extra downtime." She glanced at La-Combe. "Does he have a current reputation as any kind of troubleshooter?"

LaCombe shook his head. "Not really, no."

"But he did," Shadrach repeated. "Ten years ago, there were stories—"

"That was ten years ago," LaCombe said, shaking his head again. "These days, he's just trouble."

"Maybe he had powerful friends," Wendy said. "Maybe that's all." She picked at her pastry with one long-nailed finger and watched as crumbs piled up rapidly. "What does Caspian say?"

"I haven't asked him," Shadrach replied. "He's off-limits for my office."

"Really?" That was a surprise.

Shadrach's posture changed as he spoke, becoming stiff and awkward. "There are politics involved," he said.

"I imagine so," Wendy said, and nodded. It wasn't every day that a senior executive of one ALC partner took a job with another. "Some bent feelings, too, I suppose."

No one had anything to say to that.

"We'll worry about it another time," Wendy decided, after a glance at her clock display. It was time for an end to the meeting, and Valerie Harrada's day, as well.

CHAPTER 3

SLEEP was supposed to be easier in zero- and low-G, but that wasn't Erik's experience. Either that, or the nap on the tram had spoiled him for it for the first night in his new quarters. He spent the night in troubled dreams, hearing angry voices make heated accusations and seeing once-friendly familiar faces twist in expressions of fury and sorrow. Then—

"Good morning," his apartment said. It spoke in studiously neutral tones, working in default mode. *"What would you like for breakfast?"*

Breakfast.

At the thought, his stomach clenched, twisted, and moved about in his abdomen with entirely too much freedom. Something hot and burning rushed up his throat and into his mouth.

He staggered to the fresher, but the trip was hard going.

The lesser gravity made his movements too emphatic, and he wasn't yet awake enough to compensate. One step against the textured flooring sent him careening halfway to the toilet recess; a second frantic stumble bounced him against the neighboring wall. It was all Erik could do to regain his balance and find the commode rim before the waves of nausea surging through him crested again. He retched to almost no effect, then collapsed to the textured floor and waited for the world to quit moving.

"Mr. Morrison?" the apartment asked, still in its cool base-setting voice. No one had configured the system for him. *"Are you unwell?"*

Erik shuddered again, as another near spasm shook him. He held back the vomit and forced out a word, instead. "Privacy," he croaked.

"Privacy on," his apartment acknowledged. Shaped acoustics made the words seem to come from just above him, but Erik knew that the voice came from somewhere above the ceiling. He also knew what the housekeeper's promise meant—specifically, not much, because the thing was running in default mode. Basically, the housekeeping unit would pretend not to hear all but direct commands, at least until his behavior exceeded thresholds that the artificial brain's programmers viewed as acceptable.

On Earth, in the stand alone that had been his home the previous twelve years, he would have known what the thresholds were. Here, with his housekeeper running on default, he didn't. He couldn't. That felt wrong.

The whole world felt wrong. It felt wrong, and it looked wrong, and it smelled wrong, and he had no doubt that it would taste wrong, too.

He didn't belong here. Every movement he made in

the lesser gravity served as a reminder. Stewart might have been right. Maybe he could never get completely used to this, to the constant sense that something was fundamentally off with his world. Not after spending a lifetime in another one.

On Earth, Erik had attended hasty orientation sessions and even logged a few hours in simulators, but, like Stewart, the counselors had warned him that no amount of training could guarantee adjustment. He remembered their words now and recognized their truth.

Every step he took here was too forceful, every movement he made too emphatic. Even now, as he crouched in misery, every spasm threatened to lift him from the floor. He had to learn how to deal with that, fast, or learn if he could.

The human body was a forgiving instrument, but it had been shaped by millions of years to meet the demands of the world that had birthed it, and that world was not the Moon. Putting up with a few days of zero was one thing, but spending long years in one-sixth was a different challenge, maybe a greater one. Some could never meet it, even with artificial aids. Maybe he was among the ones who never would, who couldn't. What if he couldn't adapt? Where would he go next?

There was nowhere he *could* go.

He held that thought for a long moment, pushing it from his mind only when the last retch faded and he was able to stagger to his feet again. He stumbled into the shower stall.

"Cold," he said. "Then hot with soap, then cold again."

The water came down hard. It rushed down from most of the booth's ceiling in hard, straight streams. Driven more by pressure than being pulled by gravity, needle-thin jets pounded at him, sluicing away grime and flop-sweat and driving off some of his deep fatigue and nausea, too. At his feet, hidden pumps labored to draw the water away. When he looked down, he could see it splatter and bounce.

The splashes didn't look right, but he did his best to ignore them.

When the second barrage of cold water commenced, he opened his mouth and caught one stream. He swallowed some of the cold liquid, rinsed with the rest and spat, then drank again. Even the water tasted slightly wrong, but not so wrong that he couldn't drink it.

"Dry," he said, and warm air replaced the water.

A robe in his size but not his color and without his monogram hung from a hook in the bathroom. He shrugged into it and shuffled back into his apartment's bedroom. The water in his stomach shook and gurgled but stayed put. Erik moved slowly and carefully this time, so that his feet stayed where they belonged. The carpet felt good beneath his bare toes, but the tentative steps he had to take made him feel like an old man.

That wouldn't do. He recalled the way the bartender had moved, back at the Chrisium Port lounge, the nearly liquid combination of grace and economy. Some of the others had walked that way, too. Erik knew that he needed to be among that number.

But that could wait.

Aloud, he said, "I'm done."

"Will you be having breakfast at home today, Mr. Morrison? I'm not aware of your preferences."

"You should be," he said, irritated. "What happened to my profile?"

"The updates have been operating at less than optimal efficiency," the apartment said calmly. Everything it said, it said calmly—or at least, neutrally. It had no character. *"Will you be having breakfast?"*

"No," he said, and continued into the living area. "Not now. Not today."

This area of the apartment was somewhat triangular, narrower at one end than the other, forming a truncated wedge. The layout was common back home. If this place followed form, the wallpaper at the narrow end was made up of smaller sections and had higher resolution. He moved closer and settled onto a convenient couch.

"Get me the morning feeds," he said. "And get me Garcia. You should have her code, at least."

Two views opened on the wallpaper, still in its neutral gray default mode. One view filled with the scrolling fields of text and images that announced the latest news developments, but the other remained blank.

"Call in progress," the apartment told him.

Its words and neutral tone reminded Erik that the housekeeping system didn't know him well. Hastily, he said, "No video from this end."

Just in time, the "image blanked" announcement appeared in the view's corner. It became an overlay as Garcia's face snapped into focus.

Erik didn't wait for a greeting. "Morning, Garcia," he said. "I have some things I need done."

"Mr. Morrison!" Garcia said. She seemed pleased to hear from him. "I was just going to call you." She paused. "Is something wrong with your pickup? I'm not getting a picture at this end."

"Blanked," Erik said. Later, he could configure the

housekeeper to generate an appropriate mirage, if his preferences didn't turn up by then. "Have you arranged the review?"

"Review?" Garcia paused again, clearly confused. "Oh, the meeting. Yes, yes. For fourteen, on-site. Most of the team can make it, but—"

"I want them all there," Erik said.

"We can remote conference—"

"No virtual, no Mesh," Erik interrupted. He allowed himself a slight smirk. "We're doing it the Moon way, re-member? I want everyone there, in person."

"But Callahan—"

The name was only vaguely familiar, from a briefing or memo.

"Callahan can call in from the hospital or the crema-tory, if that's where he is. Otherwise, I want him sitting at the table with me."

It was time to show her who was boss.

"She. Callahan is a she," Garcia said.

Erik made no reply. He didn't really care.

Just as the silence reached an awkward length, Garcia nodded. "I'll see to it," she said.

"Good," Erik said. "Now tell me where I can get some groceries." As he spoke, the other view cleared itself, then presented a kitchen inventory and services directory. Clearly, the housekeeper was no longer pretending to ig-nore ambient input.

"Central can get you whatever you need," Garcia said. "Same-day delivery."

That would do to start, but not in the long run. "I want to choose my own," Erik said. "Where can I do that?"

Garcia paused, thinking. "There are a couple of places," she said. "But most people just use Central—"

"Where?" Erik demanded again.

"The Mall," Garcia said, then brightened. "Or the Concourse. Zonix Lifestyles runs a market there. Domestic and import, and it's on the main lines. Your housekeeper can give you directions."

Erik nodded. A thought struck him. "And a trainer," he said.

Garcia silently stared out from the screen, her face made blank by confusion.

"I want a personal trainer," Erik said, using patience he didn't feel. "Physical therapy, exercise, nutritional advice. Someone good, someone discreet." He felt a sudden moment of doubt. "Don't tell me there aren't any in Villanueva."

"Your apartment has a fitness unit," Garcia said. "The housekeeper can display whatever guidance you—"

He wasn't sure he wanted a brainware program telling him how to move his body. "I don't plan on walking around here like some bumpkin—"

"Bumpkin?" Garcia interrupted.

"An old word," Erik continued. "From an old world. Look it up, after you find me a trainer."

"Yes, sir," Garcia said.

"Good," Erik responded. "I'll see you at thirteen."

"The meeting is at—"

"I'll see *you* at thirteen," he repeated. "Have a complete briefing ready for me. I'll ask questions. And have Personnel send my preferences to my housekeeper again."

A moment later, with good-byes exchanged and the connection broken, he padded out into the kitchen area. He had to resist the temptation to take long, stretching steps, and realized with a bit of sadness that his striding days were probably done, at least for now. It seemed that his entire body language was wrong for this place.

"The kitchen has a full range of prepared meals," the housekeeper announced. It was persistent, if nothing else. *"Available breakfast dishes include—"*

"You talk too much," Erik told it. While the housekeeper paused to process that input, he examined the kitchen. Gleaming plastic and polished metal, the place looked like it had never been used and even smelled new. Management must have refurbished it for him, he realized.

In one corner was the integrated stove, with the freezer at one end and warming trays at the other. Its top held a single heating element, and a quick check showed that the neighboring cabinets contained only the bare minimum utensils.

"I'll need a new stove unit," he said.

There was no response. The housekeeper had adjusted itself.

"I said, I'll need a new stove," Erik repeated. He hoped that his preferences would arrive soon. "Answer me when I speak to you, and not just questions. Can you arrange the stove, or do I have to do it myself?"

"Please provide specifics," the housekeeper said. Still calm, still neutral, the synthesized voice's tones had somehow become even more detached.

"Something I can use. Auto capacity, but hands-on, too. And cookware."

"Central can provide a full range—"

"I'm sure they can," Erik interrupted. "But that's not what I want." He paused, considering, and almost smiled. He liked having something to think about. After a moment, he said, "Order a stove, five preparation surfaces, manual controls. Oven, convection, and micro. Order a standard cook's complement of cookware, kitchen utensils, dishes, and flatware. Quality stuff, but buy for utility and durability, not luxury. There should be consumer ratings somewhere on the Mesh; access them."

"Number of place settings?"

"Six, to begin with," Erik said. He would be living by himself for a while, at least, but he didn't mind entertaining, and it was expected with the job. On the other hand, he didn't care much for big dinner parties, and the apartment wasn't very spacious. "Schedule delivery and installation for working hours. Keep an eye on the personnel involved and keep playbacks for my review."

"Noted."

He turned, heading back toward the living area. "Now, let me see that grocery order screen again."

THE conference room at EnTek was shabby and low-tech, almost insultingly so. The table was dead pseudo-wood, with no Mesh connections or private views, and its laminate was cracked and peeling. The chairs surrounding it were a bit better, with pickups for the individual computers that the meeting attendees had unrolled on the table, so that they could link together in a temporary network, separate from the Mesh. The place's only real amenity was a beverage service, complete even to the colorless stuff that the Chrisium Port bartender had dispensed the day before.

Erik sipped a glass of it now, as he listened to Juanita Garcia's nervous words.

"I'm sorry for the accommodations," she said. She fidgeted as she spoke. "It's been years since the home office budgeted anything for redecoration."

"There's a reason for that," Erik replied. Seated at the

table's head, he had unfurled his own computer and configured it upon arriving. Now, he drummed the thick fingers of his right hand against the table's worn surface. "Nobody's been using this place, apparently."

Surrounding the table were eight chairs. Seven were occupied. In addition to Garcia, two women and three men stared anxiously in Erik's direction, obviously unsure of what would come next. One or two had attempted to make introductions or small talk, but Erik had managed to ignore them without seeming too blatant about it. He wanted to greet everyone at the same time.

"I made some calls," Garcia said edgily. "I was able to find—"

Erik glanced at her. "Later," he said.

Garcia fell silent.

Erik drummed his fingers some more, glanced at his computer's display. "Seventeen after," he said, without trying to hide his irritation. "We might as well begin without him."

"Mr. Kowalski's schedule is very demanding," Garcia said. "And he's off-site for days at a time. I don't know—"

"Most security officers have their hands full," Erik said. "But that's not an excuse. It's not even a reason."

He knew the way the system worked. Internal clearances were complex processes and took time. In the ordinary course of events, a local head of site security would know about any personnel transfer at Erik's level months in advance. Even with the way things had played out back home, Kowalski had doubtless known Erik was coming here even before Erik knew.

Speaking more loudly now, he repeated, "We might as well begin."

More fidgeting, more anxious glances.

"As most of you know," Erik said, "my name is Erik Morrison. I'm your new Site Coordinator. I'll meet with each of you individually in the next few days, but I thought it would be a good idea for us all to get together and introduce ourselves first. I know my assignment must have come as a bit of a surprise, and I know that transition periods are always rough. I wanted to reassure all of you that I'll do my best to ensure that the changeover goes smoothly. I'm sure I have a lot to learn from all of you, but I think you'll find I have contributions to make, too."

It was a canned speech, standard stuff for the new boss to deliver. He knew it by heart. The others probably did, too.

Erik nodded. "Names to faces, then," he said. "Left to right."

"Jee-Woo Harrison," said a wiry man with dark hair. "Acting head of production, Bio-Products Division."

"Ronda Wanderman," said an Asiatic woman with buzz-cut red hair. "Quality Control." She looked especially nervous and didn't appear any calmer when Erik nodded at her.

"I've been looking forward to meeting you," he said, and watched her look more nervous still.

One by one, the men and women introduced themselves. Erik mentally filed away their names, titles, and duties. He focused on their primary roles. Most wore more than one hat, organizationally speaking. Briefings back home had explained that. There was plenty to do on Villanueva, but much of it got done with automated assistance. Even with short work shifts, oversight personnel tended to need more than one thing to keep them busy.

Arthur Zavala ran Sales, both Domestic and Earthside; he was the first genuinely fat man Morrison had seen on the Moon, and probably didn't have much to do except review screens and sign off on orders. The unhappy-looking Amber Callahan was late middle aged, fair nearly to the point of albinism, and headed Purchasing. A burly man with an ornately coifed beard introduced himself as Seven Thomas and said that he ran Research and Development, even thought it took "more coordinating than running."

"Seven?" Erik asked him.

The big man grinned. Of all those in the room, only he seemed completely at ease. "My parents were multitarians," he said, "and they took it seriously."

Erik nodded and filed the comment away for future reference. He turned to Garcia and asked, "What about Personnel? Compensation?"

"They don't report directly to you," Garcia said. "You wanted just your line staff here today."

"Business Development?"

"No formal post," Garcia said, shaking her head. "Ad hoc committees, as the need arises."

"There's always a need for business development," Erik said, genuinely surprised. He'd had no idea that things had gotten this bad.

"Maybe so, maybe on Earth," Thomas said. "We do things a bit differently here."

Erik looked again in the man's direction, assessing him for a second time in as many minutes. The big man seemed pleasant enough, but he also didn't seem reluctant to challenge authority. "Differently?" Erik asked.

Thomas grinned again. "Just a bit. New world, new ways, and all that."

Erik didn't say anything.

Thomas continued. "Look, if you had asked us for our

titles and duties a week ago, you might have gotten a different set of answers. Most of our duties are fluid. Ninety percent of the time, my own group runs itself, so I have downtime. A week ago, I was working with Amber to resolve some Purchasing problems. I didn't contact my own staff for four days, at least."

Callahan nodded in agreement.

"It's the same for all of us," Thomas continued. "The only guy with a job cast in steel, Kowalski, isn't even here." He paused. "This isn't a rigid hierarchy, sir. Caspian knew that." Rogers Caspian had been Erik's predecessor. "He took his job title pretty seriously. He was a coordinator, both internal and external."

"That's my title, too," Erik said.

"I've read your résumé."

Erik smiled tightly. "Good," he said. "That's why I posted it." He paused. "But just in case the rest of you haven't, let me run down a few of the highlights."

The others looked at him expectantly.

"Between consultancies, subcontracts, and direct payroll, I've been with EnTek for twenty-three years, ever since Academy. I've headed work groups, departments, divisions, and subcorporations. I've held responsible positions on five continents, and I've consistently been at the lead in business growth areas. I was running EnTek Australia when Russell Watterson filed the first patents for the current generation of biological AIs, and I was on the committee that approved registering the Gummi-Brains trademark," Erik said, and paused. "Though, to be honest, I didn't vote in favor of the motion."

Polite laughter followed the comment, but none of it came from Thomas.

"At one point, personnel, divisions, and contracts under my direct supervision accounted for 12 percent of EnTek's net profit." He paused again, this time for emphasis. "Not gross, net."

"That was Alaska, right?" When Thomas spoke this time, his words were cool and remote and bore little resemblance to his earlier, amiable tones.

"Alaska, yes," Erik said. He decided not to rise to the bait. "I was director of North American Initiatives then. But that's the past. We're here to talk about the present."

No one said anything.

"Or, actually, the future," he continued. "When the board offered me this assignment, I told them I would make changes. I intend to."

"With all due respect," Thomas said slowly. "We've been running a successful program here. We've met or exceeded every projection and quota for the last sixty quarters. I urge you to consider how we're doing things now—"

"I intend to do that, Seven," Erik said. "As I said before, I'll be meeting with each of you individually during the next week or so and discussing goals and incentives, talking where we want to go and how we can get there. Part of that means learning where we are. I promise you, I have as many questions as any of you do, and maybe more."

Amber Callahan looked suddenly, dramatically, more at ease.

"But as part of that learning process, and until further notice, we'll have weekly meetings like this one. And since face-to-face hasn't worked out very well," he continued, nodding at Hector Kowalski's empty chair, "we'll do them my way, on a sub-Mesh hookup."

"Uh."

"Yes, Arthur?"

"We've usually found in-person meetings more productive," the sales director said carefully.

"Well," Erik responded. "Like I said, we're here to talk about the future. And there's not much point in having tools if we aren't going to use them."

AN hour later, after more pro forma feint and parry with his line staff, Erik followed Garcia down a short corridor and around a corner to his offices.

Erik didn't like them.

They were Caspian's old spaces, and they reminded Erik of the conference room. Just as low-tech and just as out of date, they had a worn look, as if they had seen very heavy traffic. Spotlessly clean, the place still bore the marks of much use. Nicks and chips marred the desk's surface, and round scars marked where beverages had sat. Work screens and printers huddled in one corner, all at least a generation past their prime. Most of the rest of the place was given over to a reception area that could double as conference space. Another meeting table sat inside a ring of guest chairs, none of them new. Someone had set the walls to display an archival image of what Erik recognized as the southern reaches of Anchorage National Nature Reserve.

He wondered who had chosen the view, and at the reasoning behind the choice. Was someone being considerate and hospitable, or cruel?

"This won't do," he said.

Garcia made no reply, but touched the extra bit of

jewelry that hung from her left earlobe. She had opened a recorder.

"I'm not much for visitors."

Garcia nodded.

"Switch the spaces," Erik continued. "Privacy zone where the workstation is now, new desk in the main area, dead center. Something modern, impressive. Two guest chairs, lots of open space. Bar, but mask it. I'd prefer a manual one. Open the space up as much as you can. No partitions, no walls. See about expansion, too. I want real space, if it's available." He glanced down, at the puce floor covering beneath his sandaled feet. "And for God's sake, lay some decent carpet. Get some decor examples from NorthAm headquarters and see what I mean. There's a budget for it, part of my transfer package."

Garcia nodded again.

"And get a new conference system. Whatever Caspian had, it's not going to be good enough."

"But, Mr. Morrison," she said, "we really don't use the Mesh much for meetings."

"Didn't."

"Didn't?"

"Didn't, not don't. Didn't, but we will," Erik said. "Like I said, there are going to be some changes." He paused, grimaced. "And I want something else on the walls, right now."

The office complied. Images rippled and flowed across the vertical surfaces. The forest preserve's greens and browns faded, disappeared, resolved themselves as a convincing trompe l'oeil of oak paneling and cluttered shelving. Illusory framed paintings and photographs interspersed themselves among equally illusory leather-bound old-books. Erik had seen places like this in history books and museums.

He almost laughed. "Old-fashioned," he said. "Older than old."

"Mr. Caspian's settings," Garcia responded.

"Not mine."

"I didn't think so," Garcia said. "We made a guess on the new defaults, but—"

Erik finished the sentence for her. "But the updates are giving you trouble?" he asked.

Garcia nodded.

"Give me something open, expansive," Erik said.

"We did."

Erik glanced at her, but didn't say anything.

Again, the images dissolved and re-formed, as the office manager unit presented glimpses of various selections in its library—seascapes, rolling sand dunes, even a glacier field, blinding in its whiteness. One image made Erik smile, however slightly, for what felt like the first time in days.

"That's it," he said. "That's the one."

Now, it seemed that he and Garcia stood on the Moon's bare surface. Gray dust and darker rock stretched for apparent kilometers in every direction, bounded only by the sky's black inverted bowl. Rocky peaks thrust upward, as if to stab the pinpoint stars that shone down at them. Erik had no idea of the view's specific coordinates, but he liked it. The detail and degree of lighting meant that image had almost certainly been enhanced, but he didn't care.

It seemed real, and it seemed right. A little bit pretentious, but right.

"That's good," he said. "Lighten it a bit." As the panorama faded a bit and lost some contrast, he nodded. The vista no longer seemed to swallow up the room, but even in gray, it impressed. "Good. Stop."

Garcia stared past him at the artificial view, at the curved, ragged line of the Moon's horizon. "Y-you can't work with it like this," she stammered.

"I can."

"I've scheduled courtesy calls from the other companies," Garcia said, protest in her voice. "And even if you do them on the Mesh, the visual feed—"

Her emphatic reaction to the selection was surprising. She had struck him as being more timid and restrained than that. "What's your problem with it?"

"I—I don't like it," Garcia said. She paled, color draining from her already fair complexion. "Most locals won't. I'm not a native, but I've gotten used to the walls. I *like* the walls," she nearly wailed. She stumbled to a guest chair and dropped into it.

Erik noticed that even when she was upset and distracted, Garcia's body language was more like the bartender's than his. She must have been local for a long time. She probably even tripped gracefully.

"Get used to it," he said, feeling only a faint hint of concern. "It's a good reminder."

"But the others—"

"They can learn to live with it."

"Your guests," Garcia said, pleading.

"I don't plan on having very many guests," Erik said. "Not in person." The phone would present whatever image he wanted to callers.

"I've already scheduled courtesy calls from the other companies," Garcia said. She looked from him to the ersatz sky and back again, not wanting to focus on either. "And your staff—"

"I'm not worried about the staff," Erik said. "But as long as you mention them, I want copies of their personnel files."

"Those are confidential." Garcia looked surprised.

"I want copies," Erik repeated. "And whatever you can get on my opposite numbers at the other partners."

Garcia reached for her earring, then remembered that her recorder was already on and left it alone. "I'll do what I can," she said, speaking now with extra precision and clarity. She was speaking for the record. "But the files themselves are confidential. And profiling the others could be a breach. I might be able to get summaries."

Erik shook his head. "Not summaries, full text," he said. "And let me worry about breaches. You must have done the same thing for Caspian."

"I didn't work for Mr. Caspian."

That was a surprise. He had assumed she had. Line staff typically stayed on to ensure a smooth transition, unless the new regime brought a new support team with it, and Erik hadn't; his disgrace was too thorough for that. The Home Office might have given him another chance, but they weren't offering that chance very much support.

He was a regime of one, at least for now.

"Oh?" he asked coolly. "What happened to Caspian's assistant?"

"Keith? Resigned, retired, returned," Garcia said. Her tone suggested that she wished very much that those words applied to her, too.

Erik knew Caspian's exit had been something of a scandal, but one to be considered later. Now, he gazed thoughtfully at Garcia, maintaining a silence just long enough to prompt a film of perspiration to form on the trim woman's smooth forehead. "So you've been 'promoted,' too," he said. "Like me."

She nodded again.

"It's not always a reward, is it?" he asked. Sympathy, unexpected and unaccustomed, welled up within him.

"No," she responded, then continued with a resoluteness that surprised him. "No, it's not. But challenges are good, too."

"They can be," Erik said. "If we rise to them." He sat in the chair behind Caspian's desk, his back to the Moonscape. "And that's why we're here, I suppose."

CHAPTER 4

VILLANUEVA, deep beneath the surface of its world, had no streets. The colony had conduits instead, long winding tunnels that construction teams had bored through Luna's cold, dead flesh, then insulated and lined and ventilated and lit, all for the comfort of people and machines. Construction, still ongoing, was an exercise in complexity, in planning ahead for growth yet to come, and in making allowances for any geological surprises that shared the world beneath Luna's surface. The small city's coiling territory seemed endless, and endlessly confusing.

His hasty orientation Earthside had left Erik with only a jumbled impression of the place's transit network, and local tutorials hadn't helped much. It was a complicated, three-dimensional lattice of conduits that ran at various angles and orientations, linking subterranean facilities that spread out in no obvious rational pattern. There seemed to be no way to get from one place to another in a single, straight hop. What should have been a simple jaunt from his offices at EnTek to Duckworth's primary suites had taken him through more intersections and differently angled connectors than he could count. Worse, the trip had been on foot, at Garcia's suggestion.

The conduit they walked through now was a relatively low traffic sector, roughly equivalent to an Earthside industrial park. The hollow within the Lunar crust was broad and low-roofed, built for mixed use. Display panels punctuated the walls only intermittently, and most bore nothing more elaborate than animated logos for the Big Five ALC firms, or for their contractors. Only a few dozen walkers milled around them on the pedway, which bordered a wider tramway.

"Is there any reason we're not riding?" he asked her. His tone held the faintest note of command, just enough to remind her who was in charge. Since their conversation in his office two days before, their relationship had become a bit less confrontational.

A good manager established his role and authority early. After that, he could accept another's guidance gracefully without losing face.

"I usually walk this route," Garcia said. "It's not very far, really. And this is faster than waiting for a tram or taxi."

Erik grunted. He was breathing more heavily than he would have expected. Sweat glistened faintly, briefly on his skin before being whisked away by Villanueva's low-humidity atmosphere. Right now, a tram would have suited him fine.

Walking properly in the low gravity took more thought and effort than he had expected. More than once, he had drawn up short to let another pedestrian pass and nearly fallen as his body suddenly reminded him that his mass and momentum remained Earth-normal, even if his scale-weight didn't. That had been bad enough, but such incidents only punctuated the constant need to walk carefully and at a deliberate pace. Moving too fast meant careening off his feet, and too strong a stride could send him racing toward the conduit's curved ceiling.

That lesson, he had learned the hard way.

"We're almost there," Garcia said. As she spoke, yet another low, blunt cart—open, not enclosed like the spaceport shuttle—rolled swiftly past them with its payload of passengers. Casual clothes and cameras marked them as tourists, a bit out of place in this utilitarian passage. A man seated at the tram's rear waved, and Garcia waved back, then the vehicle rounded a curve and moved out of view.

"They're making better time than we are," Erik said sourly. He hadn't bothered to wave.

"They're not from around here," Garcia said. She strode past the animated display panel of the famous Zonix cartoon cat shimmy-dancing with a milk shake. The milk shake was leading.

Erik grunted and tried not to look. He put one foot ahead of the other and kept moving.

"We're not on a tour, just a short hop. And you—*we* need the exercise," Garcia said. "Besides, practice will help you get used to the gravity."

Another pedestrian heading in their direction stepped to the walkway's edge and gave way for them. He nodded politely as they passed. Erik scarcely noticed, but Garcia returned the gesture.

"And there's more to it than that," she continued. She still seemed a bit worried about offending him, but she obviously knew what she was talking about. "It's *good* for you. The walking. You're going to lose muscle mass and bone. You've got to work against that. The gene patches help, but exercise helps more."

"Any luck on finding me a trainer?" Against his better judgment, he had tried the autogym in his apartment. He didn't like it.

Garcia wasn't blonde today. Instead, her hair was short and dark, so glossy that it looked like a black metal helmet, and hardly moved as she shook her head. "I posted the opening," she said. "We'll find somebody. But you really need to practice."

Erik grunted again. He still wasn't sleeping well, and today's jaunt from office to office, even in the lower gravity, was taking more of a toll than he had expected.

Trying not to be obvious, he watched Garcia walk. She moved with steady, efficient grace, and her feet never seemed to stray more than an inch or two from the walkway's plastic surface before gliding forward and coming down again. No movement was wasted. Over a short distance, she had built up a fair head of speed, without any apparent effort.

She noticed him watching her and slowed a bit. "It's not that difficult," she said. "It's mostly just not pushing up too hard." Her foot came up, moved forward, then down again, never more than an inch or two above the flooring. She seemed to flow, rather than step. "See?" she asked.

Erik felt suddenly embarrassed by his own awkward, hesitant shuffle and irritated that she had noticed his difficulty in finding a reasonable pace. "I'll do better once you find me a trainer," he said.

"We can still get you some smartshoes," Garcia said.

"You mentioned those before," Erik said.

"They cling when you step down and let go when you step up. It's not the same as gravity, and you still have to be careful because the rest of you keeps going," Garcia explained. "But some people say that they really help."

"How do they work?"

Garcia came to what was almost a sudden stop. "You know," she said. "I really don't know."

Erik had stopped, too, but with a bit less grace, nearly stumbling. He looked at her levelly. "You don't know how they work?"

His assistant's eyes were wide and puzzled, and, today at least, violet. "No one ever asked me that before," she said. "Magnets or something, I suppose."

"Magnets?" That didn't sound likely.

Garcia shrugged. "They work. We can get you some."

Erik felt self-conscious and uncomfortable as men and women flowed past them. "You don't know how they work, but you think I should get a pair," he said, annoyed.

"No, I didn't say that," Garcia said, nervous again. "At least, that's not what I meant. I just thought you should know about them."

"Huh."

She paused, glanced at the bracelet on her left wrist. It was flashing faintly. "Here," she said. "The lifts are working. That'll be faster." Elevator doors whisked open at their approach and Erik followed her into the car.

"Carnegie level," Garcia said in what had to be her command voice. The lift obeyed, and Erik suddenly felt slightly closer to his proper weight. He almost smiled with relief.

She looked at him. "It's only three levels up," she said. "We could use the foot-shaft, but moving up is more work than you'd think."

Erik didn't say anything, but luxuriated instead in the welcome weightiness. He wondered silently how long the ride would be, and how great a vertical distance was "three levels."

One of the most annoying things about Villanueva was how hard it had been to get a real feel for the place's basic configuration. Something about the artificial environment threw off his sense of direction, and although he was certain that the conduits and foot-shafts and enclaves were spaced according to a system, it wasn't any system he understood. Not even the animated maps had been of much help. Any that were small enough to view easily were hopelessly out of scale, and in the real world, no one seemed to apply the maps' color/number designators to the actual sectors and corridors.

According to Garcia, the conduit they had just left was part of the Trans-Carnegie run. "Here," she said. The doors opened into a short corridor that quickly gave way to a reception area under a domed ceiling. At its center, a woman with hair and dress that were the color of ingot iron sat behind a matching circular desk. Leaning closer to her than seemed appropriate, her hands flat on the spotless surface, a young Asiatic woman, short and with features that were almost boyish, spoke in tones that were low but carried well.

"Come on," she said, as Erik and Garcia glided across the thick-carpeted floor. Her words seemed to slide along the curved walls. "We could go to the Mall first, have some dinner."

The iron-haired woman shook her head. "No. I'm not interested, really."

"How do you know you're not interested?" The Asiatic

woman made a sound midway between a chuckle and a giggle. Either way, she sounded indulgent. "You ever tried it that way?"

"No, I haven't," the greeter replied. She spoke softly, too, but the same acoustics prevailed, and her firm tones carried clearly. "I'm really not interested."

"Not even curious?"

The seated woman shook her head again, but this time her features reddened slightly, and the woman standing near her laughed again. Before the conversation could go any further, however, Garcia spoke.

"Hello, Bonnie." She gestured. "This is Erik Morrison."

The receptionist was startled, but she covered it well. She nodded neatly and composed her features even as she said, "Hello, Ms. Garcia, Mr. Morrison. Welcome to Duckworth."

"We've been waiting for you, Mr. Morrison," the other woman said. She was standing at attention now and extended her right hand as she spoke. "Mr. Shadrach is eager to meet you."

Erik shook hands with her, the old-fashioned way, her palm pressed against his. "I'm looking forward to it, too," he said, keeping his voice neutral but pleasant.

At his side, Garcia started to speak. "This is E—"

"Enola Hasbro," the woman said. She cocked her head slightly. "Mr. Shadrach promised me I'd get to meet you, but I wanted to make sure." She smiled, parting flower-petal lips to show flawless and undecorated teeth.

Beside Erik, Garcia tensed slightly, and he noticed an odd expression on Bonnie's face, but he made no comment. Instead, he said, "I'm sure there are a lot of people for me to meet," he said, still using neutral tones.

Hasbro nodded. "But I wanted to be the first," she said cheerfully as she released his hand. She glanced at Bonnie. "Is the Old Man free?" she asked.

The receptionist glanced at her desk display. "He wanted me to—"

"I'll take care of it," Hasbro said. She tipped her head. "This way, Mr. Morrison, Garcia."

"Enola, really, I can—"

"This way," Hasbro repeated, ignoring Bonnie's protest. She stepped through the doorway that had suddenly opened behind the receptionist's desk.

ONLY a few minutes later, Erik was even more certain that ALC construction crews had hollowed out the Moon entirely. Hasbro, walking briskly, guided him and Garcia through labyrinthine corridors that were somewhat less distinctive than the reception area. The three of them moved beneath indirect lighting and between pastel colored walls that could have been scooped up whole from any of a hundred office buildings in Erik's experience. Featureless, drab, nondescript, the hallways ran past individual offices that were festooned with wallpaper images and furnished in the willowy, graceful style that seemed so popular here. Interspersed among them were broad common areas that were divided by partitions into semi-private work spaces, some of them decorated with still-paper images of life on Earth, a life most of the staff had left behind. The cubes faced one another across common tables.

That surprised him a bit. One thing that Villanueva had in abundance was space, and another was Mesh bandwidth. Despite that, despite the fact that there was no real reason to do so, Duckworth's work groups obviously did much of their meeting in person. At home, on Earth, the Mesh would have served the same role as conference tables seemed to here. For that matter, on Earth, he probably would have conducted this introduction via the Mesh, too.

Maybe being a quarter of a million miles from home made staff see things differently.

"Here," Hasbro said. She had slowed her pace a bit and dropped back to walk next to him, much nearer than Garcia. She had positioned herself so close that he could feel the heat of her body. That had to be deliberate, but Erik didn't make any response.

"Mr. Shadrach's office is through here," Enola said. The three of them stepped through the doorway she indicated, into a large office that had more in common with the reception area than with the more utilitarian work spaces. It had been built to impress, with gray-toned walls that were decorated with paintings rather than wallpaper. Softly lit nooks held display models of various Duckworth products, each presented like a piece of sculpture, and a triangular desk thrust up from the floor itself. Behind it was seated a tall man with ruddy features. As the three entered, the seated man rose with measured grace, the very image of a lordly host.

"Ah!" he said, stepping out from behind his desk. "Erik Morrison. Bonnie told me that you had arrived. Welcome to the land of opportunity. I'm Conrad Shadrach."

Erik extended his own hand, hooked thumbs briefly, and then released. The bluff and hearty approach wasn't one that Erik cared for. He found himself taking an instant dislike to the man, mild but genuine. He was careful not to let his distaste show; first impressions were important.

"Good to be here," he said. He gestured in Garcia's direction. "You've already met Ms. Garcia, I think."

Shadrach seemed to take no note of the other woman's presence. Instead, he looked in Hasbro's direction. "Thank you for showing Erik around," he said, his voice noticeably less warm. "I'm sure that Bonnie and I could have handled things, though."

The shorter woman smiled. "I was there," she said. "I was happy to help."

"Mmph." Shadrach made a sound that wasn't quite a word. "We can talk about it later. Don't you have an assessment cycle to review?"

Hasbro's smile widened but seemed to harden. "Nice meeting you, Mr. Morrison," she said, then turned and left.

Shadrach, still standing, watched her go. "Hasbro," he said softly, "is very hospitable. She likes to try new things." He turned to Erik, who was careful not to say anything. "Well," Shadrach repeated. "Welcome to the land of opportunity. Can I get you something to drink?"

"Nothing, thanks," Morrison said easily, but the other man had already moved toward one of the display models. An articulated miniature of the third Golden Gate Bridge, back on Earth, swung aside, to reveal a coffee service as well as a selection of gleaming bottles.

"You're a bourbon man, right?" Shadrach asked, glancing at him for confirmation. "I've got Conestega-Zonix, fifty years in the barrel, straight from Kentucky."

Erik shook his head. "Nothing for me, thanks," he said, but he filed Shadrach's words away for future reference. The other man had done some research, he realized. He paused a moment, thinking. Shadrach obviously liked to play the host, and it might make sense to let him. "Actually, new-coffee. Black."

"Excellent. It's local crop. They grow it here, in the parks." He paused. "Rather, farms—the air-recyclers. I have it roasted and ground to order."

Four guest chairs surrounded a low table supported by impossibly slender legs. Shadrach gestured, and Erik settled into one, subliminally aware that, like the bar stool in the spaceport bar, this seat simply did not feel right beneath him. Garcia followed suit, and the two of them watched as Shadrach busied himself with the coffee service. A moment later, the older man set mugs before his own seat and Erik's. The cups were plastic, but the flat gray of unfinished steel.

"This is my personal assistant," he said after a sip of his coffee. The blend was surprisingly good, a close approximation of one he remebered from Earth. He nodded at Garcia, who sat coffee-less at his left. "Juanita Garcia."

Garcia smiled gratefully in his direction and touched her earring.

"That won't work here, Ms. Garcia," Shadrach said. He seemed finally to have noticed her and gestured dismissively. "Privacy protocols."

She blushed. "Force of habit."

Shadrach nodded. "Still, I wonder if you'd give Erik and me a few minutes together, in private? To talk about old times."

Garcia shot a worried glance at Erik, but he simply nodded, then watched her exit.

Shadrach smiled faintly as the door whisked shut. "She seems very competent."

Erik took another sip of new-coffee. He considered commenting on Shadrach's manners, then decided not to. "She's being kind enough to show me around," he said. "Villanueva proper, I mean, not your spaces."

"And she's a good choice for it, too, I'm sure," Shadrach said. He gazed at Erik with eyes of a frosted blue that almost certainly was not natural. "So, Erik, tell me. What brings you to the Moon?"

A very old joke surfaced unbidden in Erik's mind. "The *Eugene Cerman*," he said. "Three hours late."

Shadrach laughed softly, the indulgent chuckle of a man who thought himself above humor. "No. Seriously. What are you doing here?"

"Are you this hospitable with everyone, Con?" Erik asked. He kept his tones casual, but the room had become noticeably more tense. "The bourbon. The coffee. You were ready for me."

Shadrach nodded but didn't say anything.

"You must have done your research," Erik continued. This was an old game, and he found its familiar nuances reassuring.

"Common courtesy," Shadrach said.

"And I don't believe we've ever met before," Erik said. "I hope you'll forgive me if we have and I've forgotten. But that raises the issue of why you wanted privacy to talk about 'old times.'"

Shadrach added more coffee to his mug and stirred it with a spoon the color of gunmetal. "You're right. We haven't met. But I was stationed in Melbourne about ten years ago, account-managing Duckworth's piece of the Mesh Pylon project. EnTek had part of the cybernetics contract there, remember?"

It was Morrison's turn to nod. The Sydney Pylon was one of ten major processing centers for the Earth Mesh. Those ten were the closest things to central repositories that the vast computer network had, and the Sydney Pylon's endo-processors had been a major EnTek initiative.

"That was a while back," he said. "And most of the contract, actually."

"You people were having cost overruns, and the Aussies were getting cranky." Shadrach smiled faintly. "They weren't the kind of cost overruns companies like."

"There was a problem with processors," Erik said. "Those were first-generation Gummis and no one knew about—"

"Three career EnTek directors lost their jobs, and another seven were demoted," Shadrach said. "That was a bad business. Not as bad as Alaska, but bad. I heard a bit about it."

"People talk."

"Yes, they do," Shadrach agreed. "So, tell me—what are you doing here?"

"Site Coordinator. But you know that," Erik said. "Is this how you receive all your visitors, Con?" For the first time, he let the irritation that had been building within him show in his voice.

Shadrach noticed. The older man settled back in his chair, and his frosted blue eyes became less intense. He smiled and become the very image of a genial host again.

"High-level turnover here is rare," he said. "And I was surprised to see someone with your kind of track record here."

"Track record?" Erik gazed levelly at him. "What does Australia have to do with anything? That was a long time ago."

What if they were talking about Alaska?

After a long moment, Shadrach nodded. "You're right," he said. He drummed his fingers gently. "And I'm not being a good host. I just remembered some stories from Earthside . . ." His words trailed off into silence.

"There was nothing special about the Pylon project," Erik said, relaxing slightly. "Management needed a fresh perspective, and I was available."

"And here?" Shadrach's gaze was frank again. "EnTek has troubles?"

Erik almost laughed. Villanueva embodied a joint effort by five companies that were largely, even necessarily, non-competitive—but when corporations got to be the size of the ALC members, they had interests in common and in conflict. It was the nature of the beast. Whatever Shadrach's concerns were, his inept probing wasn't about Alaska.

"The problem with a pyramid like EnTek—or Duckworth, I suppose—is that the higher you go, the fewer slots are open. I wanted a change, and, like you said, Villanueva is the land of opportunity," Erik lied. "And as for troubles, you can ask me that again in six months."

Not that he'd answer.

Shadrach's expression changed to a vague, generalized unease. "Well," he said. "Of course. If there's anything I can do to help you, or help you adjust, I hope you'll let me know." He glanced at a clock display. "Mmph. Ms. Garcia must be wondering what we're up to."

"I imagine she thinks we're swapping career details," Erik said, almost but not quite asking the question.

"Mine aren't very interesting," Shadrach responded. He sipped his coffee, and his patrician features flowed briefly into an expression of mild distaste. "Are you sure I can't interest you in the bourbon?"

"I'm sure."

"I went to work for Duckworth straight out of college," Shadrach continued. He set down the mug and shifted in his chair. "My father and my father's father had both worked for the company."

"Family tradition?"

Shadrach shook his head. "Not really, though I know it looks that way. Four years after I graduated, I left and moved around a bit, trying to build up my résumé. I even worked for the federales for a year, before they ran out of money. Five or six years later, I came back to Duckworth because I liked it."

"Okay. I like EnTek, and EnTek needed me here." The lie came easily, as it had so many times before. "Villanueva is a big part of the picture."

"Bigger for Duckworth, I think," Shadrach said. "Especially if Australia manages to pass an appropriation for the new space platform."

"I imagine so," Erik said. Heavy metalworks on the Moon made sense, especially for orbital projects. The low gravity did interesting things to the casting process and made larger payloads cheaper to loft. If heavy metals were harder to find on the Moon than they were on Earth, the energy to work them with was cheaper. Applied System Dynamics had a monopoly here, and a near-freedom from regulation that gave the ALC access to technologies that were effectively illegal on Earth, thanks to environmental and other regulations. Cheap fusion meant cheap energy, even on a world where water was dear.

"It's a lot to give up, though," Shadrach continued.

Erik shrugged. "It was time for a change," he said. He shifted slightly in his chair. "But tell me about your operation here," he said. "Staff, facilities. Capabilities."

Shadrach nodded. "I'll give you a quick overview," he said in a pleasant tone of voice. "There's a more detailed briefing on the Mesh for you, but the personal touch always helps."

As he said the word *touch,* Shadrach pressed one

thumb to a spot on the tabletop. Responding to his words or the gesture, or both, the tabletop darkened and a three-dimensional schematic condensed in its apparent depths. It was a version of a map that Erik had seen before.

"Villanueva," Shadrach said. He pointed. "You are here." He dragged his thumb across the table's slick surface, and the display tracked with his movements, adding detail and annotation to each sector. "Offices, residential zone, labs, foundries, studios. The ALC company spaces are mixed in with one another. Hotel—*hotels*—are here."

Erik grunted. Seeing the map now, after spending part of the day tramping with Garcia through what it showed, did a bit to make the geography more comprehensible, but the general layout still confused him.

"The layout is partly doctors' orders," Shadrach said. "Low-G makes it hard to hold on to muscle and bone mass, even with the gene patches. Good for the heart, though. About thirty years ago, the meds and the insurers worked with the city planners to change the layout and encourage physical activity."

"That means there was a lawsuit. Investors, or just personnel?"

Shadrach shrugged. "I really don't know," he said. He pointed, and more of the map displayed. "Now, here's the main foundry, just on the other side of Chrisium Port. We truck ore in from the hinterlands, smelt and work it here, convenient to the cargo launches. Hasbro would doubtless be happy to show you around there, but I advise against it. There's not much to see, unless you're interested in heavy industry. Most of our engineering work is done here."

He went on like that for the remainder of their visit, giving Erik a succinct but complete virtual tour of Villanueva.

One by one, he indicated the broad outlines of each ALC company's territories, which overlapped and tended toward the noncontiguous. It was a businessman's tour, focusing on functionality and slanted to impress, but Shadrach seemed determined to move the conversation into nonconfrontational channels. He indicated the regions belonging to the other ALC companies and gave a quick overview of their contractor spaces. When he was done, Erik felt grounded in a way that he had not before.

"Thanks," he said, meaning it. "Things make more sense now."

Shadrach nodded. He took Erik's now-empty mug and carried it, along with his own, to the refreshment nook in one corner. "You have to get out there and move around in the place some," he said over his shoulder. "It doesn't make much sense on the maps. The human-factors engineers had too much input into the design, and a lot of the empty regions are designated for future growth. It'll be more confusing when they fill."

When he came back to the table, he didn't sit, and Erik realized that the interview was over. He stood, too, and hooked thumbs with Shadrach again. The other man's grip felt a bit more sincere this time.

"Now, let's see if we can find Ms. Garcia for you," Shadrach said. "Enola probably has her."

As they moved out into the office corridors, Erik heard words drifting over a partition and into the open spaces. He caught only a few of them before the shaped acoustics of the Duckworth spaces swallowed them up.

"The cherry-jalapeño curls are imports. We don't make them here yet. That's why the unit cost is so much higher. Now, the scotch-bonnet and wintergreen—"

The familiar voice startled him enough to make him

take a misstep, and his hesitation prompted Shadrach to look at him quizzically. Erik shrugged and smiled, but didn't say anything.

He didn't see any need to renew his acquaintance with Doug Stewart.

THAT night, alone in his apartment, Erik sipped bourbon and thought, as images of the Alaskan wilderness flowed across the walls before him. Uninterested in prepackaged Zonix documentaries and dramatizations, he had found instead a stereoscopic travelogue taken by a crew in whispercopter five years before, back when it was still the Alaska he remembered. He had muted the soundtrack narrative and called up some pleasantly nonbombastic classical music from the Mesh for accompaniment. The bourbon was the real thing, imported Sony ordered up from Central for an absurd amount of money, and it filled him with a gentle warmth that was familiar, too. The water chaser tasted wrong, and sometimes when he shifted in his chair, he thought he would drift out of it, but the bourbon and the music and the movie were enough to distract him from the anomalies of his new life. Even with the whiskey in him, he could think with relative clarity.

His father had called this "unwinding." God only knew why.

It certainly hadn't been a good day, but not quite a bad one, either, all things considered. The long muscles in his legs hurt from moving in new ways, and his nose and mouth itched from breathing too-dry processed air. Garcia's whirlwind tour of Villanueva had spent too much time in the tunnels and too little in the office spaces for his tastes, but he had come to the realization that the woman knew what she was doing. She had guided him from site to site with a certain diffident efficiency and kept perfect track of to whom he was to speak and where. That was more than he could say; the names and faces had blurred together for him, lurking just below the threshold of his subconscious, waiting to be recalled. The only persons he had found specifically memorable had been the ones he hadn't liked—Conrad Shadrach, for example, and even that man had done him a very real favor.

Erik sipped his bourbon without looking at it. On the wallpaper, steel-gray waves pounded on beaches of color-less sand, and then the moving image's viewpoint moved, too, gliding in from the coastline, and above the land-scape at an apparent altitude of twenty meters or so. Five years before, the whisper-copter's track had taken it above a wildlife preserve, and now, it took Erik there, too. Below him, an Alaskan brown bear raised itself on its hind leg and waved one stubby forepaw at the intruder, either in warning or greeting.

That particular bear was almost certainly dead now, Erik knew.

"What are you doing here?" Shadrach had asked, be-fore steering the conversation into less contentious chan-nels.

Erik wanted to ask him the same thing. Shadrach was supposed to be good at what he did, but he struck Erik as lacking finesse, blunt rather than direct. His question hadn't seemed to be the good-natured probing and fence-testing of a fellow professional, but something more per-sonal. Shadrach clearly had an agenda of his own, and Erik had no idea what it could be.

Neither did Garcia, evidently. He had spent most of the day with her, even lunching at a tourist trap restaurant he hadn't liked, in a sector called the Concourse. Between bites of plastic food and cups of ghastly synthetic new-coffee, they had exchanged comments and queries about the day's progress, until he was satisfied that her read on things in general tracked with his. Then they had returned to the EnTek office suite. There, she had familiarized him with the office routine and procedures—such as they were—and discussed his calendar for the next day.

He found himself inclined to let her keep her job and perhaps even develop her for additional responsibilities.

"Messages," he said aloud, in his command voice. In the day's only development that genuinely pleased him, Personnel's systems had finally disgorged his personal settings and other files, revised them to match Lunar protocols, and loaded them into his apartment housekeeper. Filters and mirages and preferences that he had spent months refining back on Earth were in place here now, as familiar and comforting as old shoes.

"Three specific," the apartment said crisply. *"Ten status queries. Seven commercial calls."*

Those numbers were sure to rise in the days and months to come, Erik knew. "Start with the three," he said. "Sound only."

Before him, the forested mountains gave way to cloud-flecked blue streaked with the red rays of a setting sun, as the whisper-copter's images continued to unreel. Five years ago, on Earth, in Alaska, night was falling. Already, the eastern horizon was the color of slate, and Morrison could see hints of the lights cast by the cities beyond it. There had been a time when he could have seen much the same view from his home, from a real window cut in a real wall to look out on the real sky.

Villanueva, hidden beneath the surface, had no sky to speak of.

"Mr. Morrison?" The music did not die, but faded enough that he could hear the vaguely familiar voice, relayed through the housekeeper. "Mr. Morrison, my name is Enola Hasbro. We met earlier today. I don't want to seem forward, but I know that you're new in Villanueva, and I thought if you'd like some company, we could—"

"Next," Erik said. Apparently, Shadrach's underling had an agenda, too. That could wait.

"Erik. Heh. You're on the Mesh after all," Doug Stewart said easily. The recorded voice sounded serenely self-confident. "I thought I saw you earlier, at Duckworth, right?" He paused, as if waiting for a response, but then moved on.

Erik splashed more bourbon into his glass, watching the liquid from the corner of one eye. He sipped, first the whiskey, then the water and then the whiskey again. The gentle warmth inside him grew warmer, and he considered the option of just paging forward to the next call.

"Hey, I don't want to seem pushy or anything," Stewart's message continued, in an unnerving echo of Hasbro's. "But if you're not busy, and if you'd like some company, I can give you the two-credit tour." Another pause followed; either Stewart was uncomfortable leaving messages, or he had thought that Erik was auditing his calls. "Let me know; we could go to the Mall," Stewart concluded awkwardly, then broke the connection.

"You captured his codes," Morrison said in his command voice, his words almost, but not quite, a question. He couldn't imagine any reason for Stewart to mask the call.

"*Yes,*" his apartment responded.

"Low priority, but find out what you can from them," Erik said. Stewart had become a bit too familiar a presence to please him. "Run a search. Find me a public profile or something, and see if you can go any further." The problem with public profiles was they tended toward the inflated. EnTek resources could dig deeper, but he wasn't sure that the effort would be justified. He continued. "Next."

"Ralph Tanaka's office, calling for Mr. Morrison."

At first, Erik thought that the intonations were his housekeeper's own. Then he realized that the caller was another synthesized voice, similar in make and maybe even model, but not personalized even to the minimal extent of his own system. The name it spoke was familiar, but only slightly; it took him a moment to realize where he had heard it before.

Another voice continued the message. "Mr. Morrison, I asked my office to alert me when your codes became available," a man's voice said. "I'm Ralph Tanaka at Project Halo. I'd like to be one of the first to welcome you to the Moon. We've scheduled a reception and tour for Monday. Naturally, if that's inconvenient, we can—"

"Gauche," Erik said softly. It wasn't a word he used often, but it wasn't often that he encountered someone déclassé enough to use a robot receptionist to place calls like this. That's what people like Garcia were for. More loudly, in his command voice, he interrupted. "Send my apologies," he told his apartment. "And don't forward any more calls from that system, unless they're placed by a person."

A finger's width of bourbon remained in his glass. He swallowed it and looked thoughtfully at the squat, familiar bottle that sat on the small table next to him. The dark liquid tempted, but he'd had enough.

"Son," his father had said more than once. "There's a difference between unwinding and getting unwound."

Whatever that meant. Morrison shrugged and poured himself another small drink.

"Receiving," the housekeeper announced.

"Audit," Erik ordered.

A new voice continued. "Hello, Erik. Out and about? I had hoped to catch you at home."

Erik paused briefly in his breathing as the words hung in the air.

"Who is that?" he demanded of the housekeeper, even though he already knew the answer.

"Personal calling codes masked," his apartment replied. *"Placed from New Sacramento."*

Erik nodded, his guess confirmed. The familiar voice was very slightly less than he remembered it, abraded and eroded by its long passage from Earth to the Moon and through the countless connections of the two major Mesh systems. More, it had the tinny echo of a signal with multiple layers of privacy cloaking that could be peeled away only by systems with matching key codes, codes such as those in Erik's personal preferences.

The Home Office was calling.

"This is a Priority One call," his housekeeper announced.

Erik set his drink down, very carefully. He was far from drunk, but he would need to be even further before he even considered taking the call. Speaking to Janos Horvath demanded his complete attention and absolute focus.

Why the hell was the Home Office calling? More specifically, why was it Horvath who was on the line from Earth? He glanced at a clock display. It was well past midnight in New Sacramento, and that meant Horvath had planned his call to match Erik's schedule and not his own. In Erik's experience, that simply did not happen, not with people like Janos Horvath. Men like Horvath had their calls placed for them, and they had them placed according to their own schedules.

"Decline the priority," Erik ordered. He watched salmon splash and struggle as they swam against the current of the river on his apartment wall. He thought about his last exchange with Horvath, about slightly curled lips and veiled threats, followed by the cool contempt of absolute dismissal. "I'm not home to take the call."

Another pause followed. Back on Earth, Janos Horvath was waiting long enough to realize that he wasn't going to get a real-time response, and as the radio waves that passed between the Earth and the Moon brought his words back to Erik's apartment.

"I'll try again tomorrow," the man who arguably *was* the Home Office finally said. "Twenty-one and thirty, your time. I'd appreciate your making yourself available." His tone sounded light, even pleasant, but Erik knew that the words were an order.

Horvath wanted something from him, and Erik had to wonder what.

CHAPTER 5

"THIS doesn't make any sense," Erik said sourly, scowling at the wall of his office and the computer-rendered diagram that hung suspended before his simulated Moonscape. Déjà vu swept through him; the chart was almost as confusing as the maps of Villanueva. It was fairly elaborate, a maze of glowing cells linked by equally glowing lines in a dozen different hues. It mirrored the one displayed on his personal computer, which he had unfurled on his desktop, but was easier to focus on and offered greater detail.

Erik had always preferred looking at the big picture and at how he fit into it. In this particular case, he fit in near the top, but many of the lines radiating from his cell were colored to indicate coordination, rather than full authority.

He thumbed one square on the desktop display, and

the equivalent one on the wall glowed in response. He pressed harder, and the glowing cell opened, revealing a standard-format employee ID image and a dozen lines of associated text and numbers. He asked, "Who is this guy?"

Not all of Erik's new office furniture had arrived, but the guest chairs had. Juanita Garcia had neatly composed herself on one of them. "Chuck Kurilla," she said, looking at the pudgy, vaguely unlikable looking little man peering out at her from the wall. "I don't think I know him."

"Who does he answer to?" Erik demanded. Kurilla's box was one of a series arrayed along the chart's left perimeter, linked to none of the others.

"He's an independent contractor," she said, as if her words explained everything. Her computer sat folded on the front of Erik's desk, and she reached for it. "I can get his files if you want me to."

Erik shook his head. It had been a frustrating morning and promised to get worse. No one seemed very interested in giving a real answer to any of his questions. "I don't care who this Kurilla is," he said. "I want to know who he answers to."

Garcia unfurled her computer. She had configured herself again as a blonde today, and her silvered nails flashed as she worked the display. After a moment, she looked up. "Right now, he's working for Dynamo," she said. "I could find out who his line supervisor there is, if you want."

"No," Erik said. "No, I don't want you to do that. What I want you to do is tell me why he's on my org chart if he works for Dynamo."

The morning was already delivering on its promise.

"Oh. He's a contractor. When he works for us, he works for you, or at least for your office," Garcia said. She smiled tentatively, and Erik noticed that she had evidently left her picto-tooth at home today. "He's an 'available asset,' except he's not available right now. Unless he finds something we might want, and Dynamo doesn't."

Erik looked at her. "I understand how contracting works," he said. "Or how it usually works."

"He's a prospector," Garcia said, as if that explained everything.

Erik looked at her some more.

"He's a contractor," she repeated. She ran her thumb down her computer's surface, making the perimeter series flash in response. "All the prospectors are contractors. These, too." Her fingers flew again, and more cells flared briefly on the chart. These were connected to the system, linked by pale umbilici of varying hues. "These are working for us right now. Kurilla isn't. He's working for Dynamo."

Erik took a deep breath and tried to settle back in his chair, but couldn't. The cushions wouldn't yield properly, and he felt like he was floating an inch or so above the furniture's frame. "We don't have exclusive contracts with our support suppliers? Or at least priority contracts?" he said. The idea was astounding.

Garcia shook her head. "We don't need a full-time prospecting team," she said. "Duckworth does, for metals and such. Dynamo is always looking for ice deposits, but the only raw materials we need are a few rare-earth minerals and some light-metal salts, for the systems breeders. Mr. Caspian released the last of our exclusive drivers nearly a year ago and put the ones on the chart on retainer."

This time, it was Erik who shook his head, but he tried not to let the extent of his consternation show. There were ways to save money, but depriving the company completely of dedicated suppliers wasn't one of them.

Besides, from what he'd seen and heard, cost-cutting wasn't a priority in Villanueva. If anything, cheap energy had made management sloppy and indulgent. He was concerned a bit about the ultimate impact of such sloppiness on the overall brand values.

"So we use our competitors' field assets," he said softly.

Garcia looked at him with an expression that suggested he had said something impolite. "They're contractors," she said yet again. "Freelance."

"Who look first to our competitors for work, because our competitors are their biggest customers," Erik continued implacably.

"They're not our competitors," Garcia said. She was looking nervous and insecure again. "They're not."

Erik drummed his fingers softly, gazing at the wall display, trying to frame his next words. What he wanted to explain to Garcia was so basic to his way of thinking that he had a hard time believing she did not know it already.

"We don't do metalworking," the woman continued doggedly, feeling the need to fill the silence. "We don't build power plants. The raw materials we need aren't the raw materials they need. We're not competitors. That's why the ALC works."

"Alright." Erik nodded. "You've explained that." He turned to gaze at her. "Now, let me explain something." To his surprise, the words came to his lips easily, and some corner of his mind realized that they were the same words his father used years before. "The business of business is competition. All businesses are competitors."

"But we don't make—"

Erik shook his head and once again allowed irritation to enter his voice. "All businesses are competitors," he repeated. "Maybe not in obvious ways, but they compete.

All five ALC companies are partners, but they're all competitors, too. Caspian has to have known that."

"Mr. Caspian—"

"We compete because we're all after the same credit, the same money," Erik continued. His words fell into an easy rhythm now, as he recalled and tailored verbiage he had delivered many times in various briefings in countless contexts. "We compete for suppliers and customers, even when we provide products and services that seem completely noncompetitive on the surface."

Garcia looked at him, obviously confused. He tried to think of a way to explain, and then his earlier conversation with Conrad Shadrach came back to him.

"Did you know that Duckworth has its own artificial intelligence and data processing division? They own a controlling interest in Cybrotics," he said, and nodded for emphasis. Cybrotics was EnTek's biggest rival in the company's main business area. "We competed directly with them for the contract on the Sydney Pylon. Duckworth had the lead on construction and pled that they needed the AI account, too, to ensure systems integrity. They got part of it."

"But Cybrotics doesn't have a facility here," Garcia said.

"They don't," Erik agreed. "That's part of the charter. But now we're obligated to use their parent company's prospecting and supply assets. Theirs, and Dynamo's. Do you think they don't realize that?"

"All of the partners do," Garcia said.

That surprised him. "All of them?" he asked.

Garcia's fingers traced something on her computer again, and more cells joined the perimeter list. "Most of the prospector workforce have preferred-provider contracts with Duckworth and Dynamo now," she said. "But they all hire out to all five companies. I think to Halo, too, but they don't have as much to spend."

"Zonix and Biome?"

"Biome uses rare-earths, too," Garcia said.

"More competition," Erik noted. The rare-earth elements were essential for the nutrient baths that, in turn, were essential to growing the semi-organic Gummis. For that matter, so was water, which made the Moon's scarce water deposits a strategic supply for EnTek as well as for Dynamo.

"Among other things," Garcia continued. "DIS runs tours and does some producing on the surface. They use the prospectors as drivers and tour guides—some of them—and as location scouts. Most of the companies still have some exclusive contracts with certain drivers, of course, but—"

"But Caspian changed that, too," Erik said.

Garcia nodded.

"Have you talked with him since he left?"

Now it was Garcia's turn to sound sour. "He's not talking to anyone," she said. "People are still surprised."

Erik could believe that, and the distaste in her voice made sense to him, at least vaguely. Garcia seemed naive about some aspects of business, but obviously felt the company loyalty typical of someone at her level.

"I can understand that," Morrison said. He paused. "Maybe I should get in touch with him."

Garcia didn't say anything, but made a notation on her computer.

"Who conducted his exit interview?" Morrison asked.

"I don't think there was one," Garcia said. "If there was, it wasn't with anyone local. He spent hours on-line with Mr. Horvath just before lunch, and after lunch, he didn't work here anymore."

Erik thought about that for a moment, then nodded. "You've got a project," he said, and paused while Garcia tugged her earring. "Research the prospector workforce," he continued. "Use whatever resources you have to, within reason, but don't be too obvious about it. Find out who has the highest performance ratings, who's had the best strikes, who is under exclusive contract, and who isn't. Find out who we want and who we can get."

Garcia nodded.

"Flag the ones who have worked for us before and pull their records," Erik continued. "Double-flag the ones who went to Duckworth, for that matter." He paused and looked again at the wall display. "Talk to Production, but be discreet with them, too. Find out what we've been buying from field providers and how much. Get me a summary report by Monday, and we'll talk to Personnel about recruitment."

"I can do that," Garcia said, turning off her earring. "But Monday is the reception at Halo—"

"I'm not worried about Halo," Erik said. He thumbed his computer. It went blank, and the larger wall display reverted to the Moonscape. "Now. What about the production issues?"

Garcia's silvered fingers did their dance again, and tables of figures appeared on Erik's computers. Too many of the numbers were in red.

"We've missed seven major shipments," Morrison said. The delays weren't huge, but they were significant. More sloppiness. "Who's at fault?"

Garcia shrugged. "I don't know," she said carefully. "I don't work Production."

"Guess, then. Or tell me anything you've heard," Erik said. He spoke in the matter-of-fact tones of a man accustomed to giving commands.

"There are rumors," she said. "Production uses the same data-processing resources as everyone else. The brainware has burped a lot lately, and there've been datastorms—"

"Who built the underlying systems?" Erik asked. He knew what answer to expect, but wanted to hear it from her.

"We did. We grow the Gummis in-house. Ninety-three percent of the Lunar Mesh is our work. The rest is imports and proprietary modules from the other patrons."

That was a much higher percentage than EnTek could boast providing to the Earth Mesh, but the Earth Mesh had been a collaborative effort. Erik considered the percentages and studied the numbers on his display. He thought about Garcia's tardiness in meeting him at Chrisium Port and about Personnel's delay in configuring his apartment settings.

"There's been a substantial increase in message traffic lately," Garcia continued, still nervous but determined. "Tourist traffic is up and so is DIS content throughput. The system here is much younger than the one on Earth—"

Were the datastorms because of the increased info traffic, or were they because the systems weren't performing properly? Eric wondered.

"Are other companies having the same problems?"

She nodded. "All of them. It's in the Mesh," she said. "Everything else hangs off of that."

"Not a very strong endorsement of the quality of our work, is it?" Erik mused. He scanned the figures with a practiced eye, but they tracked well with Garcia's comments. Missed shipments, missed deadlines, system failures had all hit EnTek in roughly equivalent percentages that weren't spectacular but were significant. He wondered when the trend had started.

"Do you have Caspian's current addresses?" he asked. Most people got new ones when they changed employers, even men at Caspian's—Erik's—level.

"No," Garcia said. She did something on her computer. "And they aren't in the public directories, either. I suppose Heck would know how to get in touch with him."

Erik looked at her blankly.

"Heck. Hector Kowalski," Garcia said. "He's security chief."

Erik remembered the name. Kowalski had been the nonattendee at his introductory meeting. He nodded, then continued in his command voice. "Get Kowalski on the line for me," he said.

"Mr. Kowlaski is in, but declining all calls," his office responded.

"But he's on-site?"

"Yes."

Erik glanced at Garcia. "You know where his office is, right?" he asked, and when she nodded, he stood. "Good. We'll do this the Moon way," he said.

ERIK knocked on the closed door.

Erik kept knocking on the closed door.

He knocked with bare knuckles on plastic-clad steel, and he knocked with metronome-like regularity and persistence. He did not pound on the door but he knocked hard enough to be heard on the other side, despite any reasonable level of soundproofing or masking noise.

"He's here," Garcia said, at his side. "I checked his calendar."

On the door frame, a red light glowed, *Privacy*. Erik ignored it and kept knocking. He found the physical exertion, however slight, somewhat invigorating, and it was good to have found a problem he could best address by hitting something.

The privacy light flashed. Erik ignored it some more.

Still knocking, he turned to Garcia. Several days' frustration and irritation barely showed in his voice as he said, "Find a maintenance crew. I want this door opened."

"But—"

"Now," Erik said, still knocking.

As if it had heard his words, the door whisked open. Garcia in tow, Morrison glided through it, scarcely pausing as he lowered his hand and extended it.

"I'm Erik Morrison," he said to the slender man behind the cluttered desk.

"I know who you are," the man said. He was sitting at right angles to the entrance and didn't rise to take the offered hand, but he nodded his head in Erik's general direction. "Take a seat," he said. "I'll be with you."

On the wall he was facing, two warriors battled against a mountainous backdrop. One, dressed like a monstrous clown, bore an antique machine gun. Instead of bullets, however, the weapon fired laser bolts, even as, against all reason, it discharged glistening brass cartridge casings. The other combatant was an older man, clothed entirely in white. Undercutting his general grandfatherly aspect was the mirrored helm, shaped like the cartoon silhouette of a human skull. As he used the shield to parry the clown's laser, the second gladiator stabbed at his adversary with a tri-bladed sword. Muted noises of warfare sounded in the tiny office.

The man who had to be Hector Kowalaski watched the

images battle, rapt. Borscht pops and taco shells, the remnants of a fast-food meal, sat on the desk before him. Without looking, he scooped up some Snackles with his right hand and put them in his mouth. As he chewed, the clown-warrior got a shot past his rival's shield. Kowalski made a sound of dismay louder than that of either animated adversary.

Erik, still standing, said, "I want to talk to Rogers Caspian. You can help me with that, I think."

"He doesn't work for us anymore," Kowalski said. He gestured with his left hand, the one not holding the food, and the shield of the man in white came up quickly. He gestured again, and the shield swung back down, neatly slicing through the clown's striped jersey and into his stomach. The creature howled and clutched itself, but kept firing its unlikely weapon.

"Turn that off," Erik said, speaking to Kowalski in the same tones he would have used to command his apartment.

"I don't work for you," Kowalski said. He seemed unimpressed. "And I'm on my lunch break." He gestured again. The control ring he wore on his left hand glinted under light from the ceiling fixture. Responding to his movement, the warrior surged forward, driving the pointed jaw of its skull-shield into a dragon's belly.

"We both work for Janos Horvath," Erik said. "And we're supposed to work together."

The injured clown wailed from his place on the wall, but Kowalski said nothing.

"I'm expecting a call from him this evening," Erik continued, careful to speak only the precise truth. Invoking Horvath's name was not something one did lightly, but Erik managed to make his words sound serenely confident.

Kowalski's left hand and the wall-warriors froze. As he turned in his chair to face his guests directly, he stripped off the control ring and set it aside. "That's interesting," he said. "You got one from him last night, too. I was under the impression you weren't in his good graces these days."

Erik didn't say anything. That Kowalski knew about the call didn't surprise him, but it was safe to assume that the security officer hadn't heard its cloaked content. Tracking private call traffic was one thing; auditing its content was another.

Kowalski extended his hand. "Hector Kowalski," he said. "I'm pleased to meet you at last, Mr. Morrison." He sounded almost like he meant it.

"You could have done that before," Erik said. He hooked thumbs with Kowalski just long enough to be polite.

"The all-hands? I was off-site," Kowalski said. "I work very long hours, Mr. Morrison, and the nature of my work keeps me very busy."

Erik glanced at the still-frozen combatants. "So I see," he said.

"I'm on my lunch break," Kowalski repeated, but this time, he said the words in a more conciliatory tone. "I sent my apologies, and you can have them again now, if you'd like. And it's Heck."

Erik nodded in acceptance. "Heck, then. I'd like to get in touch with Rogers Caspian."

"He's not in any of the public directories anymore. EnTek cancelled his entries when he made his move, but I've got his new addresses and codes. Mind if I ask why you're looking for him?"

"Professional courtesy," Erik said. "And I have some questions about how he did things."

Kowalski nearly laughed. "Do you want me to set up things, or will you do it yourself?" he asked.

"I thought I would call," Erik said. He glanced at Garcia and then back at Kowalski, and thought for a moment. Despite his initial misgivings, the recent barrage of in-person interviews and conferences had been more effective than he would have expected. Certainly, it had worked with Kowalski. "Unless you think it should be in person."

"He'll listen harder that way," Kowalski said. "But he might not want to talk to you. There are still a lot of bent feelings."

"On *his* side?" Garcia asked, tartly.

Kowalski glanced at her and laughed softly. "Good point," he said. He looked back at Erik. "You'll like working with Juanita," he said. "She's very loyal. Not like Caspian."

Garcia blushed. She had settled into one of the guest chairs Erik had declined and was watching them both.

"Some folks at Duckworth owe me some favors," Kowalski said. "And word is that you're pretty much an unknown quantity to them. It might be better if I opened the door."

Erik decided to trust him, and he nodded again. "I'd appreciate that, Heck," he said affably. "I'd rather work with you."

"I can understand that," Kowalski said, grinning. For the first time, he seemed completely sincere. Security officers were a breed apart. They had easy access to information and insights above their station, and if there were bodies, Security almost always knew where they were buried. Kowalski would make a better ally than adversary, and he obviously knew it.

Erik wondered how much the slender man knew about

what had happened in Alaska, and then decided that he would never be sure.

Kowalski continued. "I don't mind telling you, Mr. Morrison—"

"Erik."

"I don't mind telling you, you're not quite what I had expected," Kowalski said. "I didn't really know what to expect, actually. But what Earthside gave me on you makes me surprised that you're using Horvath's name so casually."

This time, Erik nearly laughed. "Janos might be surprised, too," he said. "He knows I like to do things myself."

CHAPTER 6

WENDY Scheer took a mild, if inconsistent, pride in being a woman of modest but excellent tastes. Her office in Armstrong was small even by the federal base's standards, little more than a cubby tucked between structural members, lined and wired to the base intra-Mesh. She really didn't need much more; the unusual nature of her job at Project Halo meant that she didn't spend a lot of time there.

Within that space, however, she had made her own, neatly realized world. The walls bore a few well-chosen paintings—real paintings—and little else, except for the gray expanse of communications wallpaper. A low shelf along one wall held a half-dozen old-books and, less obviously, a triple-reinforced safe keyed to open at her touch alone. The office door was opaque, and although others used transparent panels to create the illusion of openness, she did not.

Privacy was a luxury made necessary by the nature of Wendy's work and by the nature of Wendy herself. To leave the door open was to invite an unending stream of visitors, drawn by her mere presence.

Her work surface was a neatly formed curve of cast plastic, projecting from one wall. Placing chairs one way made the counter a desktop, a reminder of formality and process and authority. Placing them in another configuration made the same curve less of a divider than a common work surface, evoking hospitality and collaboration rather than power. Just now, she was sharing that space with Ralph Tanaka, the titular head of Armstrong and the project it hosted, and a dozen relayed images on her wallpaper.

She liked Ralph. He was intelligent and dedicated, and he knew how to let her do her job. He had provided her with the bad news about his call to Morrison and then remained, as the others Meshed in.

"I may have pressed him too hard," said one of them, Conrad Shadrach. He looked rueful and embarrassed.

Wendy drew a deep breath but didn't say anything, or look anywhere but at the screens. The feed from her office was miraged. Instead of seeing her and Tanaka, seated in Halo's Security Office, the others could see only Valerie Harrada, lowly Duckworth selenologist, taking their calls from even more utilitarian surroundings. Even with the mirage in place, however, she was confident that the older man could see and read the irritation on her features.

He could. "I—I'm sorry," he said. The vaguely paternal mien he generally cultivated fell away and left something less impressive in its place. "I'd heard from other sources, in the old days, that Morrison was a cagey number, but that he sometimes responded to a direct approach."

Wendy scowled, and the conferenced images reflected her dismay, if not her anger. The Mesh connection—the very nature of remote conferencing—meant that they would be less immediately sensitive to her moods. She had encountered all of them recently in person, however, and spent enough time with them that the memory now lingered.

Tanaka wasn't as fortunate, Wendy realized abruptly. Seated across from her, he looked positively woebegone at her distress. She took mercy and favored him with a quick, hidden smile, but she said nothing, to avoid confusing the mirage brainware. As Tanaka relaxed, she returned her attention to the conference.

"I thought I told you all to be careful with this situation," she said with measured calm.

A dozen televised heads nodded in near-unison.

"I wanted to find out why he was here," Shadrach continued. "It's not like I wouldn't have asked anyway. Caspian made his move pretty abruptly, after all."

"What *about* Caspian?" Wendy asked.

Shadrach shrugged. "I haven't been able to speak with him. Either they're grooming him for something special, or he's being paid well for what he knows."

"My guess is, he doesn't know anything," LaCombe said, his nasal twang a stark contrast to Shadrach's lordly tones.

"Then he gave up an awful lot to be ignorant for a new employer," Wendy said dryly. Rogers Caspian had been a career EnTek manager who had fought hard for the job Erik Morrison now held. She had considered recruiting him more than once, but her coverage of EnTek operations had been sufficient, so that there was no need—until his known association with Ramirez had increased his potential value. It was only too bad that his sudden career change had made him unavailable at about the same time.

The two developments had to be connected.

"If he knew something—if he even knew where to find Ramirez—Duckworth would have made a move by now," LaCombe continued. "We're seeing lots of small-scale activity but no major initiatives. I don't know exactly what it is that this Ramirez has that we want so badly—"

"You don't need to know, Ralph," Wendy said. The other man's ongoing persistence continued to surprise her. She had taken very careful and deliberate steps to control the flow of information as thoroughly as she could, and strongly discouraged general curiosity. For most of the others, it was enough to know that she wanted Ramiriez found, but not for LaCombe.

For whatever reason, he obviously wanted to know *why,* too.

Wendy sighed softly. That was the real issue. It wasn't enough to find Ramirez; she had to find him before the secret of what he had found became common knowledge.

"—and maybe Caspian doesn't know, either," LaCombe said. "Maybe if he does, he's not telling. And if he is, they just aren't acting on it."

"He could be dead," Lucille Cunnard said. She delivered the words in a calm tone of voice. She seemed loathe to surrender the hypothesis.

Wendy shook her head. Reddish curls shook in unison, but she knew that the others saw Valerie Harrada's waterfall locks ripple and flow instead. She had styled her hair since the last meeting, but the mirage brainware remembered the previous coif and displayed it instead. "I'd prefer to assume that's not the case, Lucy," she said.

"Maybe he's gone home," Cunnard said. "Back to Earth. That's the official story, isn't it?"

The woman from EnTek nodded in confirmation.

"Alive or dead, he's still on the Moon," Wendy said, with absolute certainty. The five companies of the ALC held near-absolute sway in Villanueva, but travelers still had to go through Earthside Customs, and her sources had assured her that Ramirez had not. "He's here," Wendy said, "for us to find."

The rest of the meeting was largely pro forma. One by one, the participants gave their reports and those who had met him gave their impressions of Erik Morrison. Little had changed in the week since the session at Villanueva. Questions were asked, and answers were given, none of them surprising. If anything, the situation seemed to have approached a sort of dynamic equilibrium, like water at a simmer, just short of a boil. Wendy had anticipated that Morrison's advent would make the bubbles a bit larger, but when she broke the connections, she felt no better off than before.

"No one seems to know anything," Ralph Tanaka said. "I thought we had better coverage than this."

"Our coverage is fine," Wendy said. Usually, she cultivated an air of good cheer, if only out of consideration for others, and reserved open displeasure to use in manipulation. Now, however, she felt genuinely glum and did not try to hide it. "The network does its job. But this isn't why I—why *we* built it, Ralph."

"No. We did that to find out about respirant production," Ralph said. It had proven very useful to have an insider's view on activities within Villanueva. The commercial colony's larger population and well-developed infrastructure made it a dominant factor in Halo's day-to-day operations.

They were both silent for a long minute.

"This is my fault," Tanaka said ultimately. "I thought he was just a crank."

Wendy almost laughed. Moving with liquid grace, she opened the safe and drew out two items. She slid the first, a secure data module, into the equally secure port hard-wired into her desktop. An image coalesced on the wall-paper.

It was the face of Keith Ramirez, a face that Wendy's people had identified with some difficulty and only after stripping away a dozen layers of mirage encoding. It wasn't a particularly impressive face. But he had good eyes; dark and aware, they peered out from beneath heavy eyebrows.

"Everything you ever wanted," the image of Ramirez said. "Everything you're here to find." He spoke in clipped phrases and shaped his words with some care.

Wendy lifted the other item she had taken from the safe. It was a metal utility box. As with the safe, pressing her fingertips to the catch opened the small padded case; as with the safe, she knew that the action had been noted and logged by the box's inboard Gummi, even as the lid swung up and open. Inside, held by padded blocks, was an irregular piece of scrap metal, a piece of framing torn away from some larger whole. Dull and unburnished, it was a remarkably prosaic-looking prize.

"How was I supposed to know what it meant?" Ralph asked. He shrugged, clearly embarrassed. "When the package arrived—"

"If you're interested," the recorded Keith Ramirez continued, "tell me when I call on—"

"Pause," Wendy said, in her command voice, and the playback froze.

Tanaka lifted the chunk of metal and hefted it. "It didn't feel like anything special. It still doesn't."

Despite his words, he spoke reverently, and his eyes seemed to light as he stared at the find.

"You're being too hard on yourself, Ralph," Wendy said.

Ralph inverted the bit of debris. The underside had a brighter finish and showed the marks of machining. Two widely separated drill-holes showed where Armstrong's researchers had bored out samples for analysis.

"How was I supposed to know?" he repeated.

Wendy rested the tips of her fingers on the back of his free hand. "No one could have known. No one would have believed it. At least you had the tests done."

"They took too long," he said. "Someone else moved faster."

"Someone always does," Wendy said. That was why she had worked so hard to create her network of informants within the ALC companies. Armstrong limped along from appropriation to appropriation, but Villanueva was awash in cash. It had been her idea to use industrial espionage as a cover for tapping into that wealth and to access the five companies' impressive data-gathering capabilities.

She reached for the piece of metal, but Tanaka paused before surrendering it to her.

"This is the last I'll get to see it, right?" he asked.

Wendy nodded. "Probably." She tucked the metal back into its box. "I'm sorry. We still haven't found Ramirez, and now that Morrison's here—"

"Why are you so concerned about him?" Tanaka asked.

"Not him specifically," Wendy said. "I'm concerned

about the increase of interest in general, and I'm concerned about EnTek in particular." She smiled slightly. "I know a bit about Janos Horvath. Word from Earth is that he sent Morrison here personally."

Removing the data module from its desktop recess, she placed both items back in the still-open safe, then swung the metal panel shut. Molecular seals engaged with an electric sigh, as the secure cabinet became one contiguous piece of metal.

She looked around her office, at the space she had configured so carefully to meet her specific needs while seeming neither utilitarian nor luxurious. It suited her perfectly.

She was going to miss it, and she was going to miss having a door that she could keep closed most of the day.

"I'm going to have to take personal charge, Ralph," she said. "Things are heating up, and, for whatever reason, Morrison is dodging you."

The director of Armstrong Base, the man whose image and signature graced the site's official documents and publications, the face of the federal government on the Moon, nodded. "I like living on the Moon, you know. I worked hard to get here. I could probably secure a position at Duckworth. Or DIS, maybe. I could help out that way."

Wendy smiled sadly. "Your face is too public. And no one's going to be eager to hire a Fed, anyway. Especially not now. The assets I have will have to be enough."

"Fine." Tanaka said it without rancor or reservation. "You'll have my resignation in the morning."

DINNER was pleasant enough, if more enjoyable in the preparation than in the eating. The new stove had arrived from Central, and so had his groceries, so Erik was able to prepare the meal himself. As always, he found the process satisfying.

He liked doing things with his hands. He liked cutting the lean pork loin and the Granny Smith apples into thin slices. They yielded beneath his knives with familiar ease, and he could tell from the texture that the meat would be tender, once cooked. Flavor was another matter, and less certain; the pork was imported. Bought at a price that, on Earth, would have been ruinous, it had to be dear even by local standards. God only knew how long it had languished in Central's freezer.

The apples, however, were local growth, from the parks, and had a crispness that he found both reassuring and irresistible. He peeled and cored and segmented three of them, but only two lasted long enough to join the sliced pork on its bed of sauerkraut in the ceramic roaster.

While the meat cooked, he chopped vegetables for a salad, again taking pleasure in the familiar activity. The lettuce, radishes, and carrots were local growth, too, and chunks of another apple complemented them well. He tossed the salad with a light dressing, garnished it with walnuts. When he finally sat down to a meal of good food in modest portions, he could almost convince himself he was at home again.

Not for the first time, he wondered how anyone could eat the trash Doug Stewart sold.

Later, after eating, he decided to try the apartment's auto-gym again. It had a treadmill function and came with smartshoes, so that, once more, he could almost convince himself he was back home. The resistance was right, and he could move his feet in a real step, instead of the Moon's insipid shuffle. Soon, he had built up a fair head of speed and could feel the familiar burn deep in his muscles.

That was essential. Even with the patchwork that Biome had done to his genes, even with the Garcia-directed regiment of a walking commute, his body was losing muscle mass to Luna's reduced gravity. And if his muscles were shrinking, his bones had to be, too, as calcium and other minerals leached into his bloodstream. There was evidence that exercise could slow both processes.

For the second time that night, he thought of Doug Stewart. "You're a quarter-million miles from home, and you haven't gotten used to the idea yet," the junk food salesman had said. "You never will. Or your body won't."

Erik ran some more, until sweat covered him and he gulped air in deep, rhythmic breaths. He had abstained from wine with his dinner, so there was nothing to mask the gentle, satisfying euphoria that swept through him. He liked having real challenges and real problems to solve, but there was no denying the simple pleasures of good food and physical activity, or the tranquility that solitude could bring.

"What are you doing here?" Shadrach had asked him that, and Erik had offered only a fabricated excuse. Now, as he waited for Janos Horvath's call, he realized that he hadn't had any real answer to give.

He suspected that was about to change.

AT twenty-one and thirty precisely, the apartment announced, *"Receiving. Priority One call. Point of origin—"*

"Accept it," Erik said, then: "Hello, Janos."

"Erik, you're looking well," the man from the Home Office said, even as his tranquil image formed on the wallpaper. "I'm pleased I could find you in."

Erik smiled, as sincerely as he could manage. "I'm sorry I couldn't take your call last night," he said. He waited as his message made the seconds-long trip back to Earth, and as Janos's response made the return trip.

"Quite all right. I understand you've been busy, making yourself at home."

"Just getting my Moon legs, Janos."

Horvath smiled faintly, probably with as much sincerity as Erik felt. His name was ethnic Hungarian, but because of his parents' remarkably complicated marriage. Horvath himself was pure-blooded ethnic Korean, an incongruity that Erik found amusing, though far from unique. Horvath himself apparently liked the discontinuity, however, and in recent years had taken to dressing himself in a slightly anachronistic manner that evoked an outdated ethnic stereotype. He wore a black business suit, severely tailored, white shirt and black tie, and his hair was short and slicked down with styling gel. The final affectation was the most striking—he wore external lenses, set in heavy frames that hooked behind his ears.

Not for the first time, Erik wondered about the glasses. There had to be more to them than a cosmetic vanity. Those frames for example, were thick enough to hold a fair amount of processing hardware . . .

"I try to make the best of every situation, Janos," he said. He smiled again, confident that Horvath could catch every nuance of the expression. He hadn't bothered with a mirage for this call.

Horvath smiled, too. "You're known for that," he said. He spoke with a distinctive Midwestern drawl, another legacy of his many parents.

"What can I do for you, Janos?" Erik asked. He had

already tired of the niceties, but knew better that to let that show. "It's after midnight where you are; I don't want to keep you up."

This time, Horvath actually laughed, for perhaps the first time in Erik's experience. The polite chuckle echoed oddly after multiple layers of masking had been peeled away. "Tell me something, Erik," he said. "Why do you think we sent you to the Moon?"

Erik had been holding a glass when the call commenced. He sipped from it before responding, scarcely noticing the mineral water's portentous surface bulge. "There was a job that needed doing. I was qualified and available." Tactfully, he forwent citing the many strings he and his various corporate allies had pulled to prevent his forced early retirement, or, worse, outright termination. "It was a good time for a change."

"Yes," Horvath said, tranquil and low-key again. He said the word that was never far from Erik's mind. *"Alaska."*

Erik said it, too, and nodded. "Alaska."

"A bad business."

"I think we're in agreement on that," Erik said. Certainly, they had agreed on it loudly and at great length during many spirited conferences in the past few months.

"Not as bad as we thought, however," Janos said pleasantly. "Indeed, in some ways, it's proven to be an opportunity."

Erik had nothing to say to that. Alaska wasn't something that he could think about with much hope.

"I spoke today with Heck Kowalski," Horvath continued. The silly name sounded even sillier when spoken in his measured tones. "He likes you, I think. Or at least, is impressed by you."

Erik thought about saying the feeling was mutual, but decided not to lie. "He seems to know what he's doing," he said instead.

"I'd like you to provide him some backing, Erik," Horvath said. "He has a full menu, and anything you can do to facilitate his efforts would be appreciated."

"I doubt that's why you called last night," Erik said.

Horvath shook his head. "Not precisely." He paused. "I know that you view your reassignment as a last chance and a dead end, Erik," he said, and paused again. "I prefer to think of it as a reward."

Erik managed not to smile. Horvath had signed off on his assignment to the coordinator's chair only under great pressure. He had no reason to offer Erik any kind of reward whatsoever.

Finally, when enough seconds had passed to convince him that he had to say something, anything, he filled the silence with, "I'm listening."

"Villanueva runs very well, Erik. Better than the numbers might seem to indicate. Remember that energy is very cheap there, so long as Dynamo has access to water ice. The same applies to our other partners, and to EnTek herself. The majority of the assets we need are readily available in the Lunar crust."

"We wouldn't be here if they weren't," Erik said.

"We also wouldn't be there except for the colony's unique status," Horvath continued.

Erik nodded. More than half a century before, a cash-strapped United Nations had chosen to take the words on a plaque in Mare Tranquilliatis—Tranquility Base—more literally than perhaps they had been intended. "For All Mankind," the UN had read, and promptly begun leasing out Lunar territory to raise funds. The vast majority of those leases had been taken as intended, as publicity stunts and goodwill gestures, but the five companies of the ALC had viewed them rather differently. Villanueva had been a bone in the throat of certain Earthside governments ever since, and a source of constant contention.

"More hearings?" he asked, again holding back a smile. "Don't worry about it, Janos," he continued, after the other man finally nodded. "The charter's secure. We pay enough in taxes to keep it that way."

"It's easy to simplify the situation," Horvath said. "And even easier to oversimplify it." He paused again. "I would appreciate it, Erik, if your tenure in this office were uneventful."

Had he been making waves? Had there been complaints? Erik couldn't see how, not in the few days that had passed. It was more likely that Horvath was warning him not to cause trouble, rather than reproving him for anything already done.

"You were very helpful in the Australia situation, Erik," Janos continued. "But this is not a situation that calls for such an aggressive approach."

There was no reason not to speak the truth. Erik recognized that Horvath's authorities were considerable, but not without limit. "I'm here to do a job," he said carefully. "There are issues that demand my attention,"

"And discretion," Horvath said.

CHAPTER 7

ONCE, years before and early in his career, a favor-currying marketer had given Erik a novelty coffee mug that he had promptly discarded and which he thought he had forgotten. On the mug, in a panorama that had stretched almost entirely around its cylindrical surface, had been the image of the famous Zonix Infotainment animated cat, surrounded by dozens of computer displays. Each had presented a unique, distinct document image, and the cat's face had worn a look of harried desperation. When hot new-coffee filled the mug, the cat would say, "I love my job!" as his hair turned white, like poor peoples' did, and his teeth fell out, also like those of poor people. Erik had discarded the mug without waiting for its Gummi to die. He had not thought of the thing in years, but he thought of it now.

Specifically, he thought of the cat's desk.

His own didn't look much better right now. Every possible view was open and hard-copy documents littered its surface as well. His requests for information had borne abundant fruit, and now he was trying to make sense of it all, to divine some kind of system. His authority as Site Coordinator was amorphous enough to make the job difficult. It was easy enough to obtain and review information on almost any given situation, but changing that situation took strategy and effort.

The situation with the field prospectors was one of many that he found frustrating. Heaven only knew how Caspian had managed to change the policy in the absence of any real need, but now that he had, no one in Personnel or Production seemed eager to change it back. No matter how much sense it made to have priority contracts in place, no one seemed interested in making it happen. Garcia's report and supporting files, all neatly sorted and flagged, showed themselves to him from beneath his desk's surface, the words and pictures seeming to mock.

It was like that with a dozen other issues. Production runs, staffing, resources, business development—all were within "acceptable" parameters. Buoyed by cheap energy and nearly free natural resources, Villanueva was, indeed, making a good return on the ALC's mammoth investments, but only a good one.

No one seemed much worried about doing better, either. Certainly, his office seemed to lack the power and the backing to make things different. What if his intended role was to sit by and watch deadlines pass and quotas go unfilled? And then, no doubt, be discharged for allowing it to happen.

He pushed a pile of printouts away from him in disgust. The plastic sheets made a rustling noise as they slid to cover Garcia's report display.

He thought about the coffee mug again, and the animated cat.

"You were very helpful in the Australia situation, Erik," Horvath had said the previous week. "But this is not a situation that calls for such an aggressive approach."

Erik knew about aggression. After Alaska, it had taken weeks of string-pulling to get to where he was now. He'd been angling for anything that would keep him with EnTek long enough for the memory of Alaska to fade a bit, long enough at least to start rebuilding his career. The Villanueva assignment, when it was offered, had come as a surprise, and he had taken it readily enough, never considering that strings might be attached. At best, it had promised to be a transition to something better; at worst, an exile and another chance at failure.

What if he could make it something more? The thought appealed to him, but it didn't seem very likely that he would be able to do so.

"I found Caspian for you."

It was Hector Kowalski's voice. Startled, Erik looked toward the doorway to his office. It was empty, so he glanced instead at his desktop.

"Move the papers," Kowalski said. He sounded amused.

Erik slid the hard copies aside again, revealing the dedicated view beneath them. Instead of Garcia's report, however, it presented Heck Kowalski's lean features. He was smiling.

"The system didn't announce you," Erik said testily.

Kowalski's screen image shook its head in agreement. "Nope," he said pleasantly. "It didn't."

The security officer had override protocols, Erik realized. He wondered how far they went. "What about Caspian?"

"He's paying us a visit," Kowalski said. "His apartment was part of his compensation package, and when he left us, he left some personal effects behind. Housekeeping 'lost' them for a while." He smiled again. "When they turned up, I let Caspian know that he'd have to pick them up in person."

"And he agreed?"

Kowalski nodded. "Does lunch sound good to you? On your budget, of course. And not now, later in the week."

A moment later, after Erik had updated his calendar, he drew the pile of printouts back to him for additional review. As he did, however, his office announced, *"Incoming."*

Irritated at yet another interruption, but bored enough by his work to welcome it, Erik accepted the call.

"Hey, Morrison," Doug Stewart said. "It's about time."

"ANY difficulty finding the place?" Stewart said, six hours later.

Erik shook his head as he slid into the booth. "Your instructions were good."

The restaurant called Fargo's! was just off the Tesla Conduit, well-placed enough to be very crowded. Finding it had taken less time than finding Stewart among the throngs of people inside.

Stewart looked about as he had when Erik had seen him last—stocky and russet-haired, and about two years out of date as far as fashion went. As he had been then, he was drinking.

"What's your poison?" Stewart asked. He snorted, and his wide features twisted in a slight smirk. "That's an old one," he said, snickering at his own witticism. He was working his way through a squat tumbler of the pale blue liquor he favored. A single piece of logoed ice floated at its center. The piece of ice broke the drink's meniscus and diminished its telltale bulge almost to the point of making it unnoticeable.

Erik looked around for the waitperson and realized that, once again, he had found himself with Stewart in a lounge that would have been perfectly at home on Earth. But where the Chrisium Port bar had evoked memories of Earth airports, this place reminded him of something else entirely. It was one of a chain he had frequented on Earth and taken for granted, but here, it prompted sharp pangs of homesickness.

Fargo's! was patterned after the taverns and road-houses that had punctuated American back roads during the previous century. Zonix Lifestyles had spent impressive amounts of money on molded, textured plastic cast in the form of unfinished timbers and rough-surfaced floorboards. The table in their booth was heavy and substantial. Lighting flickered as if cast by burning gas, and even the seating was hard and unpadded.

Erik didn't mind that. For once, he felt as if he were sitting in a chair, rather than floating just above it.

"What'll it be?" A woman wearing a stylized version of lumberjack dress had found them at their corner table. The workpants and boots she wore clung to her like a second skin. Her blouse was plaid and textured to look like flannel. Erik hoped for her sake that it was lighter than it looked, because otherwise she would be sweltering, even in Villanueva's controlled climate.

"This is a tourist trap," Stewart said lightly. He pointed at his own drink, gesturing for a refill, the drained it. "That means you can get anything you want. People come a quarter of a million miles, they expect to find home waiting for them."

"Bourbon, no ice," Erik said. "Sony if you have it. Water on the side."

The waitress smiled and shook her head. "Not here," she said, putting the lie to Stewart's words. "Is Maker's close enough? It's the real thing, imported from Earth."

"That will be fine," Erik said, and watched her head back to the bar.

"Pretty, isn't she?" Stewart asked. Erik wasn't sure how to respond to that, but Stewart scarcely gave him a chance. "Back home, you'd give your order to brainware, but here, you get to talk to a pretty girl."

"Or not," Erik said, thinking of the Chrisium bartender. "People like human servers, if they can afford them."

Stewart nodded again. "People like being reminded that they're not alone," he said. "Had you ever been to the Moon before?"

Erik shook his head.

"I bet you thought it was going to be some kind of wonder-world, the city of the future. Flying cars and all." Stewart snickered. "But this is just a company town and a tourist trap, not that much different from home. Might was well be in San Francisco or New Sacramento, right?"

"Except for the gravity," Erik said. He could think of a dozen other factors—the lack of sky, the food that felt wrong, the damn drinks that wouldn't sit properly in their glasses—but he didn't mention them.

"People are the same wherever we go," Stewart continued. "Our world shaped us, and we take our world with us. We huddle closer to the fire here, because there are fewer of us." He paused. "Overall, I mean."

The lumberjackette returned. She set drinks before them both and asked about food, but didn't seem very surprised when both men declined. Erik waited until she was out of earshot before continuing.

"Native?" he asked, nodding in the direction she had gone.

"The girl?" Stewart shook his head. "Earthborn. Probably hasn't been here a year, my guess."

"You think she came to the Moon to work for a chain restaurant as a waitress?"

"Nope," Stewart said. He took a sip of his drink, but Erik noticed that it was a small one. For whatever reason, the other man was drinking more slowly than he had in the spaceport bar. "She's probably moonlighting. My guess is, she's a systems analyst or something." He grinned tightly. "But there's a lot of money here and a lot of worse ways to make some extra."

Erik had scarcely touched his drink, and he looked at it now, having second thoughts about being there. Stewart's call and invitation had come when he was at his most vulnerable. Erik's frustration with work and annoyance with Hector Kowalski's attitude had been enough to crowd aside his dislike of Stewart. Boredom had done the rest.

"What about you?" he asked. "What are you doing here?"

"I told you. Production consultant, Snackles." Stewart glanced at his drink. "I'd had too many of these then, I think. They creep up on you."

"The receptionist at Duckworth says you're a salesman," Erik said. He had spoken with the woman at the circular desk briefly after his visit to Shadrach's office.

He thought of iron-colored hair in an upswept coif and of metallic lips parted to reveal perfect teeth in a perfect smile. He smiled, too. "She says you're a pest, and I'm inclined to agree with her."

"I'm just social," Stewart said. "Mark of a good salesman."

"Persistent."

Stewart nodded. "The other mark of a good salesman," he said. He looked directly at Erik now, and if the whites of his eyes were slightly bloodshot, the irises were remarkably clear. There was a surprising power in his gaze. "And I *am* a production consultant," he said. "Among other things."

Erik didn't doubt it; Stewart struck him as a man with a motley career track. Rather than respond, he took a taste of his bourbon. The warm line it traced from his mouth to his stomach was welcome, but it was the smoky taste of the liquor that he savored. At some point in the past, the whiskey had been Kentucky corn, ripening beneath a summer sun. Drinking it reminded him of Earth.

"They've got Sony at places in the Mall," Stewart said. The matter-of-fact way he spoke made his knowledge of who had what alcohol for sale seem perfectly reasonable. "And a dozen more will offer you something they claim is Sony, but it isn't."

"The Mall?" The term was familiar. Shadrach had mentioned it, and so had Garcia.

Stewart's drink was empty, but he didn't seem to care. "Villanueva is what they used to call a free enterprise zone, an open town," he said. "The Mall is Villanueva's free enterprise zone. Freer? When they closed the old spaceport, ALC chopped up the open space into pods and made them available to local entrepreneurs."

"I'm surprised the shareholders let them do that," Erik said. He did some numbers in his head and didn't like the results. "I don't see how it can pay."

"Doesn't have to. Much. I told you, there's a lot of credit in flux here. People like having things to spend it on."

"I can understand that," Erik said. He had adjusted a bit to Villanueva and felt more comfortable now than he had in the spaceport, and better able to deal with Stewart. Certainly, the Snackles man seemed more engaging now. He was also more sober, at least for the moment, and that helped some, too. Even so, then man's air of smugness irritated. "You say you're social," Erik said.

Stewart nodded.

"So social you hang around in spaceport bars and franchise restaurants, introducing yourself to newcomers?"

Stewart laughed. It welled up from within him, obviously sincere and heartfelt. He shook his head and smiled. "No, no, no," he said. "Chrisium was pure coincidence, I told you. I was seeing someone off."

Erik's drink was empty now, but when the waitress drifted close, he shook his head and asked for another water instead. After she had provided it, he looked back in Stewart's direction and said, "Okay. We'll stipulate that. But you've called since then, and I'm not exactly in the snack-buying business."

"I told you, I'm social." Stewart paused, as if choosing his next words carefully. "Besides, I remember you from the old days."

The old days?

Erik didn't ask the question aloud, but his expression must have done the job, because Stewart answered. "I used to live in Australia," he said. "And I meant what

I said about coincidence. I was there when the Sydney Pylon went up."

This time, Erik nearly laughed. "Everyone used to live in Australia, Doug. And apparently, everyone lived there at the same time."

Stewart flushed, his fair skin darkening, but when he spoke again, it was still in good-natured tones. "I had friends who worked for Cybrotics and EnTek, both. You made the news feeds a few times, local business reports and such."

"That was a long time ago."

"Ten years," Stewart said. "You look about the same, too."

Erik grunted, taken aback a bit. "I try to keep in shape," he said.

"That's not what I mean," Stewart said, and shook his head. "I meant, you're not much for cosmetic appliances, are you? Most men your age—"

Erik gave him the kind of look that he used to take command of meetings. "You didn't seem to know me then," he said. "At the port bar, I mean."

"I have a good memory for faces," Stewart replied. "But sometimes it takes a while."

Stewart's comments didn't make much sense to Erik, and he wasn't sure how to respond. Instead, he waited, and watched Stewart fidget. The little man passed his empty glass from one hand to the other and back. Chatter from surrounding tables, blunted by the restaurant's acoustic fields but not obliterated, filled the gap in their conversation.

At last, Stewart continued. "You were a bit of a troubleshooter in the old days. That was your reputation, anyway. It's not a good fit to what you say you're doing here." He looked Erik in the eyes, his gaze surprisingly forceful once more. "Why would they pick *you* to replace Rogers Caspian?"

Everyone wanted to know that, it seemed.

"I don't like the way this conversation is going," Erik said. He was certain now that the meeting had been a mistake.

"I'm not sure I do, either," Stewart said. "I was trying to do some business with Caspian—"

"Sesame-chili Crackly Crawlers or cherry-jalapeño?" Erik asked. He let the irritation he felt color his words, and again, he wondered what he was doing there.

The waitress had set another round of drinks before them, without being asked; Erik's request for a water the second time notwithstanding, he got another bourbon. Stewart seized his drink almost reflexively. He swallowed half of it with a single gulp and then evidently thought better of it, because he looked slightly embarrassed when he set it down again.

"Never mind that," he said.

"Biome can help you with that," Erik said. He gestured at the half-empty glass. "Six weeks of gene patches, and you'll save a fortune on drinks."

Stewart managed to keep his features composed, but his face turned dark with anger. "Thanks for the suggestion, but I can handle my liquor." With exaggerated precision, he lifted the glass and drained it, then looked around the crowded restaurant for the waitress.

Suddenly, he turned the color of soy milk.

"Or—or maybe I can't," he said, struggling to stand. He seemed to move in slow motion, stumbling as he rose, his hand raised to his mouth.

"Stewart?" Erik asked. "What is it, man?" He tried to get up, too, but Stewart's sudden, shaky rise had included bracing himself against the table. That table slid now, pinning Erik against his seat. The two drinking glasses toppled and wheeled toward the table's edge. Erik's left a trail of bourbon as it rolled.

Stewart was on his feet, tottering. Hand still to mouth, he made a retching noise. "S-sorry," he muttered. "Sick." He retched again.

Their glasses had reached the floor now, and his foot came down on one, shattering it. That was enough to make him slip and almost fall, but he was able to correct it in time, then lurch, stumbling toward the rest room. Unfortunately, his path intersected neatly with that of their waitress, who was working her way though the moderately crowded aisle, an absurdly large tray balanced on one upraised hand.

"Hey, wait!" the woman cried out, but it did her no good.

Stewart, still off-balance, slammed into her. He recovered, and so did she, but her tray did not. The waitress bleated like a sheep as it sailed from her grip, and a slow-motion storm of plates and dishes rained in all directions.

"Hey!"

"Watch out!"

"What!?"

Other patrons cried out in shock, as the food flew, but it flew in slow motion, moving in long, flat trajectories. Pita baskets of rice and vegetables disgorged their contents on nearby tables. Erik, his attention still drawn by the suddenly ill Stewart, saw from the corner of one eye something flat and brown and spinning.

It was a breaded pork chop, coming at him fast.

Reflexively, knowing he was too late, he tried to dodge. The table, pressed hard against his midriff, pinned him and kept him from moving. Then a woman's hand, appearing as if from nowhere, plucked the entrée from midair and halted its flight.

"Is this yours?" his rescuer asked. She sounded amused, obviously recognizing the absurdity of the situation. She smiled at him, and the surrounding chaos and bustle seemed to fall away. So did the irritation and embarrassment he felt because of Stewart and the general frustration that had built within him since his arrival on Villanueva. His heartbeat and breathing slowed, and he felt lighter, but in a *good* way.

The world suddenly became a happy place.

"Is it?" the woman asked.

Erik stared, not knowing what to say, but desperately wanting to say *something*.

The woman, trim and graceful, waited a moment for his answer. When she realized that one was not forthcoming, she set the chop on his table and then wiped her fingers delicately on an unused napkin. "Well," she said, dimpling at him. "I'll let someone else take care of it."

She headed toward the exit, and the noise and clatter of the world came back. Patrons cursed and the waitress apologized. Erik braced himself and pushed the table back, then stood, but by then, the woman was gone from view.

He was checking for her when Stewart finally returned.

CHAPTER 8

TWO hours into the morning, Erik sipped new-coffee and nibbled at a breakfast pastry, more out of boredom than hunger.

He was going to have to cut back on the sweets, and probably on food in general. Too many calories, and even with his exercise program and the Biome gene patch treatments, the Moon's lower gravity made it harder to burn them away. He was already putting on mass, or at least his stomach was. He had gained enough that his trousers felt snug where they shouldn't. Unfortunately, the sticky treats waited for him each morning in his office, along with the coffee service.

"Cancel my breakfast order," he said. He pushed the plate aside and tried to focus instead on the Mesh stock market reports presented by his desktop. Behind him, the grayed Moonscape image stretched across his office wall, silent and majestic. Its presence was such a constant that he scarcely noticed it anymore.

Juanita Garcia nodded. She was seated at the table in his office. Its entire surface was lit now, given over to briefing slides that combined text with animated insets. Together, they gleamed brightly enough that even the ceiling fixtures could not mask their glow completely. Garcia's face was alight the flickering radiance. "I'll take care of it," she said, without looking up. "Do you still want the coffee?"

This time, it was Erik who nodded. A moment later, realizing that she hadn't seen the movement, he said, "Yes. I'll eat at home."

"The service offers a full menu," Garcia said. She traced something on the tabletop with her fingers. The slides shifted into new sequences, and the pattern of light and shadow coloring they cast shifted, too, accentuating her strong features. "We can arrange something more substantial if you'd prefer," she continued.

Erik thought about that a moment, then decided that it was one thing to eat a pastry at his desk, but quite another to dine on omelets or oatmeal while his staff watched. "No," he said, then repeated, "I'll eat at home. I like cooking."

Garcia looked up from her work, smiled at him briefly, and then bent her head again.

"What?" he asked.

"You—you seem to be in a good mood today," she said, hesitantly. "Relaxed. That's all."

"Good mood? Hmph." Erik couldn't deny the truth of her words. The previous night's sleep had been his best since arriving in Villanueva, deep and dreamless and completely refreshing. "You could say that."

He saw her furtive smile form again, and this time, he

realized what she thought. He had seen that same indulgent, knowing expression on other women's faces, but never on any he had known as briefly as Garcia. Ordinarily, he would have felt angry at such presumption, but today, for whatever reason, only a mild amusement came.

"Yes, I had a good night, Garcia," he said. "And I don't see that it's any of your business, but it wasn't *that* kind of a good night."

"Oh." Garcia blushed slightly. "You had said you were going to dinner . . ." she said, her words trailing off. She reordered the briefing slides again.

Erik had directed her to prepare a presentation based on her prospectors report, for delivery to the various division heads. He was far from sure that it would do much good, but the ingrained habits of a career in management were hard to shake. Garcia was having a difficult time with the assignment, pausing often to request guidance, which was why she was doing it in his office. Ordinarily, her diffidence would have irritated him, but today was different. The frustration that had been his nearly constant companion since arriving at Villanueva had taken a leave of absence for some reason.

Her words made him think, however, even as he continued to review the market reports. He had been by himself for the better part of a standard year, his most recent serious relationship swept aside by the first waves of the Alaska debacle. More recently, amid the stress of reassignment and relocation, he hadn't felt much need or desire to look for someone new.

He glanced in Garcia's direction, let his gaze linger there briefly, then looked away again before she could notice. His assistant was a woman of many different looks, all of them comely. She was his subordinate and obviously both respected and feared his authority. He was reasonably sure that any advances would be accepted, eagerly or not. Despite that, despite the convenience of the situation and all that it offered, he felt no real urge for her, only a vague hint.

For that matter, he hadn't felt any real desire for the more aggressive and obviously available Enola Hasbro.

Erik's thoughts drifted back to Fargo's! the night before. Stewart's discursive ramblings were still very clear in his memory, and so were the interesting things that the Moon's low gravity had done for the lumberjackette's figure. Even the slow-motion trajectory of the flying pork chop retained all of its detail in his mind's eye.

What was vague and unspecific, however, was the face of the woman who had intercepted the flying foodstuff. He had caught only a brief look at her, and most of that look had come while he was preoccupied with other issues, but he should have been able to remember what she looked like. Instead, he was left with only an imprecise impression of how she had looked, overlaid with anxiety, and then relief, and then, when it was too late, attraction.

For the first time since coming to this place, he felt a vague hint of loneliness and wondered why. He had always been comfortable by himself.

"I've made reservations for your lunch with Mr. Caspian," Garcia said. "It's at Fargo's! and you'll like it."

Erik shook his head. "Change them. I ate there last night."

"It's one of Mr. Caspian's favorite restaurants," Garcia said. She had paused the presentation and turned now to face him, perhaps encouraged by his general air of goodwill.

"You told me that you didn't work for him," Erik said.

He filled his mug again from an insulated pitcher of new-coffee.

"I didn't. But Keith did, and I ran across some of his files when I was loading my own desk," Garcia said.

"Keith?"

"Keith was Mr. Caspian's assistant. He's retired, gone back to Earth."

She had mentioned that before, Erik realized. The memory drifted up from the recesses of his mind, and brought curiosity with it. "Any idea why?"

"He came into some money," Garcia replied. She had finished her breakfast pastry but some new-coffee remained in her mug. She took a sip.

"Still, that's a big step," Erik said.

Garcia made a delicate moue of distaste. "I suppose he didn't feel welcome here anymore," she said. "He'd been with Mr. Caspian for a long time, and when Caspian went to—"

Erik gestured in interruption. "Never mind," he said. "I understand."

All five ALC partner companies valued employee loyalty, and they valued it especially among management members. Turncoats tended to end up ostracized, even by their new employers. Rogers Caspian's move, from En-Tek to Duckworth, was not one that he could have made lightly. Indeed, Erik was surprised that Caspian had been able to make it at all; it was one thing for a contractor to move from one company to another, but his predecessor had been a manager. Someone of that rank was a substantial investment of corporate time and money, not to be thrown away lightly. Whatever level of trust and prestige he had enjoyed within EnTek, what he found at Duckworth would surely be less. Company bones did not move without repercussions, and Caspian's exodus had doubt-less tainted his staff.

"Did you know them?" he asked Garcia.

She nodded. "Not well. I used to have lunch with Keith once in a while, and I worked on some of Caspian's projects."

"I imagine you got some attention after he left." Once, early in Erik's career, he had been part of EnTek's France operations. He remembered a junior vice president who had left the company to take the reins of one of Zonix's troubled European amusement parks. Erik had barely known the woman, but despite that, the following weeks had been filled with interviews and meetings. Management had been eager to determine why the vice president had left and what damage she might have done by leaving. That was when Erik had first come to his formulation that all companies competed, no matter what.

And that had been in a far less high-profile situation than Villanueva.

That aspect of corporate culture, in fact, was one reason that Erik had been able to negotiate the Moon assignment. Once EnTek had a firm grip on any asset, the company was remarkably reluctant to let go completely.

"Not so much about Mr. Caspian," Garcia said, surprising him. "But they were very interested in talking about Keith."

Erik thought about that for a moment and thought back again to his own experience. "They were worried about him, because he was still here," he said.

"Maybe." Garcia finished her coffee. "But he isn't here anymore, and someone's still interested. Heck Kowalski asked me about him just last week."

"Hmmm?" Erik made a politely curious sound. Another

round of market reports appeared as his desktop refreshed itself, but he paid no attention.

Garcia nodded. "He wanted to know if I'd heard from him." Again, she blushed, but more faintly this time. "When he first got here, we did more than just have lunch," she said softly. "But that was a long time ago."

Erik wasn't sure what to say. Sudden confidences tended to unsettle him.

"I suppose I should let Heck know I ran across the file copies," Garcia continued.

"Probably." Erik thought a moment. "I can mention it to him, if you'd like. I'm sure he'll still want to follow up with you."

Garcia nodded again, then changed the subject. "Where do you want to have lunch?" she asked.

"Something nicer than Fargo's!, I think," Erik said. If he was going to eat less, he might as well eat better, and the memory of the breaded pork chop still loomed large in his memory. "Not something I could find as easily back on Earth. What kind of food does Caspian like?"

Garcia looked at her computer. Her nails were red today, the color of blood, and she used one to trace something in the device's interface. "Keith's notes on Caspian star Neo-Italian, German, and Peruvian," she said, and smiled. "DiNuvio's makes its own pasta, grows its own herbs, and has vegetables delivered fresh every day."

Erik took a last look at the pastry, then dropped it into a recycling slot at one edge of his desk. Somewhere beneath his feet, hidden machinery whined briefly.

"German would be better, but that sounds fine," Erik said easily. "Make the arrangements."

"*Incoming,*" the office announced. "*Discretion requested.*"

Erik glanced again in Garcia's direction. "I'll take it on my phone," he said, and watched as the desktop market feeds gave way to a message view. From it, Heck Kowalski gazed out at him with indolent eyes.

"Can you talk?" he asked. His voice came through clearly on the earpieces of Erik's personal phone. Tiny and discreet, they rode in his ear canals. He had worn them every day since his arrival, ever since Garcia had given them to him, but they hadn't been of any use until now. Their sound quality surprised and pleased him.

"You can, at least," Erik said aloud. He used his desk's audio pickup, rather than the phone's throat mike. Garcia was doing her best to pretend not to notice the apparently one-sided conversation. "Juanita is here with me."

Kowalski nodded. Not for the first time, Erik wondered how much information was lost in an audio-only call. Even miraged calls, for the most part, preserved basic body language and expression, no matter how many surface details got rewritten in the project. Even Janos Horvath, far from the most effusive man he had ever met, had communicated almost as much by visual cues as by verbal ones.

"There's been a shake-up of some sort in Hello," Kowalski said.

"*Halo*," Erik half corrected, half prompted. The ubiquitous nickname for Armstrong's primary operation grated.

"Halo," Kowalski said. He shrugged and ran fingers though his lank hair. "I thought you should know."

The news left Erik at a loss. Information on competitors was information he could use, but Project Halo wasn't a competitor. Nor did the project have any impact on his business that he could see, other than the paltry credits

Halo staff contributed to Villanueva's economy. The federal installation had no authority over the ALC colony that he knew of.

"So?" he asked.

"Hello's a pretty stable place," Kowalski said, obviously peeved that his big news hadn't made a greater impact. "Tanaka's been running it for more than ten years, and the word was that he had at least another five to go."

"So?" Erik repeated.

"Well, his replacement is more or less my opposite number," Kowalski said slowly. "If this happened at Duckworth—"

"But it's not Duckworth," Erik said, a bit more forcefully than he had intended. "Duckworth is a business. Halo isn't." As he spoke, he noticed Garcia flinch, and paused. "Just a moment."

Garcia looked up from her work.

"Juanita," he said. "Could you give us a moment?"

"Of course, Mr. Morrison," she said. She passed a hand above the tabletop, and her slides winked out. Then she lifted her coffee mug and headed toward the outer office. After the door had whisked shut behind her, Erik continued. "Why do you think this has an impact on us?" he asked. "What's Halo to us?"

Kowalski smiled. "Well," he said, "I always like to know what my neighbors are up to."

"Who doesn't?" Erik said. "You've got a point."

"They keep pretty close tabs on us, after all," the security officer continued.

That was news to Erik. "They're not a regulatory body," he said slowly.

Kowalski nodded again. "Strictly research," he said. "Or at least, that's the story. But when Rogers Caspain transitioned to Duckworth, message traffic between Halo and Earth tripled for three weeks and then dropped back to about 10 percent above normal."

"You keep track of things like that?" The information was almost reassuring. Kowalski had known about Horvath's calls, after all. Erik decided he would rather that Kowalski knew what he knew because of a system-wide surveillance effort, rather than from monitoring him specifically.

"I track them," Kowalski said. "Or the Mesh tracks them for me."

Erik thought about that for a moment.

As if anticipating his next question, Kowalski continued. "I can't intercept them, though. Encryption is too good. Wendy Scheer runs a pretty tight ship."

Wendy Scheer. Erik had heard that name before. "Scheer," he said. "I thought she was their liaison. Some kind of public relations rep."

Kowalski snickered. "She's that," he said. "Did Seven Thomas give you his spiel about wearing many hats?"

Erik thought back to his introductory meetings with the division heads who were supposed to work with him. "He did," he said, nodding.

"From what I can tell, things are like that at Halo, but a lot worse. They're understaffed and over-tasked there. Mostly researchers, but everyone's got at least two jobs."

"My sympathies," Erik said, not meaning it. He was still in a pleasant mood, but the troubles of Project Halo interested him not at all. As far as he was concerned, the place sounded like a waste of tax credits.

"Well, Scheer's got three now," Kowalski continued. "Tanaka's going back to Earth. They've already booked his flight. Scheer's taking over as director."

"Must be a competent woman," Erik said.

"She's popular, at least," Kowalski said. "Everyone likes Wendy Scheer."

"Have you meet her?" Erik asked.

"Came close a couple times," Kowalski said. "But she's a busy lady, and Halo isn't one of my priorities." He paused. "I told you, I work long hours and my job makes me travel. She's made overtures, but not in a while. I suppose I should do the meet-and-greet, but I usually have other things to do with my time."

Erik thought of clowns locked in battle with white-suited gentlemen, but didn't comment. Instead, he said, "When does she take charge?"

"She already has," Kowalski said. "That's what's so interesting. Things *never* happen that fast over there."

"So maybe I should accept the next invitation?"

"Invitation?"

Erik nodded. "I've had at least three since I got here. For tours and meet-and-greets."

Kowalski looked honestly surprised and whistled softly. "Someone must really want to meet you. I wonder why."

"I thought you said Scheer had made overtures."

Kowalski finger-combed his hair again. "Sure," he said. "But in Villanueva, not at Halo. We were supposed to have lunch at Fargo's! six months ago, but somebody hijacked an ore cart at the Penumbra Strike, and I had to go teach some lessons." He smiled at the memory, and for the first time, Erik had the impression that Kowalski might be a dangerous man.

Most security officers were, of course.

"So you're saying they're hush-hush," he said.

Kowalski shook his head. A tumbler came into view, and he sipped something from it, then said, "I don't think of it that way. All they've really got over there is a cluster of offices and labs. It's like a factory, but they don't make anything. It's only unexpected changes that make me sit up and think."

"Keep thinking, then," Erik said. "And keep an eye on them."

"I intend to," Kowalski said. He snickered. "Maybe they're going to offer you a job."

"They'd better not," Erik said. "And I meant, keep an eye on them and keep me informed." He paused, then, since Kowalski didn't work directly for him, and continued. "Please. I appreciate your insights." Kowalski nodded, and Erik decided to change the subject. "What's this about Keith Ramirez? You've been asking about him."

"Routine queries," Kowalski said, suddenly less indolent. "He quit a couple months ago, but the system hasn't forgotten him yet. Personnel is still chasing down his files and some other people want to know why he left."

"Other people?" Erik asked.

"I can't tell you that," Kowalski said.

The honesty of his reply was refreshing. Erik nodded. "Okay. Garcia tells me she ran across some personal directories and such. I'll have her copy them to you."

"I probably have them already," Kowalski said. "But thanks. Like I said, they're having trouble chasing down everything. The last time Personnel's brainware burped, some stuff went missing."

"That's a surprise," Erik said. Personnel files were very nearly sacrosanct and typically resided on heavily secured Mesh sections. "What about backups?"

"What about them?" Kowalski replied, but from his expression, he might have been saying, "Don't ask," instead.

Erik shook his head. Sloppiness abounded, and Kowalski was beginning to look a bit defensive. He decided to change the subject. Erik asked, "Is DiNuvio's expensive enough for your tastes?"

Kowalski grinned. "Sure," he said. "And we've got a corner table. I looked it up when Juanita messaged for the reservation."

Erik had to laugh at that. "Tell me something else. Do you have anything on a man named Doug Stewart?" His apartment systems had been able to find nothing of note.

"Stewart?" Kowalski looked at him blankly, then shook his head. "That's a common name. A lot of Scots up here, you know. Do you have anything more to go on?"

"I can send you a phone code," Erik said. "But it's a public one." His apartment hadn't been able to find any information beyond that.

"Well, it would be a start," Kowalski said. "Who does he work for?"

"He says he's a contractor for Zonix Lifestyles. I met him at Chrisium, and he's been making a pest of himself."

"Okay. What's *your* interest?" Kowalski asked.

This time, it was Erik who grinned. "Maybe I want to hire him," he said.

The security officer surprised Erik then, by managing to look slightly scandalized. "You can't do that," he said. "Zonix contractors might as well be—"

"I was just kidding," Erik interrupted.

"Now, that's funny," Kowalski said. "Nothing I've read says you have much of a sense of humor." He smiled slightly. "And I've read a lot," he continued and then broke the connection.

What was that supposed to mean?

"Incoming," his office announced.

Erik shrugged. "Accept it," he said.

The world seemed to fall away as the image of a woman's face formed on the screen, compelling Erik to give her his absolute attention. She had distinctive, attractive features that were too strong for classic beauty—high cheekbones and a slightly too-long nose, a broad, unlined forehead, and a chin that stopped just shy of being sharp. Framing her face was tawny blonde hair in an upswept style that seemed to ignore what little gravity Luna had to offer.

"Mr. Morrison?" she said. As she spoke, her curved lips parted to reveal perfect teeth, and her bright eyes sparkled.

The reply came unbidden to his lips. "Please," he said. "I'm Erik."

The woman nodded. "I'm Wendy Scheer," she said. She smiled, and the world suddenly became an even happier place. "I work at Project Halo."

"You're the director," Erik said, regaining some of his composure.

She nodded, and her hair rippled like tall grass in the summer wind. "Well, I will be," she said. "Tomorrow, officially."

"C-congratulations," Erik said. He paused, appalled that he had actually stammered. "Have we met before?"

Wendy laughed, like the pealing of silver bells. "Oh, Mr. Morrison," she said. "You live in the city of the future. You'll have to find a newer line than that."

Erik shook his head, trying to focus. "No, that's not what I meant," he said. "And I'm Erik." Doug Stewart's words came back to him. "But we're the same wherever we go," he continued.

"Touché." Wendy paused. "Are you busy tomorrow, Erik?"

Erik tore his gaze from the communications display just long enough to check his calendar, at the notations Garcia had made for him. Two project reviews, with Thomas and Callahan, had red stars beside them, denoting priority. He was supposed to meet with some prospector Garcia had found after that.

"Nothing important," he said. "Are you sure we haven't met?"

Scheer didn't actually answer his question. "I'd like to give you a guided tour of the Halo facility, Mr. Morrison. If I'm going to run the place, I'd like to be a good neighbor."

"It's Erik," Erik repeated. He was thinking more clearly now. The sudden fascination he had felt had attenuated into something else, a general eagerness to please.

"Erik, then. If you're free, may I schedule you for 1000?" When Erik nodded, she nodded, too. "Excellent, then," she said. "I'll message the directions to you."

"I look forward to it," Erik said, sincerely.

"So do I," replied Wendy Scheer, and then the display went blank.

CHAPTER 9

"WENDY!" Ralph Tanaka looked up from the desk that wasn't going to be his for very much longer. He had already moved, forwarded, or deleted the majority of his files, and now he was gathering his personal effects. A standard-issue plastic storage pod rested on the blanked desktop. Into it went a hard-picture of a dog, a cat, and a parrot, neatly matted and framed.

"My sister's pets," Ralph said pleasantly. "I'll get to see them for real, when I get back to Earth." He paused and looked vaguely sad. "Well, the dog and the parrot, anyway."

"Morrison will visit tomorrow," Wendy said. She settled with liquid grace into a spun-steel guest chair. It gave gently beneath her, like a low-tension spring. "I'd like to receive him here. I don't want him in my old office, and this one is more appropriate."

The director's office was as close as Halo came to luxury, decorated in a retro-modernist mode that had been popular years before. An angled ceiling rose to twice the height of the overhead of Wendy's former space, and carpeting, worn but still deep, covered the floor, instead of the more durable padding. Halo couldn't afford the bandwidth or hardware for full-scale wallpaper visits. Instead, Tanaka himself, a talented artist, had personally rendered an expressionist mural of ragged mountains that ran along one dead wall, and then hung framed still-paper images of Lunar sites along the one opposite. Alike yet different, the Appalachians confronted the up-thrust walls of Tycho crater, to startling effect.

"The place will be ready," Tanaka said. He hefted a chunk of lunar ore that had been hollowed and lined to make a vase. A single chrysanthemum bloom, grown in Halo's greenhouses, sprouted from it. Tanaka removed the flower and dropped it into his desk's disposal slot. The water followed a moment later. Then he wrapped the vase in padding material and set it into the storage pod. "I'll give that to my sister, I think," he said. He looked at Wendy. "Unless you'd like it."

"When do you leave?"

"Not for a few days. I just wanted to make the office available for you."

"I appreciate that," Wendy said. She felt a surge of genuine affection for the man who had been her faithful co-worker for so long.

"It's funny, really," he continued. "I worked my entire adult life to get here and I've spent years making this place the way I liked it. I've loved every moment of my job, but I really don't mind leaving." He smiled at Wendy. "A moment ago, I felt some regrets, but now you're here and—"

Wendy smiled at him.

"—right now, I really don't mind. Isn't that amazing?" Ralph was one of the few who was consciously aware of Wendy's gift, but he was subject to it, nonetheless. "How did you convince Morrison?"

"I paid him a personal visit," Wendy said.

"So you've met him?" A pen and pencil set, adorned with Halo's official seal, rested near the desk's edge. He took it, wrapped it, and placed it next to the vase in the storage pod.

Wendy shook her head. "Chance encounter. I doubt he even remembers the specifics. There was a lot going on, and I looked a bit different. He only got a glance."   ·

"He remembers."

"He might. The follow-up call certainly made him happy." Tanaka was probably right, Wendy knew. Though the specifics of her gift were maddeningly elusive, even to her, the end results were reasonably consistent. Her charm and appeal worked on everyone, to varying degrees, but only if there had first been an in-person encounter, however brief.

"He may not realize that he remembers, but he remembers," Tanaka said. He clicked the first storage pod shut and started filling a second with old-books. Most of them were ceremonial and presentation volumes, gifts from staff and the occasional visitor. One bore the five interlocking seals of the ALC companies.

"I'd rather we not talk about things like that, Ralph," Wendy said. Wendy didn't worry about very many things, but her own privacy was one. "And I'd rather *you* not talk about them at all."

"Not to worry," Tanaka said. More books went into the pod. "I'm taking home about seven times as much stuff as I brought with me," he said ruefully.

"You can afford the freight," Wendy said. "What's next for you?" She felt some honest affection for the man who had posed as her superior for ten years, and was not at all happy to see him leave. He was one of the very few, anywhere, who had any inkling of her secret.

"Florida. The Cape. I'm going to run the data processing centers. My people will crunch the numbers your people send us."

Wendy brightened. "We'll still be working together, then," she said. "You should have your hands full, soon enough. Especially if we find Ramirez."

"And if he's not nuts," Tanaka said. He pressed something, and the data slot on his desk whirred. A module popped out, and he offered it to Wendy. "Personal stuff. Do you need to review it?"

She shook her head again. "Nope. I trust you. All I need is this office."

Or the recognized authority that came with it, actually. Clearly, the time had passed when she could do her work with the discretion she preferred. By Halo standards, at least, Tanaka's job was much more public than her old one had been. She needed the additional prominence for the current initiative, but worried about what it would do to her network within the ALC companies.

As if he had read her mind, Tanaka reassured her. "Don't worry. Things almost always work out." He grinned. "Especially for you."

Wendy hoped he was right.

CHAPTER 10

"ARMSTRONG?" Juanita said, the next morning. She stared blankly at Morrison. His words had made no sense. "You're going to *Armstrong*?"

Morrison nodded. Casually, so casually that he didn't even appear to realize what he was doing, he glanced at the polished chrome steel of the convenient desk lamp. After looking briefly at his reflected image there, he ran his fingers though thick blonde hair that was just beginning to gray.

Juanita blinked. This was the first time that she had seen him demonstrate any deliberate awareness of his physical appearance, she realized with slight surprise. Until now, he had struck her as being consistently blasé about such things.

"I should be there most of the day," Morrison said. Now he looked at a calendar display and began thumbing appointment blocks, one after another. "You'll have to handle the project reviews by yourself. Ask questions if you see the need, but don't answer any if you can avoid it. Don't let Thomas or Callahan skip anything, either."

"But—no one goes to *Armstrong*," Juanita said. As he spoke, she used her personal computer to pull up the meeting agendas she had worked so hard to develop. Dozens of items, neatly sorted and iconed, looked back at her, but her thoughts were elsewhere. "There's nothing to see there, nothing to do."

"Ms. Scheer seems to think otherwise." Morrison was adjusting his tunic now, still moving with an utter lack of self-consciousness. He had already tucked his folded computer into one pocket.

"I—I'm not sure I'm ready for this," Juanita said. Seated at the table, she scanned the schedule that had been his but was now hers. She tried to keep all expression from her face, as she watched Morrison lock down his desk computer for the day then glance in the lamp's mirror finish again.

He looked like he was preparing for a date.

Juanita thought back to her own suspicions of the day before, when Morrison had guessed—and dismissed—her thought as to what kind of "good night" he had enjoyed. She wondered how sincere he had been then. He was a good-looking man and his physicality hadn't yet been eroded by the Moon's low gravity. He carried himself with an air of easy authority that Juanita knew many women would find attractive.

Enola Hasbro, for example.

"You'll do fine," Morrison said. "Make sure you record everything, and we'll review it when I get back." He paused, ran one knuckle against the line of his jaw, checking for beard stubble. "No. I'll be back this afternoon, but too late to do anything here. Scheer says the tour should take all morning, and then there'll be a reception of some sort."

"You're spending the day at Halo," Juanita said, still not finding it easy to believe. Morrison had declined and dismissed enough invitations from the federal site that it was hard to believe he had decided to take one.

Morrison nodded. "You can handle things here. I've set the office to take most calls, but flagged some IDs for you. Don't commit to anything, and you'll be fine."

"You're going by yourself? Is someone going to meet you?" Juanita asked. "They usually send someone—"

As casually as he adjusted his dress sandals, Morrison interrupted her. "I thought you said that no one ever goes to Armstrong." A trace of the genial quality that had colored his comments had faded now.

She felt the heat of a sudden blush spread across her face. "I've been there. Once." She paused, embarrassed. "I didn't come to Villanueva as EnTek staff." Even now, years later, the admission made her feel disloyal.

Morrison didn't say anything, but she could tell he was waiting.

"Oh, I worked for EnTek on Earth," she said. "At the Oklahoma assembling site, in Purchasing. But after my parents died, there was some money, and I thought I'd make a fresh start. Zonix was recruiting, I wanted to act—"

He was smiling at her now, but she was sure that if she went much further, his expression would become a smirk. It was a very old story, after all.

"That didn't work out," she said. The reason it hadn't worked out was that Zonix's Lunar productions were

primarily docudramas, with an emphasis on drama, and
their casts were almost always people who led exciting
lives. Being pretty wasn't enough. "I interviewed for other
positions," she continued. "One was at Halo. Just admin."

"Did they make you an offer?" Morrison looked like
he found the subject mildly distasteful, and she could understand that. Who would *want* to work for the Feds?

Juanita nodded. "But I didn't take it. There's nothing
to see there," she repeated. "Nothing to do. That's why
they come *here*."

"The shuttle." Morrison tapped the folded computer in
his tunic pocket. "At the trans-Carnegie terminal platform." He spoke the words easily and with surprising familiarity, considering how briefly he had been on the
Moon.

Juanita nodded again. "The shuttle," she said. She fidgeted in her chair, folding her computer and then unfolding
it again. She wasn't sure why she thought it mattered, but
something was wrong here. "You say there's a reception?"

Morrison nodded.

"You'll probably come back for that, then. I don't
think they have facilities there. I could do some research,
find out where—"

Morrison shook his head and ran his fingers through
his hair one last time. "I'm meeting Scheer at the station," he said.

Juanita blinked again. Halo wasn't a very extensive
operation these days, but surely its newly designated head
had other things to do with her day than meet visitors at
the train station.

Morrison continued. "I'll be back late this afternoon.
See to the reviews. We'll talk tomorrow."

Juanita watched him leave and gazed at her computer

screen for a long moment, thinking. Then she thumbed the phone icon.

ERIK stood in a nook just off the trans-Carnegie run's terminus. Discreetly partitioned from the rest of the station, the space served as a tiny waiting area for transport to Armstrong. At one end, two metal panels, like elevator doors, occupied most of the nook's wall. Behind him, from back on the main platform, Erik could hear bustle and chatter of other travelers as he waited.

He glanced at his watch. Nine and thirty.

Softly, but in his command voice, he recited Garcia's phone codes and told the system who was calling.

"Yes, Mr. Morrison?" Garcia's voice sounded in his ears. She sounded anxious, but that didn't mean much. Garcia nearly always sounded anxious, at least when she was speaking with him.

"I'm waiting for my guide," he said. Sometimes, it seemed to him that waiting for guides and being guided were all that he had done since arriving on the Moon. "What do you hear from Thomas and Callahan?" He had not been eager to delegate the project reviews to her, but it was the only way he could see to make his schedule work.

Garcia spoke hesitantly. "Well—"

"Be honest."

"Ms. Callahan wasn't very happy that I would be at the review instead of you," she said. "Seven doesn't seem to care."

Erik had exchanged some harsh words with Amber Callahan from Purchasing, about her near nonattendance of his first meeting. He wasn't surprised to hear that she was irritated now.

"Just sit there and be attentive," he advised her again. "Take notes—"

"I'm wearing my recorder," Garcia said.

"Take notes," Erik repeated. That was a lesson his father had taught him. "Even if you don't need them. It shows you're paying attention, and people like it when other people pay attention to them."

"Yes, Mr. Morrison."

A train passed through a nearby tunnel, one that ran somewhere below Erik's feet. The closed trains here used electric engines and rode on narrow steel wheels along tightly spaced traces. The metal surfaces sang as the trains accelerated and decelerated, but the acoustic fields on the platform damped most of the noise. All that survived was what got downshifted by the lunar rock, muted to a nearly subsonic rumble that he felt more than heard. The effect was particularly striking in the semienclosed waiting area, and he waited until it had subsided.

"I think you should start calling me 'Erik,' Juanita," He finally said. "If you're going to represent me at reviews, that is."

"Yes, sir!" The sudden confidence in his assistant's voice made her sound years younger.

"Yes, Erik," he said.

"Yes, Erik," she repeated.

"Good," Erik said. He heard a chime and a whisper of metal in plastic guides as the doors behind him opened. "Now, I think my ride is here, Juanita," he said, and then broke the connection.

"Erik?" A familiar voice said as he turned. "You're on first-name with Ms. Garcia now? It's about time."

The newly opened door framed a woman. Tall and lean, with features that were strong and distinctive, she was not beautiful, but Erik found himself staring at her. She wore a light tunic and slacks, cut along utilitarian lines that suggested a uniform without quite being one, but he scarcely noticed that. Instead, his eyes were drawn to her face, which wore an amused expression he found oddly familiar.

"I'm Wendy Scheer," she said.

"I know," he responded. He extended his hand to take hers, hooked thumbs, and smiled. All tension, all uncertainty, all worry seemed to flow from him. He felt as if he were in the presence of an old and dear friend. "I'm pleased to meet you at last," he said.

She laughed and tossed her hair back. Coming from anyone else, the movement would have been hopelessly affected, but from her, it seemed as natural as water flowing. "At last?" she said as she took his hand. "You've had plenty of chances. How many invitations have you turned down now? Three? Four?"

Erik wasn't sure what to say to that. He remembered his own advice to Garcia and just listened, instead.

"So," she said again. "First names?"

"You know Juanita?" he asked.

"She's taken a few of my calls," Wendy said. "Which is more than I can say for you." She stepped back through the doors and gestured for him to follow. As he did, she led him down a staircase.

Without knowing why, he felt the need to justify himself to her. "My schedule's been pretty full since arriving," he said. "And I have to give my first attentions to the other—"

"Silly." Wendy laughed. "I'm just kidding. Watch your step. You're in Armstrong territory now. That's another way of saying, 'grubby.'"

She overstated things. The platform section behind the

doors was noticeably more utilitarian than the main concourse, bordering on Spartan, but it was clean and neat. If the corridors Garcia had led him through on the way to Duckworth had reminded Erik of an industrial park, this space made him think of factories and manufacturing concerns. Unfinished gray slabs of native rock stretched away from the entrance under a gently domed ceiling— also unfinished—that held low-hung electro-luminescent fixtures. The surrounding walls were of block construction, again of the same unfinished gray stone, and punctuated by doors bearing signs that identified them as leading to maintenance cubbies and storage spaces. The air was cool but clean, free of even the faint scent of perspiration that came with human traffic.

"We don't have the budget for pretty," Wendy said, noticing his quick survey of the place. "And this is hardly a high-traffic area."

He shrugged. A phrase drifted up from his memory, the legacy of an engineering aesthetics course he had taken in college. "Form follows function. The place does the job."

Wendy nodded, smiled, and led him farther forward.

He decided that he liked it when she smiled, and followed.

Rather than an escalator or even a foot shaft, simple stairs led to a lower platform level. The risers were edged with steel cleats to prevent wear, and condensation made them slick. Erik took some care as he negotiated them. Low gravity or no low gravity, this was not a staircase he would care to tumble down. His bones would break before the steps would.

Wendy noticed his caution. "It can take months to adjust to the lower gravity. You're doing fine."

She took the steps in a liquid ripple that made even Garcia's grace seem clumsy, and Erik found it difficult to take her assessment seriously. "I had some help. But—why did you say this is Armstrong territory? We're still in Villanueva."

"Not really," Wendy said, flowing from the bottom step to the lower platform, which faced out onto a single set of tracks. On those tracks a compact auto-train waited. She gestured again, and its doors whisked open.

They settled into facing seats in the open car before she continued. "Villanueva's charter requires that the ALC provide reasonable support and accommodation to 'local federal activities.' Emphasis on 'reasonable,' and the ALC gets to define that. That means we provide our own train and tracks, and the ALC lets us connect to their system." She paused, and then corrected herself. "Your system, really."

If anyone else had offered him that explanation, Erik would have thought the terms reasonable, even generous. Hearing about the situation now from Wendy, he felt a sudden sympathy for Halo and its staff.

"That must make things difficult," he said.

"Not really," she said. "It makes them possible, actually. The federal government can't afford to make Armstrong self-sufficient, but as an adjunct to the commercial colony—"

The train lurched slightly as its motors engaged. Once more, Erik felt more than heard a rumble, and he found himself being pushed back into his seat as the vehicle accelerated.

"Officially, we're an industrial facility," he said. He didn't have to deal very often with federal officials, but he knew the preferred vocabulary when doing so. The word *colony* carried legal ramifications that made ALC management nervous.

"That's a polite fiction," Wendy said. "But I don't mind being polite."

The train continued to accelerate, metal on metal singing as it sped forward. The welcome illusion of additional gravity, however misdirected, faded as they reached cruising speed.

"Thirty minutes," Wendy said. "It's a more enjoyable ride with company."

The passenger car's interior held seats for ten. Where the Villanueva train's interior had looked clean and new, this vehicle had plainly seen better days.

Wendy saw him looking, and smiled. "It's never very crowded. Other cars are available, but there are only sixty of us at base. Ten seats are almost always enough."

"You must not entertain much," Erik said.

"There's not much to see," Wendy replied. Her words echoed Garcia's oddly. "Unless you're a radio astronomer or theoretical xenobiologist."

"Why the invitations, then?"

Wendy, opposite him, shifted slightly in her seat, looked at him with coolly appraising gray eyes. Like storm clouds, however, they seemed to be lit from within, with flecks of color and energy. "Good neighbor policy. We rely so much on Villanueva's infrastructure assets that it only makes sense. We don't even have our own hospital on-site, for heaven's sake. And if you think we're moving fast now, try riding this when it's doing duty as an ambulance."

Erik listened to the miles go by while he thought about that.

"We use EnTek processors," Wendy continued. Her words, as banal as they were, fascinated him. "When I saw that EnTek had assigned a new Site Coordinator, I extended the invitation."

"Tanaka invited me first," he said. "Then Tanaka's office."

"Tanaka extended my invitation. My idea, in my old role as liaison. With my promotion, I get to act on my own recommendations." She smiled. "Streamlines things a bit."

More miles passed, and neither felt the need to speak. Erik, for his part, felt far more comfortable in her presence than in any other he had experienced since his arrival. Some corner of his mind wondered why.

He didn't think he was *attracted* to her, in any but the most general sense of the term. He knew himself well enough to know that. She was pretty, with a good face and a good body, and her manner of speaking suggested a bantering intellect that he could learn to like, but that was all. Despite his earlier anticipation, he now felt no particular desire in her presence, not even the vague, almost knee-jerk reaction that Enola Hasbro had provoked.

What he felt was at ease. He had known her less than half of an hour, but it was as if he had known her for years, and he liked being around her. He had never felt this way before, especially not on such short acquaintance.

He liked her, and he wasn't sure why.

The train braked, then slowed, then shuddered to a halt. Wendy led him up a flight of stairs like the ones at Villanueva.

"Walking is good for you," Wendy said this time. She paused. "Do you want the grand tour first?"

"Whatever's easiest," Erik replied.

"Grand tour, then," she said with a nod. "Then lunch."

* * *

GARCIA had been right, Erik realized: There wasn't much to see at Halo. Most of the place was like Villanueva, tunnels and corridors and anonymous offices. Wendy Scheer led him from door to door, pausing now and then to introduce him to this nondescript analyst or that nameless researcher. Science, as such, didn't interest him very much, nor did the names of the people and the roles they played in pursuit of the facility's nebulous enterprise. He hooked thumbs and traded names. He nodded politely and feigned interest, as men and woman showed him various instruments and displays that he really didn't understand. Through it all, with Wendy as his patient guide, he felt not even a hint of the impatience or irritation that usually came with such boredom.

Only Armstrong's main data processors interested him even slightly. The big banks of white-finished cabinets held EnTek Gummis, semiliving tissue yoked in service to Halo's agenda. The Gummis were recorded with government-commissioned brainware, designed to analyze the endless telemetry gathered by Armstrong's array of radio telescopes and antennae. They were host to the place's private version of the Mesh, an in-house data sharing and storage system.

They were also hopelessly out of date, at least seven years old and four generations behind what Erik's employers offered now.

"A bit behind the times," he said to Wendy as she led him from the low-ceilinged room that held the heart of that network. It was the first critical comment he had made during the tour.

She nodded. "It's been a long time since we've been able to get more than a maintenance appropriation," she said, then gestured. "Through here."

The corridor had come to an end, and as they approached, the doors of a foot-shaft opened and Wendy climbed in. She moved quickly along the shaft's wall-mounted hand- and footholds, so quickly that Erik had a hard time keeping up with her. Yet again, his body reminded him that it had evolved to meet the demands of a much larger world; climbing was easier than it would have been on Earth, but not as easy as he had expected.

"Exercise is good for you," Wendy said, over her shoulder. "And these are easier to maintain than powered lifts. Cheaper, too."

Erik didn't reply. He concentrated on placing his hands and feet on one set of holds after another. The shaft was too broad to inspire claustrophobia. Its confines were close enough, however, that the air smelled of the sweat and exertion of the many who had used it before him. He was pleased when Wendy led them both through another opening and onto an upper level.

It was a garage. Ten bays waited, seven of them dark and empty. Two held tarpaulin-shrouded masses, vague and bulky in the shadows. One bay was brightly lit and nearly filled with a vehicle similar to ones that Erik had seen in Garcia's reports.

Like an ant with wheels, it had a long, low fuselage made up of three segments that came together in flexible joints, the distinctive features of a prospector's utility vehicle. Each segment was flanked by a pair of huge, knobby-tired wheels and studded with antenna and lamps. Neatly folded along its sides were probes and extensors, remote-control arms for the benefit of the vehicle's passengers. Its doors were open, and padded contour seats were visible through them, and through the lead section's domed roof.

"We're going outside?" he asked, surprised.

"Unless you don't want to," Wendy said. "The tour won't be complete, otherwise."

"Do we need to suit up?" Two nearby racks held rows of pressure suits, neatly arrayed, like soldiers awaiting orders.

Wendy shook her head. The garage's multiple light sources cast shadows on her face, and the movement did interesting things to them. Erik thought briefly of skin-diving off the California coast, of the rippling display of light and shadow beneath the sea.

"We shouldn't need to," she said. "It's just a short jaunt, a run around the installation and we won't be getting out."

Erik shrugged. Zonix Lifestyles operated charter surface tours from Villanueva, using more luxuriously appointed craft, but he had never even considered making the trip. Mesh feeds and wallpaper were enough for him.

"You'll have to drive," he said, and climbed into the passenger seat.

Minutes later, the Moon-buggy had rolled up an exit ramp, through the inner and then the outer doors of the garage airlock, and out onto the Moon's surface.

Erik saw the sky again and realized that Mesh feeds and wallpaper images *weren't* enough.

It was dawn, or nearly dawn. Low on the horizon to his left was the Earth's shadowed bulk, and peering out from behind it was the Sun, searing in its brilliance, but not enough to light the black sky. Instead, the darkness drank up its light, giving way only to more stars than Erik had ever seen before. Cold and unblinking, they gazed down on a stark landscape that was as white as bone.

"The dome cuts the glare a bit," Wendy said, after giving him a moment to take in his surroundings. "Smart filters adjust the contrast, too. But it's still impressive, isn't it?"

Erik nodded, at a loss for words.

"That's what I wanted you to see," Wendy said. For the first time since they had arrived at Armstrong, she used a tone that wasn't purely and politely businesslike. Instead, she spoke with something like reverence. "The frontier. It's why we're here, really."

Erik didn't say anything, as the tractor lurched forward, knobbed wheels digging into the lunar soil. He heard a clattering sound overlay the whine of the tractor's electric motor, audible as it resonated through the vehicle's structure. Gravel, lofted by their progress, was ricocheting from the tractor's hull.

Wendy's hands moved, and the steering yoke moved with them. She pushed down with one booted foot, and the pitch of the electric motors shifted. The buggy turned right, moving away from the nearly eclipsed sun and toward the darker horizon.

"This is a very old design." Wendy spoke with polite detachment. "They had working prototypes of these tractors more than a century ago. The motors work better and the fuel cells last longer, but the idea is the same."

Erik didn't say anything. He stared at the ragged Moonscape, so much more imposing than the wallpaper image in his office. It had a kind of majesty, of intensity, that no image could duplicate. He had seen nearly identical vistas on wallpapers and in old-books and had looked out on space during the passenger run up from Earth, but this was different.

"Let me get you a good view."

The buggy motors changed pitch again, and the clatter of bouncing gravel ended as she guided it up a rise in their ragged surroundings. For whatever reason, less gravel littered the incline, but its surface held cracks and gaps that made the buggy bounce as it rolled. On Earth, this formation might have been a river bluff, but Erik knew that on the Moon, there had to be a different origin for the thirty-meter incline. When they reached its top, he could see that the selenological ramp came to an abrupt end, giving way to a sharp drop-off. Beyond it, in the deeper darkness, the hints of something darker could been seen, blocking the stars from view.

"Lights," Wendy said in a commanding voice.

In instant response, the buggy's headlamps activated. The beams they emitted were effectively invisible, of course. The Moon had no atmosphere to speak of. No atmosphere meant no floating dust motes to catch the light and throw it back at them. Instead, that role was left to the small forest of structures ahead, as Wendy shone the light on them.

They looked stark and unfinished, like skeletons without skin. Pylons crafted of girder latticework rose from the lunar surface. Buttresses and guy wires stabilized them, but they still looked absurdly ethereal for the burdens they bore: huge antenna dishes, mounted on motorized pivots, trained at the blackness above. Scores of antennae stretched into the distance, but Erik could see only a portion of each, as the oval pools of light slid over them.

"These, too," Wendy repeated. "They were building dishes like these more than a hundred years ago, and for pretty much the same purpose. They will never look much different. Like you said, form follows function."

"This is Project Halo, then," Erik said. Not too many days before, he had dismissed the concept as a waste of taxpayers' money. Here, seated in a Moon-buggy atop a lunar crest, the reality seemed more impressive, even if still wasteful.

"Good distinction," Wendy said. The fingers of her right hand had coiled loosely around a lever on the control panel. She moved those fingers now, and the headlamp beams moved in response, playing across one antenna after another. "This is really all Halo is, when you get down to it," she said. "Ears. Passive listening. We monitor in a range of one thousand to three thousand megahertz, and we've got the resolution down to point-five megahertz." She paused. "Computer imaging can take it further down, of course. We look for regular patterns, signals, anything that even suggests an artificial signal not of Earthly origin."

"I'm surprised you get anything useful out of them," Erik said.

She glanced at him, surprised. "Good point. We don't, really, not anymore. Signal traffic interference from Villanueva has gotten too great in the last ten years or so. That's why we've gone to remote dishes for most data collections, with smaller sites positioned over a broad area, and a relay network. Mobile units, too."

"That's not what I meant," Erik said. "Not useable, useful." Wendy flashed him a glance then, and he wished he hadn't said anything. "What I mean, is—"

"I know what you meant," Wendy said. She spoke now in clipped bursts of syllables. "There's no profit in it." She did something to the buggy controls and pulled back on the steering yoke again. The buggy began moving backward in a curving track.

"Well, there isn't," Erik said. He spoke mildly, but with heartfelt sincerity.

"Call it research," Wendy said, still terse. She brought the buggy to a halt, twisted the steering yoke to her right, then shifted to forward gear again. They moved back down the rise. "In its purest form."

"Pure research is a luxury," Erik said. He had uttered the same phase many times over the years, but usually from a position of authority.

"It's not a luxury," Wendy said. "It's something people *do*. It's like art, like music, like exploration, like love." She sounded surprisingly idealistic for a government functionary.

Erik could think of a dozen arguments to counter each of hers, but he didn't voice any of them. He didn't like the tone of her voice, and he didn't want to aggravate things by disagreeing over an issue as trivial as this one. Instead, he nodded, and asked, "Have you gotten anything?"

"Some leads," Wendy said. "Nothing that we're ready to talk about. Security concerns."

"SETI is classified?" Erik almost laughed.

"SETI has serious public-relations issues and is widely perceived as a waste of taxpayer money," Wendy said with some asperity. The crack in her professional demeanor opened wider, and defensiveness spilled out. "The Search for Extra-Terrestrial Intelligence doesn't have very many friends in Congress, and Congress doesn't have very much money to spend. The federal government isn't fat with money like the ALC and corporations like it. We don't need the embarrassment of a false announcement. We'll wait until we're sure."

Erik didn't want to disagree with her for some reason, but he had had this kind of argument with others, many times, and the appropriate response came almost reflexively to his lips. "You've been waiting a long time."

Wendy didn't say anything. They were near the bottom of the rise now, and the reverse hail of up-tossed gravel rattled again against the buggy's hull, making her silence all the more noticeable.

Actually saying the words was like swimming in glue, against the current. "SETI runs back at least a century, right? You said the listeners date back that far."

Wendy nodded.

"When's it going to pay off?"

"It doesn't have to pay off, not in credits," Wendy said.

Erik had no idea what to say to that.

The buggy's motors changed pitch again. More gravel kicked up, and the bumpy ride continued. Wendy guided the utilitarian vehicle on a tour of Armstrong's surface facilities, directing his attention to one low structure after another. Utility sheds, testing equipment, and supply dumps all dotted the Moonscape, mute evidence of mankind's presence. Most of the area had been cleared by earlier traffic, but at one point their progress took them through a patch of micrometeorite dust. It rose in a little puff, and for a brief moment, the buggy's headlight beams were visible from inside the compartment, pale lances on light against the darkness.

"We've been here a while," she said, finally resuming their earlier conversation. "Funding was more generous in the old days, and we could do more."

"I thought you looked a little understaffed," Erik said. Many of the offices and work areas in Halo's lower levels had been closed and dark.

"Sixty-three on-site now," Wendy said. "At peak, it was a hundred and forty-seven. We don't have the luxury of your budget. We almost didn't get funding this year, at all. I don't suppose we can expect it next year."

Erik thought about the news feeds he had studied since arriving here, about how hard Armstrong's sponsor had fought to secure even a token appropriation for the government site in the current budget. He supposed that she was correct in her pessimism, but aloud, he said, "Things might get better."

Wendy made no reply, but steered the buggy back toward Halo's garage airlock.

LUNCH in Wendy's office was pleasant enough. In the brief time since Tanaka's evacuation, she had redecorated. Wanting Morrison to feel more or less at ease, she had requisitioned the best of the old-furniture from storage. Staff had reconfigured the former site head's space to include a discreet dining area, neatly but not elaborately appointed. The commissary chef wheeled in a cart laden with gleaming covered dishes—more reminders of better-budgeted days—and left the two of them to dine together.

"I hope you don't mind eating in private," Wendy said. Deliberately, she feigned a delicate shudder. "I don't take guests to the commissary."

Morrison laughed politely and lifted the first of the dish covers. The aroma of fresh-baked bread wafted through the unfortunate Tanaka's former office. "This looks very nice," Morrison said. He lifted another cover, revealing sautéed chicken slices in a cream sauce. "Hmph. *Rahm-geschnetzeltes vom Huhn*." When he named the dish, he spoke the words in a musical cadence that Wendy had never associated with German.

He glanced at her. "Do they raise poultry here?" he asked.

She nodded. "Villanueva does. Zonix, actually. The pasta is local, too."

Local and good. Wendy had expected nothing better than high-end auto-stove meals, but, plainly, the commissary chef had gone further than that. She didn't need Morrison's expertise in German cuisine to know that someone had done an excellent job of balancing spices and other seasonings. Even the chicken itself was better than she would have expected, with a texture and character that belied its local origin.

"Are we civilized?" she asked, after a last bite.

Erik nodded, setting down his fork. "Cuisines are interesting things. They evolve in new environments. This is a traditional dish, but using local foodstuffs makes it new again. I'm impressed. I wish we ate this well at En-Tek. You'll have to introduce me to your chef."

Laughter, easy and sincere, came uninvited to Wendy's lips. "You've met her," she said. "She was wearing a lab jacket and monitoring a scintillometer, but you met her."

"A scintillometer?" Erik looked at her blankly.

"Scintillation counter," Wendy said. "It measures rapid changes in the brightness of celestial bodies. We process data from—"

Morrison still had a distinctly blank look on his face. "I'm not a scientist," he reminded her.

It was not the best opening that Wendy could have asked for, but it was good enough, and the time had come to be direct. "What are you, then, Erik? What are you doing here?"

The muscles in Morrison's face tensed, and his lips became a straight white line. His eyes took on a sudden intensity, and the graying brows above them drew together. It wasn't an expression Wendy saw very often, but it looked at home on her visitor's face.

"You're the second—third person to ask me that here." He gestured at the remnants of his meal. "And my guess is, you've done at least a little bit of research into the matter."

Taken aback, Wendy said, "I'm not sure what you mean."

"I like German food," Morrison said. He still spoke pleasantly—everyone spoke pleasantly in Wendy's presence—but his tones held a new wariness. "Not very popular these days, but it's in my publicity bio. You've done some research."

"I have," Wendy said, nodding. She felt suddenly, uncomfortably close to losing control of the conversation. "Nothing more than what a good hostess should do, though. Especially regarding someone with your reputation."

A fragment of fresh bread remained on the small saucer next to Morrison's plate. He raised it, bit, chewed, and swallowed. "Reputation?"

"People say you're a bit of a troubleshooter," Wendy said.

Now, it was Morrison who laughed. "Used to be. But that was a long time ago."

Wendy stared at him. Had she guessed wrong?

Morrison continued. "If you talking about Australia," he said, "I—"

Wendy shook her head. It was time to be direct. "I'm talking about Ramirez," she said. "And what he found."

Once again, Morrison stared at her blankly. Utter confusion marked his features as he said, "I have no idea what you're talking about."

He was sincere, Wendy realized, and she felt the world seem to fall away as she realized the magnitude of her mistake. Morrison didn't know about Ramirez or his find.

Or, more precisely, he *hadn't* known.

CHAPTER 11

BY the standard clock, late afternoon had come by the time Erik made his way back to Villanueva proper. It was too late in the Moon's arbitrary day for him to go back to work. The world seemed to move in slow motion as he retraced much of his earlier route in reverse.

Had he paused to realize, he would have been surprised at the casual ease with which he made his way from the discreet entrance on the trans-Carnegie platform and back through the looping sprawl of trains and gray tram tunnels that led to the EnTek sector. He moved with rapid confidence, shouldering his way through crowds, yielding right of way to no one, barely noticing the occasional tourist or local who didn't get out of his way promptly enough. His footsteps fell, one after another, in the rapid, shuffling pace he had practiced so hard, faster than they ever had before. For perhaps the first time since coming to Villanueva, he walked without conscious deliberation, and with an air of purpose.

His mind was elsewhere. The remainder of his interview with Scheer had been awkward, to say the least. After her question about Ramirez and his find, his hostess had hastily changed the subject, with a certain rhetorical ineptitude he had found charming at the time. Now that he was away from her, however, now that he was out of her presence, the remembered clumsiness of her verbal feint was too great to ignore. He had to wonder how Wendy Scheer had ascended to her present status and what she had meant by her question.

Who was Ramirez? What had he found?

"Juanita," he said, in his command voice, then waited a few seconds for his phone to make the connection. When she acknowledged, he continued, without greeting or pleasantry. "Find Kowalski. Tell him I want him in my office tomorrow at oh-eight."

"He's supposed to be—"

"He's supposed to be in my office at oh-eight," Erik said, interrupting. The tram he was riding slowed and braked, but he didn't wait for it to stop completely before stepping lightly onto the substation's platform deck. He bounced a bit as his feet struck the rubbery surface, but he made the momentum work for him as he moved quickly toward a foot-shaft. "Tell him that, and put it that way," he continued. "He'll show, if only to tell me he didn't have to."

"Yes, Mr. Morrison," Juanita said.

"Yes, Erik," he corrected her.

"Yes, Erik."

Seven matching women had somehow gotten between him and the foot-shaft. All were beautiful. Their heights differed, but hair, eyes, and picto-teeth were all precisely the same, and they carried matching shopping bags. They even moved in perfect unison, and the low gravity did interesting things for their generous figures. Their tunics all bore the logo of a Zonix casino. Heaven only knew what they did there, and right now Erik didn't care.

Still moving with a fluid grace that would have been beyond him even a week ago, he threaded his way through the cluster of femininity, scarcely noticing barely stifled comments or grazing contact with warm flesh. He was still thinking about Scheer and what she had said. One of the women winked at him, but he ignored her.

"What do you know about Rogers Caspian?" he asked, as his hands found the foot-shaft handholds and he began moving upward. This was a broader, heavy-traffic shaft, with multiple ladder-ways and even a powered section that some corner of his mind dismissed as being pointless. The walls of the shaft moved rapidly past him as he climbed. He found the rhythm again quickly, the exercise soon became oddly comforting.

"Well, I—" Garcia had reverted to her typical diffidence and hesitation.

"I need a backgrounder on him," Erik interrupted. "Not the canned release stuff, but something from people who knew him. Can you put together a list of staff and known associates?"

"I told you, I didn't work for Mr. Caspian," Garcia said.

"I can get something official, if I go through channels," Erik said, responding only obliquely. "I just don't want to wait."

"It would only take—"

"Horvath can get it for me, but I don't want to bother him," Erik said. He chose his words carefully and made his tone deliberately casual. It was a safe bet that Horvath's interest in him was office gossip by now. If it wasn't, it would be, after he broke the link. "Get me what you can. Ask around, but be discreet." That shouldn't be too difficult; Caspian's change in employment must have prompted a fair amount of gossip, and if Garcia were careful, her enquiry would seem to be more of the same.

"I'll do what I can," Garcia said.

"When is my lunch with Caspian?" Erik asked. He released the last handhold and stepped out into a familiar corridor. He was midway between office and home.

"Tomorrow, noon," she said. "DiNuvio's. I put a map and menu in your directory."

"Good. Now call Kowalski," he said, and broke the connection.

"I don't work for you," Heck Kowalski said twenty minutes later, sprawled on the couch. The lights above had been dimmed, and the Mesh wallpaper had been set to prerecorded images of the Amazon rain forest. The result was a riot of color and vegetation that looked as if it belonged to a world other than Erik's habitual Alaska wallscape. Kowalski had apparently pumped the intensity, too, to levels high enough that the walls cast a greenish-yellow light into the room. The dappled radiance played along the contours of Kowalski's face as he sat, unmoving, in the midst of Erik's private quarters.

Erik paused as he stepped through the door into his own apartment, but only briefly. Recovering, he nodded and almost smiled. "Very dramatic tableau," he said. "Dialogue, too. Did you get that from one of your games?"

"I don't work for you, and I don't take instructions from Garcia," Kowalski continued. He spoke with a calm assurance and barely glanced in Erik's direction as the door whisked shut. "Except maybe to DiNuvio's."

"She called you already?" Erik asked, more surprised by that than by Kowalski's presence.

Kowalski shook his head, moving it only a fraction of a degree in either direction. "I was listening," he said. He was carefully watching something in the wallpaper scene, and it apparently commanded most of his attention.

"That's a surprise," Erik said. "You must have a lot of free time, after all." That Kowalski could monitor his voice traffic was a given, but that the other man would do it in real-time was a bit of a surprise. Erik wondered if he were under continual surveillance.

Kowalski shook his head again. "This is really nice," he said idly, and pointed. "The wall setup, I mean. I can't afford feeds like these. Or screens. I wish I could. This is what the human eye evolved for, you know."

"High-res wallpaper?" Erik asked.

"For yellow sunlight filtering through green foliage," Kowalski said. He was focusing on something in the recorded image, and Erik craned his neck to see what. A patch of color shifted, and he realized that what commanded Kowalski's attention wasn't just another of the many tangled vines that hung on the imaged trees.

Or if it was, it was a vine that could move.

"Anaconda," Kowalski said matter-of-factly, as the ropy mass of green and brown slithered along a tree limb. "They used to grow to almost ten meters in the wild. This must be old feed."

"Thirty years old," the apartment housekeeper interjected. *"Archival footage from the—"*

"Shut up," Kowalski said, before Erik could. The apartment fell silent.

"It's a jungle out there," Erik said. "Can I fix you a drink? Or have you taken care of that, too?"

Kowalski looked away from the snake to face Erik and then looked back again. "I wanted to ask you about Armstrong," he explained. "I wasn't sure when you were coming back, so I let myself in and set my phone to monitor yours, so that I'd know when you were on your way. That's just in case you were wondering."

Erik nodded. That made a certain kind of sense, even if he didn't like it. "Just like the wallpaper," he said. "Rank has its privileges."

He stepped to the kitchen and opened a cabinet. "Sure I can't get you a drink?" he asked.

"I don't drink when I'm working," Kowalski said.

"You're working now?"

"I'm always working," Kowalski said.

Erik nodded at that, too. "It's a good policy, but I'm at home," he said. Finding the bottle he wanted, he poured vodka into a squat tumbler, then added ice and orange. "Local stuff, but I might as well get used to it. How about coffee?" When Kowalski nodded, Erik grabbed a can of instant before he returned to the living room.

On the wallpaper, the snake was eating something. Its jaws were open, and the last of a pair of brown-furred legs were twitching desperately as the serpent's powerful muscles drew something inside.

"Lemur. I moved the feed ahead," Heck said, and caught the coffee as Erik tossed it to him in a long low, arc.

"Make yourself at home," Erik said again, a bit grimly this time. He settled into a chair and waited.

"This is an EnTek guest facility," Kowalski said. He peeled back the lid of the new-coffee and took a sip of the now-steaming contents. "I have access codes and overrides. If you want privacy, you can rent a place of your own."

"My guess is, that would cost a lot more and I'd still likely find you in my living room," Erik said.

"If I wanted to be there," Kowalski smiled. He was dressed more neatly and looked more official today, but a brief grin undercut that. He sipped some more new-coffee. "This is a company town, Morrison."

There wasn't much Erik could say to that, but, mentally, he filed the other man's words away for future reference.

"Tell me about Wendy Scheer," Kowalski continued.

"Attractive," Erik replied. He thought for a moment. His visit at Halo had left him with half a dozen contradictory impressions that were hard to reconcile, and harder to articulate. Plus, he wasn't sure how much he wanted to tell Kowalski. "She seems knowledgeable, but somehow, slightly naive," he said. "No, not naive. Guileless. She strikes me as someone who usually gets her way, but doesn't know how to work consciously for it." He paused again, and smiled. "I liked her."

"Everyone likes her," Kowalski said.

"You said you've never met her before."

Kowalski shook his head, more emphatically this time. Whatever the wall-snake was up to, it no longer commanded his attention, and he focused on Erik as he spoke. "But I've met people who've met her. They all liked her, and they all say she's smart. You're the first one to make the guileless comment, but that doesn't contradict anything else I've heard."

He paused, sipping. "What did you want to see me for, anyway?"

"See you?" Erik asked, startled by the change of subject.

"I told you, I monitored your call to Garcia," Kowalski said patiently. "Or do I have to wait for tomorrow at oh-eight?"

Erik set down his drink. He would have preferred time to put a bit more thought into the matter, but Kowalski's presence, unexpected as it was, had forced the issue. "I want you to work with me on something," he said carefully. "*With,* not *for.*"

"I'm waiting."

"Scheer's hiding something," Erik said. Saying the words aloud crystallized the situation in his mind, and he found himself suddenly able to set aside the Halo woman's undeniable charms.

"I thought you said she was guileless." Kowalski had finished his coffee and set the disposable can aside. "Do you have anything to eat?"

"Ready meals in the kitchen," Erik said, reasonably sure that Kowalski knew about them already. "Help yourself," he said, but Kowalski was already halfway there. "And she is guileless. Guile is deliberate, and this was accidental. She made a slip when we were talking," he continued. "Do you know anything about a man named Ramirez?"

From the kitchen, he could hear a brief, muttered exchange between Kowalski and the apartment housekeeper. Something clicked and whirred. Then Kowalski continued in a louder voice, "Ramirez. It's a common name. You ask about a lot of common names."

"Scheer is looking for him."

"Any idea why?" Kowalski asked, returning. He had another can of new-coffee in one hand and a tray of fast food in the other—meat rolls, dip, and Snackles.

"He's found something," Erik said. "That's all I know. But she thought I knew more."

"Thought?" Kowalski was eating, rapidly and efficiently, and scarcely paused between bites to speak. He still spoke like a trained investigator, though. "She doesn't think that anymore?"

"I told that her I had no idea what she was talking about," Erik said.

Kowalski grunted. "You couldn't bluff?"

"I didn't want to bluff," Erik said, and, again, saying the words crystallized the thought. "I didn't want to lie to her." More to the point, he had wanted to answer every question he could, but there was no point in giving Kowalski that kind of detail. Instead, he gave a quick summary of his visit, and of his conversation with Scheer.

Kowalski grunted again. "She is attractive," he said.

"It wasn't like that," Erik said, and shook his head. Away from Scheer, her presence was easier to describe, if increasingly difficult to remember clearly. "She had some kind of effect on me. *Charming,* that's the word. She was charming."

"Everyone likes Wendy Scheer," Kowalski said again. He sounded as if he were quoting a truism.

Erik thought back. He had been attracted to and involved with more than a few women, and he had been seriously, deeply in love twice. Scheer didn't fit into either of those categories. He liked her, pure and simple, with almost no overlay of sexual attraction or romantic feeling. He tried to remember a match for the kind of magnetism he had felt in Scheer's presence, but could find none. The closest he could come was the undeniable charisma of certain politicians and powerbrokers—like

Janos Horvath. But, whereas those men and women carried with them an air of command, Wendy Scheer's presence had been something gentle and persuasive, so low-key that he had been almost unaware of it at the time. Even now, the effect lingered.

"Good thing she's not a politician, isn't it?" Kowalski asked, then put a Snackle in his mouth, chewed, and swallowed.

"I wish she were. I'd vote for her," Erik said, without humor. "For any office." He paused. "Can you look into the Ramirez thing for me?"

"I don't work for you," Kowalski said, yet again, like a mantra.

"I'm not asking you to," Erik said. "But I think I'm on to something, and I think that it might be something big." He spoke carefully. "I can't make any promises, and I'm not exactly on the golden track these days, but these things have a way of changing. Work with me, and I might be able to do things for you in the long run."

"Horvath says I'm to cooperate, but I'm also supposed to keep an eye on you." Kowalski continued, with surprising directness. "I'm supposed to use my judgment. He thinks I have some."

That was another surprise. There had to be more to Kowalski if Janos Horvath had any regard for his judgment at all, Erik realized. "I don't plan to give Horvath anything to worry about," he said.

"You already have, I think," Kowalski said coolly. He set the snack tray aside. "Or maybe *worry* is too strong a word. He's certainly interested in what you're up to."

Erik nodded. "I know." That raised even more questions, but he didn't feel like pursuing them just now.

"He wouldn't tell me why, though, and I know better

than to ask," Kowalski said. "It's funny," he added. "Half the people I talk to think you're in exile, but I think he had you sent here to do something for him."

Erik had no response to make to that. Instead, he said, "I still need help with this Ramirez."

"Like you did with Stewart?" Kowalski asked.

Erik had almost forgotten about Doug Stewart, but he nodded. "Like with Stewart," he said. "Any information on him?"

Kowalski shrugged. "Just that he doesn't exist," he said easily, then grinned at Erik's reaction. "Heh. That's the other reason I'm here. I wanted to see how you took that, in person."

"He doesn't exist?" Erik asked, dumfounded.

"No one by that name exists in the Zonix's contractor rolls." Kowalski opened his computer and read from it. "There are seventeen Doug Stewarts in the general populace, but none work for Zonix, neither contract nor staff. Another eight have come and gone in the tourist trade over the last three weeks, but I don't think any of them is the guy you're looking for."

"How is that possible?" Erik asked. He had long since assumed that Stewart was hiding something, but this was a surprise.

"We're a closed society, but we don't micromanage," Kowalski told him again. "There's no reason to. The five partners look out for their own, and we all look out for tourists. There are cracks, though, and people can fall through them." He looked at his computer again. "I ran the phone code. It was public, from a third-party reseller. He probably got it at the Mall for hard currency. There's a good market for stuff like that. He paid with third-party credit at the restaurant, too."

"Why?"

Kowalski took a deep breath. "You're married," he said. "Hypothetically, I mean. You've been in a marriage for ten years, and you're tired of your wives and want some variety. The missuses think that means a vacation on the Moon, but you think it means a night with the Clone Sisters, over at ZonixWorld. So you buy third-party credits and take a little vacation of your own, without telling anyone. Maybe one of your wives does the same thing." He grinned tightly.

"But why?" Erik asked again. The idea of not being able to trace personnel as they moved about the facility was anathema. "Why does the ALC allow it?"

"Tourist trade."

"Stewart isn't a tourist. He's gone to some trouble to make himself a nuisance," Erik said.

"Maybe he's looking for a job," Kowalski said and snickered. "You said you were interested in hiring him."

Erik waived in dismissal. "That was a joke," he said, irritated. "And I can't hire someone who doesn't exist." That prompted a thought. "No one else can, either. He must have a real name, real accounts," Erik continued. "Any way you could track those down?"

"Maybe, but not without a lot more reason than you've given me," Kowalski said. "I've got a budget, and I have to account for how I spend it."

"I could give you a description. If he's staff, his personnel file would include images. And if he's a visitor, his passport—"

Kowalski laughed at that. "A description wouldn't be enough. I'd need a high-res picture to make a reliable match against the Personnel and Customs files. A good picture, nothing miraged. Even then, it might be tough.

I don't have access to everything," he said. "And there's something else to consider."

Erik looked at him blankly.

"Juanita doesn't look the same two days running, does she?" Kowalski said.

He had a point. Juanita's gallery of new looks was impressive. Apparently, cosmetic appliances were cheaper here, or at least more popular. The image of seven identical women wearing the ZonixWorld logo drifted up from Erik's memory. They had to be the Clone Sisters. He wondered briefly if they still matched so precisely at the end of the day.

Or night.

Kowalski continued. "If I had a reliable image, I could run it against the files, but that would take time, too. Recognition brainware is good, but not as good as people think it is. And time is credit. Unless you can get me a budget boost—"

"I can't do anything about that," Erik said. "At least, not yet."

Kowalski stood and stretched. "Reset," he said in what had to be his command voice, and the walls reverted to blank. "I'm about done, then," he said. "We'll have to wait until Stewart makes another call."

"We?" Erik said.

Kowalski nodded. "I've got some downtime," he said. "And I looked over your files. You've been able to do people favors before, and I'm guessing that someday, you'll be able to do favors again. I like favors." He looked suddenly more serious. "But I'm not going to do anything to cross Janos Horvath."

That seemed reasonable enough, so Erik nodded in agreement. Of course, it was entirely possible that

Kowalski's definition of not crossing Horvath would be to report every development to upper management first. There might be nothing Erik could do about that, but it was a fact that he had to keep in mind. Part of the game was remembering never to trust your allies completely.

"I don't want to cross Horvath either," he said aloud, almost meaning it. "Not again."

"Yeah, I head about Alaska," Kowalski said easily. "Tomorrow at noon?"

Erik nodded. "What about Ramirez?" he asked.

"I'll do what I can. Like I said, it's a common name. I'll start with my Halo records. Did you get anything else?"

Erik thought, picking through his memories. Here, at home, he could be a little bit more objective about what Wendy Scheer had said, but she really hadn't said very much. "Ramirez is a *he*," he said. "No first name. He's found something, and I had the impression that Scheer was looking for him, only because she wanted *it*. She quieted down as soon as she realized that I didn't know what she was talking about."

"That's not much," Kowalski said. "Maybe I'll get lucky. Anything else?"

"I'd like to know Wendy Scheer better," Erik said. "More about her, I mean."

"You've met her, I haven't," Kowalski reminded him. "Everything I have is secondhand."

"I'd still like to see it."

"I'll put together a backgrounder," Kowalski said. "It'll be in your private directory tomorrow. Just use your mail access code to read it."

"That's supposed to be confidential" Erik said.

Kowalski smiled. "See you at DiNuvio's tomorrow," he said.

* * *

"HE'S eating lunch at DiNuvio's tomorrow," Wendy said, as the last syllables of the audio feed faded.

Old habits died hard. She had returned for the evening to her preferred office, the secluded nook on Halo's lowest level. It hadn't been reassigned yet and wasn't likely to be, any time soon, so the security systems were still in place. Steadily declining budgets for Armstrong had resulted in a surplus of space, and not many found the place's other amenities as attractive as Wendy did. Right now, seated at her familiar desk, she felt at home again, surrounded by unfurled computers and hard-copy documents. Except for her paintings, now hung in her private quarters, it was as if she had come home again. Even the guest who sat opposite her was familiar.

"That's too expensive for my account," Ralph Tanaka said easily. He looked out of place, perched in a guest chair in what had been his own office. "Not that I plan to make the Villanueva run anytime soon."

"Tomorrow, I think," Wendy said.

"Tomorrow?"

Wendy nodded. "I made a bad mistake, Ralph. I thought Morrison was already on the trail, and he wasn't. Not until I set him on it."

Tanaka shrugged. He scrolled back through screens on his own computer to check his notes and nodded. "Morrison was asking about Caspian before he had any idea who you were," he noted. "The man was his predecessor as site coordinator, after all. And he quit. That raises eyebrows."

"It's more than that," Wendy said. Here was one drawback to her gift. It blunted the best judgment of others, sometimes in her favor and sometimes in what they perceived as her favor. Ralph wasn't trying to disagree with her; he was trying to soothe her. "He's having lunch with Caspian, at a restaurant that no one but tourists can afford, with his security chief for company. We have to act."

CHAPTER 12

AFTER Kowalski had left, Erik decided that he was hungry, after all. He went to the kitchen and looked for the appropriate components to a light meal.

The apartment had come pre-equipped with a modest complement of ready meals and prepackaged foods, and his grocery orders had supplemented them considerably. One cabinet yielded a brand of vegetable spread he had enjoyed in Australia. That prompted memories of happier times, so he made a sandwich, using the spread and some heavy, chewy bread that was labeled as being made from locally grown grain. Another refrigerator compartment offered up hybrid lettuce and radishes that he sliced thin and combined with bottled dressing to make a light salad. Taking a quick glance at the freezer inventory, he was delighted to discover that someone had stocked the place with the expensive luxury of real coffee, even if the beans were of a variety that was new to him. He measured out a reasonable portion and dumped them in the stove's appropriate slot.

For engineering and economical reasons, Villanueva's artificial environment operated at an atmospheric pressure that was only about 80 percent of Earth's sea-level normal. Given a chance to adjust, the human body didn't mind much, but the reduced pressure lowered water's boiling point correspondingly, so that certain kinds of cooking required special measures. Brewing coffee was especially tricky, and best left to the apartment housekeeper's brainware.

"Coffee, strong," he said. "One cup, to start with."

A minute or so later, the stove vented the brewing coffee's aroma to the air, and Erik smiled. Much of the flavor was actually defined by aroma, he knew. Now, even in this strange place that would never really be his home, the coffee smelled robust and real, and familiar.

He moved to the kitchen's small dining area. In response to a murmured command, a table and chair unfolded themselves from wall recesses, and Erik arranged his sandwich and salad neatly on a decorated place mat. After a moment's thought, while he waited for the coffee to finish brewing, he went to the appropriate cabinet and found the imported Sony bourbon.

With Kowalski gone, there was no need to drink the cheap stuff.

A horizontal panel on the stove's cooking surface slid back, and his coffee rose into view. Erik took the mug and tasted its contents, nodded to himself in satisfaction, and then sat.

As he ate and drank, he thought.

There was plenty to think about. The fact that Kowalski

could enter his quarters unbidden wasn't surprising and even made a certain kind of sense, but he was surprised that the other man had been so obvious about it. That merited some consideration.

It could have been as simple as Kowalski had said, Erik knew. He had wanted to meet Erik and hadn't wanted to wait in the corridor, and it was Erik's experience that people who had privileges and authorities tended to use them, and use them more casually as time passed. On the other hand, the way that Kowalski had made himself completely at home suggested that he had wanted to make some kind of impression on his host. Overriding the house-keeper and even selecting dramatic wallpaper feeds went far beyond simple territory marking.

Erik bit into his sandwich. The vegetable protein tasted precisely as he remembered it tasting on Earth and could have been from his own kitchen there. But not the bread. It tasted right, but it chewed wrong, with a texture that probably spoke to its local origins. It was good, though, and filling. He swallowed and sipped his coffee, which tasted so right and so familiar that its richness was almost overwhelming.

If Kowalski had wanted to impress Erik, he had a reason. By dodging Erik's earlier overtures, he had already demonstrated and emphasized his role and outsider status as security chief, so today's visit was probably something new. Erik's best guess was Kowalski had been responding to the interest that both Wendy Scheer and Janos Horvath had shown in Erik, which Kowalski had to see as unusual. Horvath's evidenced interest probably meant more to Kowalski than did Scheer's, if only because Horvath was, ultimately, Kowalski's boss.

Erik found Scheer more interesting, though.

He finished his sandwich and turned his attention to the salad. He had spent years assigned to EnTek's European markets. Dining there had led him to the habit of eating salad at the end of a meal's main course rather than before it, and he had extended the practice even to such casual dining as this. The radish slices crunched between his teeth as he chewed.

Scheer was new, but Horvath was a familiar factor in Erik's life. At various times, he had counted the man from the Home Office as an ally; at others, as a disinterested, even enigmatic onlooker. EnTek organizational politics tended to move in long, slow cycles, as operating philosophies evolved and market trends changed, but Horvath had been a near-constant through all of it, operating under multiple titles. Even now, even in exile, the knowledge that Horvath thought him worthy of his personal attention was more a cause for caution than for outright concern. Horvath had been part of Erik's life for a long time.

Not Scheer, though. Scheer was something different.

Having finished his salad, Erik checked his mug. Half the coffee remained. He poured bourbon into it and stirred, then sipped. He smiled as two kinds of warmth flowed through him. He let the sensation linger for a moment, before gathering up his plates and utensils and feeding them to the appropriate appliance.

"Give me the rest of the coffee," he said, and nodded as the stove presented him with a vacuum flask. Using the same tray that Kowalski had commandeered earlier, he took it, the bourbon, and his mug to the living room.

"Exercise," he said sourly, and watched as a wall panel opened. Coffee and bourbon and calories, along with his body's memory of Villanueva's foot shafts, had made him oddly restive. He didn't like the apartment's auto-gym, but the hidden cluster of exercise equipment was convenient. He guided a stationary bicycle into the living room's open area and locked it down. Clips on the handlebar accepted his beverage tray, and then he settled onto the thing's padded seat. In the low gravity, it was surprisingly comfortable, and he sat there unmoving for a moment, sipping coffee and bourbon and wondering what came next.

"Find me something to watch," he told the apartment. "Anything."

Abruptly, the python and its hapless meal returned to his walls, as the housekeeper again called up its most recently displayed image.

"No, no, not that," Erik said hastily. He thought. "Find me something about Halo."

"Factual or dramatic?" his apartment asked.

"Dramatic?" Erik responded.

"The Mesh offers multiple dramatizations of the founding of Armstrong Base," the housekeeper replied. *"It was a highly rated genre during Villanueva's early days and has been revived several times since."*

A bit of trivia drifted up from Erik's memories, placed there by Wendy Scheer during his tour. Armstrong was actually older than Villanueva, a last gasp of the federal space exploration program. He smiled slightly. Armstrong had led to Villanueva, in an indirect and roundabout way, so the federal site wasn't a complete waste of tax dollars.

"That's fine," he said. "Choose the one with the highest ratings."

The snake and its unfortunate dinner vanished, replaced by Zonix's elaborate, animated logo, which struck Erik as no less serpentine. The image lingered for nearly a minute as the ceiling illuminators dimmed, and then it gave way to program credits.

"Hello, Earth—Space Is Calling!"

The title came in glowing letters that nearly filled Erik's field of view, and brought with them roaring, pompous music. It was followed by cameo images of people he didn't recognize, labeled with names that were equally unknown to him. The credits continued for much longer than Erik thought necessary, but he knew better than to ask the housekeeper to page past them. Production credits and related indicia were inviolate. Even the cast—the performers whose heavily miraged images would be on display—had contractual rights that the Mesh could not deny.

Erik began to pedal. The bicycle measured his pace and matched it, gradually building resistance until he had reached a comfortable pace and told it so. He pedaled rapidly, taking deep breaths and building up enough of a sweat that the air circulators clicked on. He didn't hear them; the program soundtrack was much too loud for that. Instead, he felt the ventilators do their work, as artificial breezes cooled his perspiring skin.

Taken as a whole, the situation was pleasant enough, but it wasn't what he wanted.

That realization, always in the back of his mind, surged to the forefront now. Coffee or booze or physical activity had set it free, and it commanded his attention like a lonely child.

This wasn't the life he wanted. Artificial food, recycled air, living in an apartment that was just like hundreds of others—he'd had his fill of all those things in the early days of his career. As the years passed, his slow-but-steady upward trajectory had carried him into management. Now, even with what was technically a promotion, in many ways, he was back where he had begun.

He could thank Alaska for that.

Still pedaling, he freshened his coffee, added another measure of bourbon. His pace slowed some as he sipped, and the world's edges became just a little bit softer.

"*. . . the human adventure!*" some idiot on the wall said, drawing his attention. Clad in white and surrounded by systems displays and lab apparatus, the speaker was evidently supposed to be a scientist, but he looked like no researcher Erik had ever seen. He had chiseled features, and his tunic was cut close enough that sculpted muscles showed. In real life, no doubt, the actual performer was 20 percent heavier and not nearly as well-featured, but Zonix's theatrical mirage systems did amazing work.

"*It's there that we'll find the answer to why we're here at all,*" the idealistic nitwit continued, and then pulled an equally idealized woman to him. She wore an abbreviated lab jacket of her own and joined him in an embrace that was just short of pornographic, as background music swelled.

It was easy to see why *Hello, Earth—Space Is Calling!* had been so popular. Even with only a cursory viewing of the first few minutes, Erik could tell that it was packaged, formula entertainment of the most one-note sort. Zonix might not have intended it as propaganda for the Project Halo program, but the idealized treatment of the subject matter had the same end effect. Erik had seen similar programs on countless other subjects. One had been a murder mystery set against the construction of the Sydney Mesh Pylon, a time and place with which he was intimately familiar, so he knew all too well just how inaccurate this entertainment was likely to be.

Still . . .

"The answer to why we're all here," the astronomer had said, his words an echo of Wendy Scheer's, earlier in the artificial day.

"It's not a luxury." She had put it that way, talking about scientific research. *"It's something people do. It's like art, like music, like exploration, like love."*

Something about her manner made the words linger in his memory, as clear and precise as words on a printed page.

Her words were his most distinct memory of Halo, in fact. His tour of Armstrong had been complete but hasty, and many details were sketchy in his mind. Utilitarian hallways, banks of anonymous equipment, lab functionaries clad in white—the broad strokes of the picture were there, but not the details. Erik liked to think he had a good memory, but his recollection of Armstrong, only hours later, was a jumble of impressions instead of a collection of specifics.

Wendy Scheer was a different matter. Her, he recalled with remarkable clarity. Every movement, gesture, and comment lingered, so clearly that he could remember hearing her explanation of the scintillometer better than he could remember seeing the scintillometer itself. He remembered her lean figure and businesslike manner, her rippling hair and her smile—

The stationary bicycle's mechanism chirped in protest, and Erik nearly dropped his drink as he brought his pedaling to a sudden halt.

He had seen that smile somewhere before, Erik realized. Clear and distinct in his thoughts of the day, it also had a half-recalled echo hidden somewhere else in his memory. He had seen Wendy Scheer somewhere before, in person and not in a picture; he was sure of that.

But where?

The world lurched slightly as he stepped off of the bicycle, either because the reflexes of a lifetime had kicked in, or because he was slightly drunk. He didn't really care which.

"Turn that off," he said in his command voice.

"*Off,*" the housekeeper agreed, and the Halo dramatization faded back into the Mesh.

"Find me something else about Halo. Fact, not fiction," Erik said. He paused, thinking. "I want a historical overview and capsule news feeds for the past six months." He paused again. "No, make that six weeks. And give me anything you can find on Wendy Scheer."

Erik had left his personal computer rolled up on an end table. Now, he opened it again, thumbed it back to life, and pulled up his business mail account. The title-lines for the dozens of messages sent to his Mesh address greeted him, most marked as having been responded to by Garcia. Even without opening them, he knew what they were—invitations to meet-and-greets, the courtesy calls that a newcomer manager could reasonably expect from his contemporaries. He sorted the list by sending organization, then highlighted the ones he was looking for.

Thirteen messages from Armstrong Base and Project Halo addresses greeted him, all sent and received since his advent in Villanueva. All but the last one had been sent from a man named Ralph Tanaka, Armstrong's exiting head. The last message was response-addressed to Wendy Scheer, and it was a follow-up regarding the phoned invitation he had accepted.

Erik gazed at the lines of text for a long moment. They said nothing that Wendy hadn't said to him on-line or in person, except to offer some detail on where to rendezvous.

In text, as strings of characters on a computer screen, the words and invitation were nothing special. He wondered why he had responded as he had—and then realized what the answer had to be.

He hadn't responded to the invitation, but to Wendy Scheer's transmitted image. He had accepted the offer only after declining others very much like it from Ralph Tanaka, relayed by Juanita.

Again, he thought back to the attraction he had felt in Wendy Scheer's presence, her undeniable charisma. She hadn't seemed to be aware of her charms, but it was always possible that she was less guileless than she seemed. As head of an operation, even just a federal base, she would almost have to be.

He didn't know much about such things, but it didn't make sense to him that he would respond to her presence, however charming, over a communications link. Certainly, talking to Janos Horvath over a phone essentially eliminated that man's considerable sense of presence and left only an echo of a memory in its place.

Why would Scheer be any different?

"You'll like her," Juanita Garcia had said about Wendy Scheer. *"Everyone does."* And Kowalski had echoed that.

Still thinking, he opened his appointment log and pulled up the social screen. It was effectively empty, except for his dinner with Stewart at Fargo's! Without really needing to, he verified the time and date and then paged back to the most recent message from Halo.

Wendy Scheer's personal invitation had come the morning after his tiresome meal with the tiresome Doug Stewart.

Erik's mug was empty now. He filled it again, this time with just coffee, and sipped. He was trying to focus on the events of the evening at Fargos!, but what he remembered most clearly was the irritation he had felt regarding Stewart.

"Receiving," the housekeeper said. *"Priority One call, from Earth."*

"I'm unavailable," Erik said. He spoke almost casually, most of his mind focusing on other things.

"This is a Priority One call," the housekeeper repeated.

"Tell Horvath that he can leave a message," Erik said. "I don't need to hear it right now."

As he spoke, he looked up from his personal computer and saw that the wallpaper now listed the files he had requested. The most recent one was a canned publicity release from Halo.

"Let me see the transition announcement," he said.

Thirty seconds of blather followed, as Ralph Tanaka made his good-byes to the population of Villanueva, addressing an audience that was scarcely aware of his existence. Only the final two seconds were of interest to Erik, as the screen flashed a brief, soft-focus image of Tanaka's successor, Wendy Scheer.

"Pause that," he said. "Capture the image." When the housekeeper had obeyed, Erik continued. "Good. Cameo the image and enhance it."

Wendy Scheer came into focus, in a badly composed image from an awkward angle. She had the look of a woman who did not want to be on camera, no matter how brief an appearance protocol required.

"Mirage the hair," Erik said, his suspicions crystallizing. "Make it longer. And red."

The housekeeper complied.

"Make her smile," Erik continued. "Just a tight little smile. Lips together, with no teeth showing. Dimples."

The image changed again, and a newly familiar version

of Wendy Scheer gazed out at him from the wallpaper. This wasn't the hospitable, pragmatic hostess whom he had met at Armstrong, nor the sympathetic, friendly presence at lunch who had suddenly turned inquisitive. Rather, this was the woman with fast reflexes, who had plucked a breaded pork chop out of midair in a crowded, noisy restaurant, then flashed him an impish smile.

"Save that," Erik said. He felt suddenly cold. "Personal files, my eyes only."

The artificial stimulation of alcohol and caffeine seemed to vanish now, their place taken by a new clarity as the situation and its ramifications presented themselves to him.

Wendy Scheer, for whatever reason, was looking for a man named Ramirez, and she had thought that Erik was looking for him, too. To that end, she had engineered a chance encounter and arranged a second, more formal meeting, to work on him in person.

Scheer had a gift of some sort, an attribute or aspect that charmed and enticed. He had no idea how it worked, and it almost didn't matter—he had felt it in action, and knew that it was real.

Ramirez, whoever he was, had something, too. And Scheer wanted it. She had thought Erik was also looking for it—and no doubt had to assume that he was, now.

Erik sipped coffee again. He wondered how far the situation extended. Certainly, the other ALC companies had been aggressive in their proffered hospitality. How much of that attention was simple professional courtesy, and how much of it was something more?

For that matter, Janos Horvath's repeated calls from Earthside made a bit more sense in this context. He might be warning Erik off, for real—or hinting at a chance for career redemption.

A thought struck him suddenly.

"Get me Heck Kowalski," he said. "Audio only, secure, and make it a priority call."

Even with that order, it took nearly three minutes for his housekeeper to fulfill the command. Erik used the time to return his stationary bicycle to the auto-gym cubby and to dispose of the coffee and the Sony. He finished and settled onto the couch when Kowalski's irritated voice filled the air.

"This better be more than important," the security chief said. He sounded slightly out of breath, as if he had been running or exercising. "You interrupted something pretty special."

"Never mind that," Erik said. "You've never met Wendy Scheer, right?"

Kowalski made an angry sound.

"Right?" Erik repeated.

"Right," Kowalski agreed. "Is that why you—"

"Don't." Erik made the word a command. "Don't meet her. Don't accept any invitations to meet-and-greet."

"You interrupted my social calendar to tell me how to conduct my social calendar!?" Kowalski asked angrily. In the background, someone giggled. "I keep telling you, Morrison—"

"You don't work for me," Erik interrupted again. "But take my word for it—if you get any invitations from Wendy Scheer, turn them down."

There was no way to explain his increasing suspicion that Kowalski might find himself working for Scheer, if ever he met her.

"Should I expect to hear from her?" Kowalski asked, more calmly now.

"You might." The thought had occurred to Erik after he had identified Scheer as the mystery woman at Fargo's! "She wants to find this Ramirez more badly than I had thought. She certainly went to a lot of trouble to ask me about him."

Kowalski grunted.

"More trouble than you realize. Just believe me," Erik said. "I don't understand the entire situation myself, but if the head of a government facility is doing her own snooping, it has to be big. There has to be some credit in it." He paused, considering his next words carefully. "I'm not making any kind of a move against Horvath, Kowalski. At least, not as far as I know."

He didn't mention the declined call.

Kowalski grunted again, then said, "Okay. I'm in the middle of some fieldwork, but I'll still see you tomorrow. I hope you can give me more to work with, then."

"I hope so, too," Erik said, and broke the connection.

"You have one message, logged and filed," the house-keeper announced. *"Priority One."*

"I'm sure I do," Erik said. "But hold it. I need another Mesh search, first. Keep the report on Halo files, but find me something on parapsychology. I need something that's authoritative, but in layman's terms. Nothing lunatic, but no textbooks, either."

He stood again and stretched. Two rounds of exercise— one in the foot-shafts and one on the bicycle—had left his muscles with a mild ache that he found oddly pleasing. Despite the fatigue, he felt a certain energy, a readiness and even an eagerness to address the new challenges the day had given him.

He shuffled back into the kitchen and dumped another measure of real coffee beans into the auto-stove's brewer. The bourbon bottle, he left in the cabinet. In many ways, Erik was something of a traditionalist. When it came to euphoriants, his preference was alcohol; when it came to stimulants, caffeine would do.

"Coffee," he said. "Very strong. I expect to be up for a while. I have some reading to do."

CHAPTER 13

JUANITA was wearing the blonde hair again today. She liked it and liked the way she felt when the random accent mirrors placed about her apartment and workstation caught her golden-tressed image and threw it back to her as she readied herself for the office. The blonde hair, the Nelson Rockefeller tooth, and the tastefully accentuated eyebrows that had cost her half a week's pay gave her the vague look of a feed star without making her look like she wanted to look like the star of a Mesh feed.

This was the kind of look she liked best. Many men and at least one woman on the trans-Bessemer run obviously liked her appearance, too, and she had basked in their admiring gazes. One had even offered her his personal feed code, an act of surprising directness that she declined as gracefully as possible.

She thought about that now, seated in the spiderweb

chair in her nook off of Morrison's main office, as she scanned through one report screen after another, for what seemed like the thousandth time. The walls around her were blanked, free of any distracting image. That was going to be the biggest thing to get used to, when she finally became famous, she decided. She would have to deal with persons instead of people, and the very thought of it made fine beads of sweat sparkle on her brow.

It would be one thing to be wanted by many, but quite another to deal with being wanted by one.

Earthside, as a teen, she had performed in a variety of amateur Mesh productions. She had played roles of every type, from Shakespearean heroine to post-Crash debutante. Posing as a blonde stranger made her feel the way she had felt then, and the appreciative gaze of fellow passengers served as a welcome reminder of what it had been like to have an audience, even an audience as eclectic as an amateur production attracted. When the nice man with the red hair had approached her directly, though—

The delicate shudder she made now was a faint indicator of the almost pathological nervousness she felt in such situations. Not even years of therapy had been able to suppress it completely. She needed something else to think about. She took a sip of new-coffee, nibbled the remnants of a light, casual breakfast, and turned her attention again to her report screens. They held quantified extracts from the previous day's project review. Absent the overlay of Seven Thomas's sardonic tones or Arthur Zavala's jovial commentary, the numbers and facts were cold and stark, the way she wanted them. They were easier to consider and compare. Nutrient consistency, genetic drift, precursor mortality rate, processor yields—she had learned just enough since taking her current job to know which data were likely to be of interest to a better educated analyst. Those were the bits of information she copied into her own report. It was early in the process, with more than an hour to go before Morrison was due at the office, and she soon fell into an easy rhythm that made the work pass quickly. She murmured numbers and hard data from the reports she read, barely vocalizing at all, and letting her phone's mike feed the syllables to the template that waited on her personal computer. Simultaneously, she listened with one ear to playback from her earring recorder, listening not simply for words but for intonations and turns of phrase that seemed germane. Those, she keyed into the same computer template via the worn finger pad in the center of her desk's working surface. Experience had taught her that some kinds of data lent themselves better to manual input, and the work gave her something to do with her hands. Together, the complementary tasks of speech and dictation kept her mind occupied. Nervousness and worry had receded into the background, and it took no conscious effort to keep them there.

Even to her relatively untrained eye, the data was interesting. Datastorms were trending up and had been for a while, but that was just a symptom. The fact that their frequency increase didn't track with data throughput trends suggested that something was wrong with the Gummis themselves. Grown in chemical media and bred from thoroughly troubleshot genetic masters, the semiorganic processors should have been nearly immune to quality control problems; at the very least, they should have performed with near-perfect consistency within any single generation.

They weren't, though.

"Ten minutes," the office said, using the deep, masculine rumble she had requested. When they were alone

together, the office management system spoke like a feed star.

"Thank you," she responded without thinking.

She worked faster now, choosing data with a bit more discretion, being more selective as to which recorded comments to integrate into her own summation. Ten minutes remained until Morrison's personal schedule said he was due, but the new coordinator had shown himself to be a man who did things with more than promptness. After seven minutes of steady, assured work, she entered a last comment of her own, then she closed out the report and saved it to her own Mesh directory.

Speaking clearly and precisely now, in her own command voice, she said, "Send report. Private."

"Sent," the office responded. It had changed its voice back to a cool, neutral default, and she knew what that meant.

The single syllable had scarcely faded when she heard the door whisk open. Turning, she saw Erik Morrison in the doorway. He looked tired and worn. His eyes were half-open, their whites shot through with red, and dark shadows hung beneath them.

She wondered if he had been out drinking the night before. Morrison had a weakness for alcohol. That was in his backgrounder, and his behavior at the spaceport bar had confirmed it, at least as far as Juanita was concerned.

"Good morning," Morrison muttered. His voice was a rustling murmur.

"Good morning, Mr. Morrison," Juanita said, and then corrected herself. "Good morning, Erik."

He smiled at that, something she hadn't seen him do very much. It made him look younger and less tired, but did nothing for the dark hollows under his eyes.

He nodded, then moved past her toward the beverage service that was, even now, extending itself from its wall recess. Even with an apparent hangover, he was moving better. Juanita noticed that and filed the observation mentally for future consideration.

"Any luck on Caspian?" he asked, sitting down gingerly. He glanced at the blank walls and said, not to her, "On."

For the briefest of moments, the question confused her. Then, as an austere Lunar panorama coalesced again on the walls, Morrison's afternoon request from the day before came back to her and she shook her head. "No," she said. "Not yet. I've made some calls and sent some queries, but—"

Morrison grunted. "Why are you here so early, then?" he asked.

"The project review," Juanita said, nervousness welling up from somewhere inside her. "I was preparing a report."

Morrison grunted again. He had filled two small cups already, one with orange juice and the other with the stomach-settler that she'd seen him drink before. Now, he filled a heavy stoneware mug with new-coffee, took a sip, and said, "Is it done?"

"Finished," she said, nodding.

"We can talk about it later," Morrison said. He put the three beverages on a small tray and headed to his desk. "But give me a chance to read it first."

"I'll send you your copy right now," Juanita said.

FOUR hours later, as he released his last handhold and then quickly drop-stepped out of the way so that the next foot shaft occupant could do the same, Erik paused to take in the sights. The Mall, Villanueva's center in more ways than one, was more impressive than he had expected.

It was hard to get a good measure of the place, even from the elevated vantage of the shaft platform. Basically, the Mall was a hole, punched deep into the physical structure of its world and then roofed over. Easily one of the largest single enclosed spaces he had been in, anywhere, it was by far the largest he had seen on the Moon. The Mall had easily the volume of a forty-story office building Earthside and perhaps much more, but there were no continuous lines or structure members to guide the eye and provide a sense of scale. The only exception was the closed curve of the walls, and even they were broken up by staggered levels—a dozen, that he could count—of shops, theaters, restaurants, galleries, casinos, and only Property Management knew what else. Between them, crowding much of the roughly cylindrical space, was a jumbled chaos of service systems, display panels, and installations that combined solid elements with three-dimensional images.

The Zonix cat was still locked in a pas de deux with its milk shake partner, this time with different, vaguely erotic animation. This particular display's enormous size made the effect all the more unsettling. The square-jawed hero of a current Mesh blockbuster waved at some patrons and fired illusory ray-blasts at others. An animated lumberjack-ette pointed with a shapely finger at one Fargo's! restaurant, then another, then a third, alerting potential diners that they could get their preprogrammed meals at any of the three restaurants, all on different levels. Long, looping helical escalators linked the various floors. Transparent elevator cars drifted up and down inside transparent shafts that threaded through the gaudy clutter. Seven segmented footbridges ran from one side of the cylindrical Mall to the other, hanging from silvery cables that looked too finely spun even for the Moon's lower gravity. They rocked and swayed as pedestrians trudged along them. Far below them, the terraced floor level wasn't much better. Kiosks, booths, and even motored carts fought for space there, islands of entrepreneurial spirit amid a sea of humanity.

Erik gazed out at the colorful matrix of solid-looking light and swarming commerce, of gleaming metal balconies and walkways that snaked between curved terraces and walls. Sections of those walls had been left naked and unadorned. The ragged outcroppings were basalt reminders of the world somewhere above them. Unbidden, memories of that world came back to him, clean air, focused images of craters and peaks, and the Halo telescope array. The dead world above was harsh and barren, but utterly tranquil, and he missed that tranquility now.

Why was that, he wondered. And was it the Lunar landscape he missed, or the comfortable sense of companionship that had been with him as Wendy Scheer operated the surface craft?

He wondered if he could ever truly know, and he wondered if it mattered. Either way, the Mall was never going to be his favorite place.

"Impressive, huh?" Heck Kowalski said. Only the damping fields made it possible for him to be heard over the surrounding chatter and noise. Even they were almost overloaded, so his syllables were clipped and slightly distorted. "And this isn't even a busy day. Like being home, isn't it?"

For a moment, Erik said nothing. The five sister corporations of the ALC had, in fact, made a bit of Earth on the Moon—but there was nothing here that he could not have seen at home, without making a quarter-million-mile journey.

"This is the busiest place I've seen since I got here," he finally said. The conduits, foot-shafts, transit stations, and even offices of his recent experience now made a degree of sense, and so did the somewhat more densely populated trains and trams. If most of the Moon seemed nearly empty, it was because everyone was at the Mall, or on their way there.

Kowalski nodded, as if guessing his thoughts. He was holding a black pseudo-leather briefcase, and he paused to pass it from his right hand to his left. It held personal effects left behind by Rogers Caspain, one justification for the meeting. "Ninety percent of every consumer credit is spent here," he said cheerfully. "Ninety-eight percent of every tourist credit."

"Impressive," Erik said. There didn't seem to be much else to say.

"Come on," Kowalski said. "I just wanted to give you a look at the big picture. DiNuvio's is this way."

The two men plunged into the tide of humanity that surged through the Mall. Kowalski moved gracefully, with intuitive ease, dodging this patron and blocking that one, sighting openings and moving to fill them, as he moved from terrace to walkway to elevator. Erik followed, less surely, taken aback by the sudden congestion and ambient clatter. He felt something that was new to him on the Moon, the sudden increase in temperature that came with many moving bodies crammed into a limited space, and his nostrils filled with the acrid odor of abundant perspiration. There was no doubt about it; this would never be his favorite place.

When they reached a second bank of elevators, Kowalski waved his hand at a brushed brass panel. He grinned mockingly at the other Mall patrons as the utility elevator's doors slid shut behind them. "With great power comes great privilege," Kowalski said. "And nobody wants to jack with a company cop." He snickered as the car began to move.

"The original idea was to use the space when they closed down the old spaceport," he continued. "The commerce came later. This was supposed to be like a park, give people something like a sky. Same as the wallpaper, same as those ceilings at Duckworth. But most people, you give them space, and all they want to do is fill it up."

Below them, viewed through the elevator car's transparent floor, the world receded slowly. The crowded floor of the Mall, itself terraced and dotted with kiosks, slowly became smaller and smaller.

"We could have entered from the top, couldn't we?" Erik asked. Garcia, as promised, had provided directions, but Kowalski had insisted on being the guide.

"I told you, I wanted you to get the full effect," Kowalski said.

Past the lumberjackette, past the square-jawed matinee idol, past the dancing cat the car rose. Erik, still gazing down at the crowd below, felt an odd sense of detachment. Kowalski's voice, even absent the blanking fields, now sounded hollow and artificial to his ears.

What the hell was he doing here? Why was he on the Moon?

"This all used to be the old spaceport," Kowalski explained again.

"I heard you the first time," Erik said.

A long moment passed in silence, and when Kowalski spoke again, it was in a very different tone of voice.
"That Scheer woman," he said. "She really got to you,
didn't she?"

Erik nodded. "Is it that obvious?" he asked.

Kowalski nodded, too. "I can tell when people are paying attention to what I'm saying," he said.

"You aren't. What about her?"

"I'm not sure," Erik said.

Kowalski sighed, dramatically and obviously for effect.
He gestured again, and the elevator paused in its path. "We
have a minute or two," he said. Through the elevator car's
transparent floor, the leering Zonix cat seemed to peer up
at them. "And no one's listening here."

"Why are you suddenly so concerned?"

"Why are you?" Kowalski asked. Without waiting for
an answer, he gave his own. "Your call came pretty late
last night. Scheer's came early this morning."

"An invitation?" Erik asked, his thoughts racing. Whatever Scheer's agenda was, she had obviously made a misstep in her fumbled interview with him. Had he been in
her position, he would have been doing his best to control
the damage.

Securing new allies was one way to do that.

"You didn't talk to her?" he asked.

Kowalski shook his head. "I told you, she called early.
She left an invitation with my housekeeper, though."

"Don't take it," Erik said. The words were a command,
but Kowalski didn't seem to mind. "Stay away from her."

"Why?" Kowalski asked.

"I'm not sure," Erik said again. The theory he had so
painstaking formulated after long hours of study seemed

embarrassing and foolish now that he tried to put it into words, but it was the only one that seemed to fit the facts. "I did some reading—"

"*Subliminal Cues in Interpersonal Discourse,*" Kowalski said, nodding yet again. "*Pheromone Manipulation. Charisma: Applied and Practiced.* But you started with parapsychology."

Erik scowled faintly as he realized what Kowalski's words meant. "You accessed my accounts," he said accusingly.

"I accessed the public Mesh library logs," Kowalski corrected him. "The other end of the transaction." Beneath him, the cat had paused its dance to drink some of its milk shake partner. "What's she up to, Morrison? What are *you* up to?"

"Everyone keeps asking me that," Erik said, irritated. "I'm getting tired of it."

"Scheer, then. What about her?"

"I don't know," Erik said honestly. "But there's something about her. She's too—" He paused. "Too *likeable*."

"Too likeable," Kowalski said flatly.

"There's more to it than that," Erik said, well aware of how foolish he must sound. "If you meet her, you like her. A lot. I don't know how she does it or what the mechanism is, but the effect is there. And she knows it." A name drifted up from his memory, the legacy of a half-remembered history class. "She exploits it," he continued. "Just like Hitler."

"Hitler?" Kowalski asked blankly.

"Never mind," Erik said. Quickly, he summarized his experience of the past few days—the dodged calls from Scheer, the anonymous encounter that he was certain now she had engineered, and his own near-infatuation with Halo's new head. "It's very subtle," he said. "If she hadn't startled me with the wrong question, I never would have realized what was going on."

"So you like her," Kowalski said. The words were not quite a question. "That's no crime. If you want company, there's plenty to be had."

Erik shook his head. "It's not like that," he said. "She's charming and attractive—literally attractive—but you can work against it. My guess is, she has to meet you in person first, for the effect to take. After that, she's your best friend, unless you know enough to tell yourself she isn't."

He felt a pang as he spoke. Scheer had been nothing if not gracious and considerate during his visit to Project Halo. Now, here he was, making wild accusations about her to a man he didn't even particularly like or even trust. There was still time to pass it off as a joke, however clumsy—

Just in time, he caught himself.

Kowalski must have seen it on his face. "Okay," he said. "She's off-limits. For both of us." He gestured again and the elevator car came back to life. The world below began to move away again. "I'll see what I can find out about her."

"I think that's a good idea," Erik said. "See if you can track her movements, find out who she calls on in Villanueva."

Kowalski grunted, and Erik could tell that this favorite phrase was about to come to his lips again.

"I know you don't work for me," Erik said hastily.

With a slight smile, Kowalski nodded. "I can try. It might be harder than you think. We've got plenty of security cameras, but a lot of personnel traffic, too. And personal cosmetics make things hard on the recognition brainware. But I've got some other queries running, and I might be able to combine things."

"I might be able to get you more brainspace," Erik said. "This is important. I'm not sure why, but it is."

Kowalski grunted, then changed the subject. "Caspian is meeting us at the restaurant," he said. "Don't expect much."

"You've met him?"

Kowalski shook his head. "He wasn't much on face-to-face. Neither am I." He grinned. "But I did work for him. And I've been researching him."

IF the Mall as a whole looked alarmingly familiar, it served to make DiNuvio's exotic appearance somehow reassuring.

That was Erik's first impression as he stepped through the logo-decorated doorway. The cavernous space looked as if it had been designed by Duckworth's architect, but with a much bigger budget. The gray stone of the ceiling arched even farther into the distance above, and something about it told his practiced eye that this was real space, not simulated. Black plastic tables, conditioned to look and feel like marble, hung from that ceiling, at the ends of long, stoneware-clad poles that evoked stalactites. Elegant wait staff in formal attire drifted from table to table. Low, wheeled drones followed them, shouldering the more physical aspect of their work without undercutting the luxury of a fully human-staffed restaurant.

The accident that had happened at Fargo's! wouldn't be repeated here, Erik realized, as the hostess showed them to their table.

"Corner table," Kowalski noted as he settled in. "I was right." He slid the briefcase he carried beneath the table, but kept it near him.

Erik didn't see that it made much difference. He could see images of Tuscany through ersatz windows shaped to look like ragged breaks in cavern walls. The contrast was striking, but the images were unimpressive. He could call better ones on his home wallpaper.

"This is all nonsense, of course," Kowalski said. "The Moon never had enough water to grow stalactites. They hung the tables this way because gravity let them, and worked backward. Pretty, though." He looked at Erik. "What are we doing here, anyway?" he asked.

"I'm curious, more than anything else," Erik said. It was nice to have the shoe on the other foot. After being asked again and again why he had come to EnTek's Villanueva facility, he was looking forward to asking why Caspian had left it. "I thought Caspian might provide some insights about the job."

Kowalski started to say something, then caught himself and gestured. "Here's our man," he announced, indicating a third party being led by the host to their table.

"Let me take the lead on this," Erik said softly.

Kowalski's reaction reply was to call out, "Hey! Rogers! Over here!" He had a loud voice that carried well, cutting neatly through the dining room chatter. He grinned as other patrons made whispered comments and shot poisoned glances in his direction.

Rogers Caspian settled into the empty chair. He was the very caricature of a career functionary—neatly groomed, appropriately dressed, not in very good shape, and obviously nervous. He did not look like the kind of man in whose footsteps Erik Morrison was accustomed to following.

"Hello, Heck," Caspian said. He did not offer his hand. "Could we be more discreet?"

"Hide in plain sight, Rogers," Kowalski said. He was cheerful, almost boisterous, for Erik's benefit or Caspian's, or both. "No one who works for the ducks can afford to eat here, anyway." He made a soft quacking noise and moved open hands together, miming a beak.

"I know but—"

"And your privacy stopped mattering to me when you turned coat," the security officer said. "Say hello to your replacement. I worry about him now, instead."

For Erik, Caspian was willing to extend his hand. "You must be Morrison," he said. "I'd heard—"

"Erik's the new site coordinator, Rog," Kowalski interrupted. He seemed determined to keep Caspian ill at ease. "Just up from EnTek Earth. You remember EnTek, don't you?"

Erik decided to take mercy. "Caspian," he said, hooking the other man's thumb. "Good to meet you. Are they taking care of you over there?"

"So far," Caspian said.

"What are your duties?" A water service and three glasses had been waiting for them at the table. Erik filled one for himself and then offered a second to Caspian, who accepted.

Erik decided that Kowalski could serve himself.

"Duties?" Caspian seemed to smother a laugh. "I'm running a historical research committee. Someone wants to write a social history, and I'm to make sure that they get the right facts."

"Right, or accurate?" Erik asked.

"Right."

"Sounds like dry work," Erik said.

"It is," Caspian responded. He sipped his water.

"Well, they must think you'll do well, or they wouldn't have recruited you." Erik sipped water, too. "They did recruit you, didn't they?"

Caspian didn't reply, but one eyelid twitched.

Erik continued. "Juanita Garcia sends her regards. She misses you."

"She does?" Caspian seemed pathetically pleased. "I'm surprised that anyone's willing to say that."

Erik nodded. The lie had been a harmless one, and seemed to have soothed the other man a bit. "We're professionals, Rogers, not barbarians," he said. "I appreciate your meeting with me like this."

"Why are *you* here?" Caspian asked. "I know that Heck has my—"

"Stuff," Kowalski interjected. He turned to face the waiter who now stood before their table. "What's the most expensive lunch you have?" he asked cheerfully.

The answer turned out to be farm-raised calimari rings, with what DiNuzio's management claimed were spring vegetables and pasta with red sauce. All three placed the same order and shortly were working their way through plates piled high with food.

"This is really very good," Caspian said. He raised a laden fork to his mouth, chewed, and swallowed.

Erik had to agree, for the most part. The squid was almost ethereally light, covered with only the thinnest coat of breading and then perfectly fried. The vegetables were good, too, and crunched nicely as he chewed. Only the pasta disappointed, even in the least. Something about it was gummy, almost sticky, as if it had been undercooked.

"The flour's not the same. More gluten. And pressure here's not as high as at sea level on Earth," Kowalski said with surprising expertise when Erik commented on his meal. "Think high altitude. They have a hard time boiling the pasta right. You get used to it."

"That's the kind of thing my people get to research," Caspian said. He sounded disgusted. "The impact of environment on cooking and the anthropology of food."

The meal progressed pleasantly enough. Caspian never relaxed completely, but he seemed pathetically eager for news about his former staff. After a few more conversational volleys, even Kowalski seemed willing to chat. News of marriages, health problems, commendations, reassignments—in less than an hour, Erik learned more about the day-to-day lives of his team than he had in the long days since his arrival. The atmosphere soon become comfortable if not congenial.

Only once did their conversation pause. Halfway through the calimari, DiNuvio's lighting flickered, and the air circulators paused briefly in their work.

"Burp," Kowalski said, as the system stuttered. "Datastorm."

"They're getting worse," Caspian said, pleasantly, but with no particular interest. "Nothing to worry about. The backups are super-redundant, but—"

"We can talk about that later," Erik said easily. He had reviewed Caspian's records on the brainware glitches and wasn't eager to hear more.

Finally, as the waiter brought them a payment key and a small plate of segmented oranges, he asked the real question—the one that had been on his mind throughout the entire meal.

"Why'd you do it, Rogers?" he asked gently.

Caspain paused in mid-chew. His lips parted to reveal

sweet orange pulp for a moment, and then he swallowed hastily. "Do it?" he asked.

"Make the change," Erik said. "You've been around. You had to know it wasn't going to be easy. What did they offer you?"

"A chance to do something new," Caspian said.

"History is new?" Kowalski asked, barely managing not to sneer.

Erik shot him a glance, then turned his attention to Caspian again. "That's the story, but there must have been a better reason. What kind of package did they offer you?"

"Package?" Rogers suddenly stiffened in his chair, and the fingers of one hand tapped nervously on the black stone-finish table.

"Compensation package," Erik said, surprised by the other man's reaction. "I know credit is loose up here, but to recruit someone at your level to write a history presentation—"

Caspian had placed the restaurant's heavy cloth napkin in his lap before eating. He retrieved it now, still spotless, and folded it neatly, then set it on the table. "It's more than that," he said.

"And are you enjoying it? Is it challenging work?" Erik asked. The words rung hollowly in his own ears. There was nothing about the Site Coordinator slot that he found challenging, and it seemed almost hypocritical to ask the question of the nervous man seated opposite him.

"Will anyone even talk to you?" Kowalski asked suddenly. For the first time, his voice held a faint note of sympathy. A man could spend his entire life working for one subsidiary or affiliate, or move back and forth between a dozen, as long as he remained loyal to one ALC partner. Leaving one of the superconglomerates for another was a major transgression, not easily forgiven. Even moving out of and back into the private sector was viewed more kindly.

Caspian unfolded his napkin and then folded it again. He seemed determined to ignore both men's steady gazes. The silence stretched for more than a minute before Erik finally broke it.

"What if you could come back?" he asked, surprising himself. The offer wasn't his to make.

"Hey!" Kowalski interjected.

"Come back? Can I?" Caspian asked, with sudden intensity.

Erik shook his head and made himself look regretful. "A rhetorical question. I was thinking about another situation like this, back when I worked in Australia."

"If I could come back?" Caspian rolled the words on his tongue. "I'm an EnTek man from way back. My family is EnTek. Of course I'd come back."

"Why did you leave then?"

Again, Erik waited, and again, he broke the silence. "I can't make promises," he said. He chose his words carefully. "But Horvath has taken an interest in the situation."

Caspian stared at him with the faint beginnings of hope.

"That's right," Kowalski said. Now his voice was free of feint-and-parry, and he spoke with an easy matter-of-factness. "He's been on-line to Morrison half a dozen times."

Erik nodded. "I can't make any promises," he repeated. "But I'd like to know why you left."

"Wait a moment," Kowalski said, and gestured for silence. He reached into a tunic pocket and pulled out a small metal device. He set it on the table, next to the plate that held the orange rinds from their dessert.

"You don't need to record this," Erik said, looking at the apparatus.

"I'm just making sure no one else does," Kowalski said, with a head-shake. "It's a damper."

Caspian nodded at that. "You're serious," he said. "Both of you. Even after I left, after all I've—"

"Never mind that," Erik said, interrupting. He glanced around the restaurant. DiNuvio's was apparently too expensive to be crowded, at least at lunch, but other patrons still lingered at their tables. If Kowalski wanted privacy, it made sense to look for familiar faces, too. He did, and found none.

"Just tell me why you went."

Caspian almost smiled then. The tension finally drained from his body and his face, and he settled back in his chair. He looked as if a burden, heavy even on the Moon, had left him.

"Because I was stupid," he said. "And because of Keith Ramirez."

CHAPTER 14

"HELLO, Erik." Janos Horvath's words the next evening were as cool as the air in Erik's apartment. He sounded composed and totally at ease, and his features were equally calm on the long wall imaging system. "I'm returning your call. I apologize for the awkwardness of the hour. You must be preparing for dinner."

Horvath smiled slightly. The expression spread across his placid features like oil on water, making just enough difference to give the hint of a lie to his words and lingering just long enough that Erik was certain to see it.

This was a game Erik knew how to play, too. "Quite all right, Janos," he replied, equally easily. With an overstated casualness that was just shy of elaborate, he settled back in his recliner and sipped cold carbonated water. The glass he held was etched with the EnTek logo. "I'm at your convenience, after all. I know that you have a busy schedule, and this place almost runs itself."

It was late standard evening in Villanueva, but Erik hadn't bothered to determine Horvath's local time. The man from the Home Office traveled often and took much of the Home Office with him when he did. Horvath could be anywhere, from New Sacramento to Hong Kong. Wherever he was, local facilities would have conformed their schedules to his, rather than the other way around. That was the kind of authority he wielded.

There had been a time when such things would have impressed Erik. Now, he gave them little thought, and sipped domed water instead. It sparkled and hissed, and droplets from the bursting bubbles rained on his upper lip, reminding him faintly of ocean spray. Briefly, he wondered if he would ever see the oceans again.

Horvath seemed attentive enough just now, but that could be illusion. The same mirage brainware that tailored images to the caller's requirements could do much more than that. Tenor, body language, setting—all could be massaged easily enough by the appropriate systems. On the wallpaper, Horvath appeared neatly groomed and attired in his usual black business-wear. In reality, it was entirely possible, if unlikely, that Horvath was nude and calling from the rumpled sheets of his bed, making obscene gestures rather than smiling pleasantly at the video pickup. It was barely conceivable that Horvath wasn't on-line at all. Erik could be speaking instead to some functionary, cloaked deep in illusion.

Erik, for his part, opted for a clean feed, whenever practical. It was one thing to blank the image completely, but he was a reasonably direct man, and confident in his own ability to lie, unaided. Horvath, at his end, would see Erik as he was, less two seconds or so of delay, as the signal made its way between the Earth and the Moon and through the maze of Gummi brains and satellites.

"I had lunch with Rogers Caspian," he said. "DiNuvio's, in the Mall. You may have been there, yourself." He knew that Horvath's travels had taken him to the Moon more than once, and the upscale restaurant seemed to him very much Janos's kind of place.

Horvath's neutral expression brightened a bit. "How was the calimari?" he asked. "They raise it locally, you know."

"I was more impressed with the wine," Erik said. "I wonder if they call it a cellar here?"

The man from the Home Office made the barest hint of a shrug. "I don't drink alcohol, Erik. You know that. It's too addictive."

Horvath didn't *approve* of alcohol, either, Erik knew, and preferred other euphoriants for himself and for his staff. They had had that discussion more than once, even in person, under more openly formal circumstances.

"Wine is traditional with Italian food, and at business lunches," Erik said. Now it was his turn to make a feint, however minimal. Whatever Horvath knew of Caspian's story, it was likely that he knew less than Erik did. "Caspian drank more than I did," he continued. "He talked more, too."

"Caspian's a traitor," Horvath said. He spoke the name with what sounded like genuine annoyance. From somewhere off-screen, he raised coffee or new-coffee—Erik couldn't tell which—and drank. Horvath preferred to drink the stuff Russian-style, hot and steaming from a heavy glass more typically used for beer or spirits. That glass bore the same, familiar logo as Erik's did. "Associating with disgruntled ex-employees isn't going to do your reputation much good," Horvath continued.

Erik grunted. "I don't worry much about my reputation these days," he said, realizing the truth of his words even as he spoke them, and with a bit of surprise. "I'm still working for EnTek, even after all that's happened. That means that you think I'm an asset."

"Or that management appreciates your past contributions," Horvath said. The emphasis he placed on "past" was almost too faint to be noticed. "Or that you have friends," he continued. "Or that you had strings you could pull."

"Or all of that," Erik said, still calm. He raised his drink again. More carbonated water flowed across his teeth and tongue. "But being seen as an asset strikes me as more likely."

"You are," Horvath said. "Or were. You greatly expedited things in Australia, and I have a long memory."

"What happened in Australia was mostly chance," Erik said, not for the first time.

Horvath continued as if Erik had not spoken. "But Alaska is more recent, and I remember that, too."

"I told you then, that was too close to home," Erik said. He tensed. Too easily, too quickly, irritation welled up from within him, prompted by the memories that Horvath's comment prompted. "*My* home was there, dammit. I wasn't the hired gun from out of town," he said. Irritation flared, and he spoke with an edge in his voice. "I used to live there, four months a year. Not anymore."

" '*Hired gun?*' " Horvath's interruption came later

than he had probably meant it to. Transmission delay wreaked havoc on the natural rhythms of conversation. "That's an odd term."

"An old one," Erik said. He spoke in measured tones, consciously coaxing tranquility back into his demeanor. This was an important conversation; he had to maintain control of it. "An old turn of phrase, out of United States history."

"Yes, history. You studied history. I remember now," Horvath said. He nodded.

Memory had nothing to do with Horavth's comment, Erik was sure. Men like Horvath didn't spend time familiarizing themselves the academic records of line staff, not even staff with Erik's prominence, or notoriety. No, that bit of information had surely come from Erik's employment record, which was equally surely being fed in discreet bits to Horvath as they spoke. Either a hidden earpiece or wallpaper display overlay at his end would do the job nicely.

Erik said, "You always know the right thing at the right time." He smiled.

Horvath smiled, too. "Do you know who Henry Ford was?" he asked. "Why he was famous?"

"Industrial pioneer from the last century," Erik said, startled by the question but able to answer it. "Transportation specialist. We own his name."

"He made a statement." Horvath smiled again. " 'History is bunk.' "

Erik flushed. The conversation was slipping away from him again. "We don't need to talk about Australia or Alaska, then. God knows, we've talked enough about both of them."

"Tell me something new, then," Horvath said. "Something I don't know."

"You know some of it, I think," Erik said. "A man named Keith Ramirez, working as a prospector for Duckworth, found something on the surface." He paused and sipped water, counting the seconds as he waited for a response.

"Something?" Horvath said, and some subliminal cue told Erik that he had the complete attention of the man from the Home Office, perhaps for the first time.

Erik nodded. "Whatever it is, Duckworth wants it, badly. That's why they recruited Caspian."

He paused again, but this time, Horvath said nothing.

"As near as I can tell, Ramirez approached us first. He had a connection with Caspian and spoke to him about it. Caspian didn't give me any details, but my guess is that he made inquiries within EnTek before changing sides." Erik paused. "If he did, I suspect you heard about them, Janos."

This time, when he paused, the silence bore fruit. The other man nodded and smiled tightly. As had seldom happened in Erik's experience, Horvath's expression seemed genuine and not intended for deliberate effect. "He did, indeed," Horvath said. His tone, like his expression, was mildly rueful. "Rogers Caspian made overtures about Ramirez and his find. We—*I* dismissed them," he said. "I may have made a mistake in doing so."

His last words were ones Erik had never heard him speak before. Erik sipped water to cover his surprise, then said, "Did he provide you with specifics?"

"Caspian was only an envoy," Horvath said. He looked disgusted. "I never spoke with Ramirez."

"Did *Caspian* provide any specifics?" Erik asked, with a tone of authority he had never used with Horvath before.

"No specifics," Horvath said. "Only hints and extravagant claims." He paused. "They seemed to think that Ramirez had found evidence of life on other planets."

That fit, Erik realized, but he merely said, "Not on the Moon."

"No, of course not. That's ridiculous," Horvath said. "I can assure you, our installation—installations are the only life on Luna. You and Halo have no neighbors."

Erik continued to speak with studied casualness. He knew that the best voice stress analysis systems available were studying his every word, eager to feed Horvath any hint of duplicity on his part. "Then what's the problem?" he asked. "Some mold spores on Titan—"

"*Intelligent* extraterrestrial life," Horvath interrupted. "Ramirez seems to think he had found evidence—I don't know what or why—of intelligent life on other planets."

This time, it was Erik's turn to say nothing.

"Can you imagine the impact such a discovery could have on our business?" Horvath asked. His image abruptly rippled faintly and lost some of its enhanced definition. He looked older now, fatigued, and his voice had lost much of its urbane polish. "Can you?"

Horvath had canceled his mirage fields, Erik realized with genuine shock. Gazing out from the wallpaper was the same face he had seen in his few face-to-face meetings with the other man. The effect gave a new immediacy to Horvath's words.

"I'd think there would be opportunities," Erik said stiffly. "Government construction contracts, research grants, packaged entertainment." He thought a moment. "Tourism, maybe."

Horvath nearly laughed, which made him all the more human. "Small change, all of it. There may well be some way to make credit from such a discovery," he said. "But there would be far more opportunities to shut down Villanueva, or at least take it over."

"We have a charter," Erik said. "It calls for near-autonomy. The U.N. will honor it."

"We have that charter because we spend almost endless credits fighting for it," Horvath said. "Every year."

That was true. The court battles over Villanueva's charter had begun before the first blueprint had been drawn and continued to this day, almost without pause. What was left of the United States had ongoing, open action items about the U.N.'s authority to issue leases and charters, even for fund-raising purposes. The South-Pacific Union had mounted similar objections, and so had Mother Russia. Over long decades, the ALC had arrived at a state of turbulent balance. The profits, tax revenues, usage fines, import duties, and plain old-fashioned graft that Villanueva brought to the table were enough to keep her there, and keep her there exclusively. As long as the ALC indulged nonsense like Project Halo, that dynamic equilibrium remained the status quo.

"And even if the charter holds," Horvath said, "Our monopoly won't. There will be too much interest. We don't need the competition."

"You seem to be taking Ramirez's claims more seriously now," Erik said.

"Duckworth is," Horvath said. "And whatever interests a partner company has to interest us. They may know more than we do, too. Ramirez was working for them, after all. What did Caspian tell you?"

Kowalski apparently hadn't forwarded his recording to

the Home Office, Erik realized. That was a surprise. Aloud, he said, "Not much. Ramirez wasn't very forthcoming with him, either."

"Caspian wanted to come home. Back to Earth," Horvath continued. "We didn't have anything for him."

"Duckworth did," Erik said. The carbonated water was gone now, and he wanted more, but this was not the time to interrupt the flow of conversation.

"Not what he wanted, I think," Horvath said. "Not Earth."

"Or maybe they want him on deck locally until they find Ramirez," Erik said. "They seem to think he's important."

"The other companies think so, too," Horvath said. "They've formed search committees of their own, according to my sources. That's another reason that I think my original reaction may have been a mistake."

Erik thought about that for a moment. Today was the first time he had ever heard the man from the Home Office explicitly acknowledge an error, and he had done so twice in the space of a short conversation.

"What about Halo?" Erik asked.

"What about them?" Horvath's words were cool, but some faint note of concern colored them.

"I paid a site visit to Armstrong Base," Erik said. He was careful to speak the literal truth. "Lunch and a tour. The new project head, Wendy Scheer, mentioned Ramirez."

The two-second lag lengthened into a longer silence as the man from the Home Office considered Erik's words. "I don't think Halo is a concern at the moment," Horvath finally said. "At least, not in and of themselves."

"I don't see how they can't be," Erik said, certain that Horvath was wrong. "If this is true, it's what they're here for."

"Their out-year funding is gone, and our cost-of-service contract line item is being contested," Horvath continued. His gaze shifted, then returned to meet Erik's. "I'm checking their budget now. Even if it's true, they can't do anything about it. They certainly don't have the resources to field a full search."

"Scheer mentioned Ramirez," Erik said again. "They're looking."

"That means you have to look harder," Horvath said. "I concede the point. Find him first, though, and Halo won't find him at all."

Erik took a deep breath before answering. "You'll need to be more specific," he finally said.

"I opposed your assignment to the Lunar post," Horvath said. "I pushed hard for mandatory retirement."

Erik doubted that. Very little happened within EnTek that Janos Horvath actively opposed. He said nothing, however.

"Not strongly enough to prevent it, but I didn't endorse it, either," Horvath continued. He drank more of his tea, or whatever it was. "But since you're there, I'd be foolish not to take advantage of the situation."

Erik made no response. He knew what Horavth wanted, but wanted the other man to be specific about it.

"I don't want another Alaska," Horvath said, almost gently. "But if it meant protecting our interests, I wouldn't mind another Australia."

* * *

HALF an hour later, the connection broken, Erik took another shower. Speaking with Horvath, and keeping himself calm while speaking with Horvath, was more exhausting than almost any physical exercise. He stood under the stinging spray for long minutes, letting it drive the tension and fatigue from his body. With conscious, deliberate effort, he thought of other things.

Instead, as the water sluiced away into the powered drains at his feet, he opted out of the dry cycle and stepped still dripping from the stall. Central had finally disgorged a robe in a color and cut he found acceptable, and his housekeeper had found someone, somewhere, willing to earn extra credit by hand-embroidering his monogram where it belonged. Now, as he shrugged into the loose, comfortable garment, he felt somewhat at home.

But the smallest bathroom in either of his houses on Earth had been twice the size of this one, and in neither of them had mist-droplets from the showers hung in the air so long.

None of that really mattered, he decided, and pushed the thought from his mind.

Heated slippers waited for him just inside the bathroom exit. He stepped into them and the door took the hint, whisking open so that he could amble into the living area. Today had been long, but not particularly fatiguing, and what fatigue he felt had vanished with the shower water. The Moon's lower gravity, or Villanueva's exercise-encouraging architecture, or both, had given him a new general energy. It was one thing about living here that he did not mind.

"You're looking good," Heck Kowalski said, emerging from the kitchen. In one hand, he held a plastic food storage container, and in the other, a glittering pair of silvered chopsticks. One after another, he lifted bits of homemade chili-fried tofu to his mouth, then chewed and swallowed. He ate the leftovers—Erik's leftovers—and spoke with equal, studied nonchalance.

"Kowalski," Erik acknowledged, unsurprised but non-plused at the other man's presence. He pushed those thoughts from his mind, too, at least for the moment. "What do you think?"

Kowalski shrugged and kept eating. "You're moving pretty well for a guy your age," he said. "Who's been here for less than a month. File says you played football and surfed as a kid, and that probably helps."

"American football," Erik corrected him.

"The surfing probably helps more. More three-dimensional, and the body remembers," Kowalski said. He kept eating.

"But that's not what I meant. What do you think of the tofu?" Erik continued.

"This?" Kowalski asked. He speared a piece of bean curd, made a show of examining it carefully, then popped it into his mouth. It crunched between his teeth. "Good. Central?"

Erik shook his head. "Just the raw components," he said. "I did the rest."

"That's right. You cook," Kowalski said, and nodded. "There's ginger in it, right? And some kind of mush-room."

Erik nodded. The robe and air had worked together to dry him. When he ran his fingers through his hair, they came back only slightly damp. "Music," he said softly, and was pleasantly gratified when the apartment complied by playing back something light and instrumental. It was a pseudoclassical file chosen to meet his tastes, not his visitor's, and that made him smile slightly.

"I had a lady-friend who absolutely condemned my eating habits," Kowalski said, still eating. He had made substantial inroads on the tofu, and the scent of spices hung in the air with each bite he took. "I told her she underestimated me. I told her that I have low-brow tastes, but that I'm not illiterate, about food or anything else."

He stabbed the remaining food with the chopsticks, left them in the container, and used his now-free hand to reach into a tunic pocket. "Here," he said, and tossed a black case toward Erik with a lazy, underhanded motion. "You wanted this. Just don't kill anyone. The reporting requirements are unbelievable."

Erik intercepted the black pseudoleather case's flat trajectory easily enough. It was a smaller version of the case Juanita had given him weeks before and, like that one, opened to a touch from his thumb. Inside were a small dart pistol and three ammunition clips, each in its own padded recess.

He tugged the small gun free and hefted it. Compact and elegant, it felt better in his hand than he would have liked. When he closed his fingers, only the automatically telescoping barrel protruded beyond his grip.

"I'll be careful," he said. He indicated the magazines. "I thought you said these were stunners."

"They are. That doesn't mean they can't kill. It's an imprecise art. If nothing else, we've got more than our quota of heart patients up here, and a jolt from that wouldn't do any of them any good." Kowalski glanced at him. "Is this your dinner?" he asked, gesturing again with the chopsticks. "*Was* it, I mean?"

"Last night's," Erik said. "I have other plans for this evening." He was still preoccupied with the case and its contents. He tugged one of the magazines free and examined it. The folded fléchettes were yellow.

"Those are live. The third set, the red darts, those are dummy loads. Practice with them." Kowalski looked at him levelly. "And do it before you start carrying that thing."

"Practice?"

"Get the range of it, the feel. Gravity makes a difference, but not much. Almost everything's short-range here," Kowalski said. "Still, I'd rather you shoot some holes in this place before you fire it in public." He looked serious again. "And I'd really rather you not fire it at all."

Erik slid the clip of red darts into the small pistol's grip. A telltale light lit as the clip clicked into place and the gun recognized its ammunition. He nodded, peripherally aware that Heck Kowalski had tensed suddenly, and then he thumbed the release and unloaded the gun. Kowalski relaxed again. A moment later, with the gun and its magazines back in their nests, Erik closed the case again. "Thanks," he said.

Kowalski had relaxed a bit, but he didn't look very happy. "I'd really rather you not fire it at all," he said again. His tone was neutral. More than a day had passed since the lunch with Caspian, and their conversations during that period had been brief and perfunctory. Much of the rapport Erik had built with him seemed to have evaporated in the interim.

Erik knew what was on the other man's mind. Kowalski was thinking about the question he had asked as they left the Mall restaurant, and about the answer Erik had given him. The response had surprised both men, actually; Kowalski, by its content, and Erik, by its honesty.

There were things he wasn't accustomed to telling anyone, much less someone he had known as briefly as he had the security officer.

"That's not why they sent me here," Erik said. A thought crossed his mind, limiting himself again to the literal truth.

"Did you talk to Horvath," Kowalski said. The words should have been a question, but the flatness of his tone and the expression on his face made them something else.

"I did. You probably know that already, though," Erik said. "Even if you don't know what we said."

Kowalski nodded.

His monogrammed robe had deep pockets; he tucked the gun case into one of them. As he spoke, he smiled slightly. "What did Horvath tell *you*?"

Kowalski smiled, too. For the first time since entering Erik's quarters, he seemed fully at ease. "Quite a surprise, really," he said. "I thought I'd grow old and retire to Madagascar without talking directly to Mr. Horvath."

"I sometimes wish *I* had," Erik said. The shifting fortunes of his career ran briefly through his mind. He had worked for Janos Horvath for much of his career, whether directly or indirectly. After Alaska, that history, and the cachet it lent him had given much validity to his last-ditch efforts to save his job.

He had thought himself done with Horvath's patronage once he came to Villanueva, but clearly, he had been wrong. The man from the Home Office's reach extended even to here.

He said it again, "What did he tell you?"

"Take my lead from you. Work closely with you and trust you. You're a good man and have his implicit trust,"

Kowalski said. He smiled again. "That was a surprise, too."

"Janos can surprise," Erik said. "What about the part where he asked you to report regularly on my activities and keep me from doing anything foolish?"

Kowalski shrugged. "I expected that," he said.

"So did I," Erik said. He looked at Kowalski. "What about the gun?"

"What about it?" Kowalski asked.

"Does Horvath know about it? Or doesn't it count as me doing something foolish?"

Kowalski nearly laughed. He upended the container and poured the rest of the tofu into his mouth. He smiled as he chewed. "There are some things that don't get recorded, anywhere," he said pleasantly, still with his mouth full. "Stunners are allowed, technically, if you can justify them. You probably shouldn't have one, though, given your history. I took that one off a drunk tourist two years ago, and I didn't report it. Horvath says to trust you, so I will, but if the gun goes in my report, it goes in your file, and then it goes in mine, too. So, no."

That was good, assuming that Kowalski spoke the truth. Erik saw no reason to give Horvath any more insight into his actions than the considerable amount that the other man already possessed. If complete privacy was impossible, reasonable discretion was not. The same reasoning applied to Kowalski, of course.

"You don't have to do this anymore," Erik said. He stepped to the bar and reached past the bourbon decanter it offered him. Instead, he took the glass of carbonated water it dispensed at his murmured command. He glanced at Heck and asked, "Drink?"

"Hm?" Kowalski said. "Beer, if you have it. The Shulzheimer is fine. I don't need a glass."

"You know I have it," Erik said, pulling one of the familiar green bottles from a refrigerated recess. He tossed it casually at his uninvited guest, and the beer spun lazily in midair for a moment or two before Kowalski caught it. "You've been in here at least twice without my permission, and you've helped yourself to the refrigerator. You can't convince me you haven't investigated the bar, too."

Kowalski didn't say anything, but tried to cover for his silence by opening his beer and taking a long draw. Then he set the tofu container and utensils on a convenient end table.

"That's what I mean," Erik said, continuing. You don't have do this anymore. You've impressed me. I know you can get in here when you want to, and I know that you're keeping an eye on me. You've proved your point."

He drank. The water had been distilled, carbonated, and mineralized here, but drinking it brought back a rush of memories from his stay in Europe.

"I'm not proving anything," Kowalski said, but he sounded uneasy. He twirled the beer bottle in midair, balancing it on his fingertip and spinning it on its vertical axis.

"I think you are," Erik said. "It's a tactic I've seen before. Hell, I've done pretty much the same thing—changing schedules, reassigning desk space, delaying expense payouts. Subtler stuff, too, like talking soft so you have to listen. I'm just telling you that you've made your point."

Kowalski drank some more beer.

"Do you know what shaking hands means, Kowalski?" Erik finally asked.

"Hello, nice to meet you, my thumb's just as strong as yours, so don't try anything," Kowalski said rapidly.

Erik shook his head. He settled comfortably onto one

of his easy chair's padded arms. "That's what it means now," he said. "But not originally. There was a time when men traveled armed, routinely. In Western cultures, shaking hands was one way to demonstrate that you weren't a threat, at least for the moment. You kept your weapon, but the hand you were most likely to use it with—your right hand—was busy doing something else."

"So everyone's friends?"

"Or not enemies, at least," Erik said. He drank some more mineral water. "We're working together now, and you've made your point. I respect your authority, and I'm not going to try to get between you and Horvath. You can handle him as you see fit, and I'll do the same. Okay?"

After a moment, Kowalski nodded. "Okay," he said.

"We both work for the same company, after all," Erik continued. "And I don't want to work for anyone else."

Kowalski finished his beer and nodded again. "Horvath said to trust you," he said. "And I like to follow orders." He extended his hand. "I'll trust you as far as he does. And you're right—we're both EnTek men. Shake?"

Erik stood and took the other man's hand. They shook hands the old way, palm to palm. Kowalski's grip was firm and dry.

After Kowalski had left, Erik gathered up the container that had held the tofu and the bottle that had held Kowalski's beer, and went to the kitchen. The bottle he placed in a rack for pickup and refill; the container and chopsticks he rinsed and deposited neatly in the washer.

For a moment, he stood before the sink, thinking. The conversation with Kowalski had gone as well as could be expected, and he found himself almost liking the man. Certainly, they had arrived at a degree of mutual trust; the dart pistol in his pocket was proof of that.

The music was still playing when he returned to the living room. He opened the case in his pocket again and loaded the pistol with the red darts. "Give me a target," he said, speaking in his command voice.

It didn't do much good to have a gun if you didn't have a place to point it. He wondered if Horvath understood that.

"Additional guidance, please," his apartment said.

"I want something to shoot at," Erik said. He moved as far away as he could from the main wall. "A gaming screen will work."

The wallpaper seemed to ripple and flow. When the pixels coalesced again, they formed a detailed, high-resolution image of a shooting range. Ominous-looking figures peered out from behind doorways and windows.

"Fine," Erik said. Standard specifications for spaces like these called for ruggedized wallpaper, and he was confident that the place could take anything he fired at it without permanent damage. "Now, I want to place a Priority-One call, with as much security as you can handle."

"Visual preferences?"

Erik looked down at himself. He was still wearing his robe, still holding the pistol in one hand. "Mirage me with something casual but not sloppy," he said. "Do as best as you can, consistent with the security requirements. I want to talk to Wendy Scheer."

CHAPTER 15

WENDY Scheer looked very different now than she had the day before, but the change had been gradual. When Rogers Caspian had arrived home from lunch with Morrison, he had found Scheer and her friend, Tanaka, waiting for him in the corridor near his apartment. There and then, the Project Halo head had been blonde, vivacious, almost effervescent. Now, some thirty hours later, her face and entire demeanor had changed. Here, seated across from him in the Halo conference room, she looked almost like another person.

The metamorphosis had been like a tree's growth, continuous and ongoing, but too slow to actually notice. He had completed three interviews before he had recognized its effects, but now that he had, the change was impossible to ignore.

Sheer's hair was still blonde, but the highlights had

faded. Instead of letting it form a flowing halo around her head, she had pulled it back to form a bun at the back of her neck. The severe styling made the strong lines of her face look even stronger, and she had done nothing to off-set the effect. The eyes that had been electric sapphires the day before were cool and pale now, a color midway between blue and gray. They made him think of frost on a winter morning. She wore no picto-tooth or jewelry, only a single recorder earring on her right ear. Even that was stark and functional, scarcely more than a dot of satin-finished metal. A casual glance, under different circum-stances, and he would not have recognized her.

He liked her better this way, Rogers realized, with a vague feeling of surprise. Already, Scheer's current look had become his mental image of her, and his memories of how she used to look were fading around the edges.

He wondered why that was.

"I've heard from Earth. We found the funding," she said, in a crisp, businesslike tone, and her comportment matched it. Her full lips were narrow and drawn as she paused between sentences, set in a straight line that held no hint of the laughing smile he remembered from be-fore. She wore a plain jumpsuit, undecorated except for a stenciled logo on the left breast pocket. The garment looked almost like a uniform, pragmatic and functional. "Budgets are tight this year, and I don't mind telling you that most people who go into this work do it because they're believers," she continued. "There isn't very much profit in the kind of research we do here."

"Why do it then?" Rogers asked, but Scheer didn't re-spond, so he tried again. "I know credit is tight," he said. "I've seen the spreads."

Scheer smiled faintly, and a tiny spark lit her eyes. "For EnTek and Duckworth both," she said. "I imagine you've had access to the budgets."

"I can't talk about that," Rogers said. He drummed his own fingers on the conference tabletop, then stopped, embarrassed. He didn't like acting nervous in front of Wendy Scheer; she deserved someone who was confident and assured. "Even if I *do* make the change, confidentiality requirements in my old contracts—"

Scheer waved one hand in casual dismissal of his words. Rogers found himself watching her fingertips attentively. The nails were unpainted and neatly trimmed, cut straight across. They looked almost masculine. The path they traced through the air was mildly hypnotic.

"You're going to make the change," she said, as if his objections were beside the point. "And you know that what we're looking for isn't covered by that kind of agreement. Not really. If it were, and if you really thought so, you wouldn't have gone to Duckworth"

"That's right, I suppose," Rogers agreed easily.

Agreeing with Wendy Scheer was always easy.

"Like I said," his hostess continued, "people who do this kind of work don't do it for money. Other people make the profits. And they don't do this kind of work on Earth, for the most part." She paused. "That was the hard part. We'll have to eliminate two positions to meet your salary and associated expenses."

Sympathy rushed through Rogers at her words, but honest surprise came with it. "I'm not asking for much," he said. When asked the day before for his requirements, he had given the question some thought and named a low figure and minimal benefits, at least by corporate standards.

To only a single point had he clung stubbornly and without relenting. His new responsibilities, whatever they were, would be on Earth.

He was sick of the Moon. If he was going to stoop low enough to work for the government, he could damn well stoop in normal gravity, and under a real sky.

Scheer nodded in agreement. "And we don't pay very much. I mention it only to show that we're taking you seriously," she said. "We want you working for us. You have a place with the federal government."

Rogers Caspian had never in his entire life imagined that his career could ever go this wrong.

"Here," she said. "It's approved, the whole package. All I have to do is countersign and log it."

Again, her fingers arced in a lazy trajectory through the office air. This time, their path was a shorter one, ending on the matte plastic surface of her computer, unfolded and spread on the table between them. The movement brought her hand within a dozen inches or so of his. He watched with unaccustomed attention as one of her perfect fingertips traced an interactive display. In the display, credit sums, benefits specifics, and projected escalations lit then faded, one after another, as she indicated them specifically.

"And, believe me, there will be plenty to do, once we have what Ramirez found," Scheer continued. She turned the screen so that he could read it more easily. "Once we find Ramirez."

"I don't know where he is," Rogers said. The words came out in a desperate moan that combined absolute sincerity with absolute despair. "I don't know! I haven't seen him in—"

"No," Scheer said. Her words remained businesslike,

but she spoke more gently now, as if warning to him. "Maybe you haven't seen him," she continued, "but you can help us find him."

Rogers stared at the compensation package she presented to him. There was nothing in it that wasn't modest, really, and the work that Scheer could offer didn't promise to be of any interest. The only thing that made it attractive was that it would be on Earth. That mattered more than the money, more than the numbers, more than anything else ever could, even more than the faint promise that Morrison had held out that he might be able to return to EnTek.

"I told you, I don't know," Rogers said. "I told you, and I told Shadrach, and I told Morrison and Kowalski. I don't know anything."

"Hush," she said. Much to his surprise, she reached across the table and touched him, first patting one of his trembling hands and pushing his hair back from his forehead.

Rogers's tremors eased, and his heart slowed. He felt tension ooze from his body.

"You know more than you think you do, Rogers," she said. "Everyone does. I've read your résumé and backgrounders," Scheer said. "I've accessed your Personnel files." He made a sound of surprise. In response, and for the first time since their conversation had begun, she smiled openly. "Never mind how, just listen to me. I've seen what EnTek taught you about brainware, and about the brain."

Rogers nodded, for lack of any better response. The general sense of well-being that her touch had inspired faded slightly now, and he felt the faintest hint of distress.

"You don't know what you know," Scheer continued.

"But you're still our best lead on Ramirez." She paused. The heel of her palm still rested on his forehead, and her skin felt nice against his. "You're not a technician, but you know what a memory flush is, don't you?" she asked. "We have a system similar to that."

"Gummi maintenance," Rogers said placidly. The question was an easy one, and the words came readily. "Final measures, strictly salvage. The brainware degrades over time, there's memory and data loss, especially after datastorms. After enough burps, the techs purge the system, then—"

He stopped speaking abruptly and reared back in his chair as realization struck. "You're not going to do *that* to me!" he said, panicked. "The transfer protocols are all wrong! You *can't*—"

"Of course we can't," Scheer said. "We *won't*. But the principle is the same. You've spent more time with Ramirez than anyone else we know, before and after he made the find. He *must* have said something, given up some clue, even if you don't consciously remember what. But those memories are still there, Rogers. We can get at them, if you'll let us."

Caspian's heart was beating like a trip-hammer, and he licked his lips nervously. "A brainware flush," he repeated. "No, you can't—"

She touched his hand again. "No," she said firmly. "Not a brainware flush. Call it deep interrogation, if that makes you feel better. We have experts, with drugs and monitor systems. You don't have anything to worry about, especially if you cooperate."

"That's almost the same thing," he said. "A brainware flush." He had seen the reports from flushes that had failed, and the damage estimates for Gummi-Brains that had undergone them. Systems were never quite the same afterward, and even a successful flush could be ruinous. He shuddered at the idea of something like that being done to him.

"It's deep interrogation," Wendy repeated, soothingly. She took his hand again and squeezed his fingers. "We can find what you can't. If nothing else, a total download will help us improve the psychological profile we've developed. And when it's done, you can go back to Earth. I promise."

"I—I don't know," Rogers said. "I can't—"

Sympathy drained from Scheer's voice, just as glamour had drained from her appearance. "You can, and you will," she said, in matter-of-fact tones. She gazed at him with stern eyes. "EnTek doesn't want you anymore. We've already announced that you're joining Halo, so Duckworth won't have a place for you anymore, either. You need this."

Rogers wanted to say something, but voice didn't seem to work anymore.

The door to the small conference room opened, and Ralph Tanaka ambled in. Tall and graceful, he looked tired, but otherwise no different than he had the day before. He smiled pleasantly at the two of them, displaying strong, regular teeth that were as white as gypsum deposits. "Hello, Rogers," he said. "Wendy tells me that you're joining our team. I'm glad to hear that. I've got some people waiting who are very eager to talk with you."

Scheer did something then that Rogers had never seen her do before. She looked annoyed and spoke with obvious irritation. "Ralph," she said. The single syllable sounded ominous.

Tanaka nodded at her.

"Ralph, Rogers and I aren't quite done," Scheer continued. Her frost-colored eyes continued to gaze at Rogers's troubled ones, but she was not speaking to him anymore. "If you can wait—"

"No, really," Rogers said, eager to please. "I don't mind. I'll do whatever it is you want. Just give me the agreement, and I'll certify it."

"Rogers and I aren't quite done," Scheer said again. Now, she looked at Tanaka with an expression that was almost but not quite a glare. "And interruptions like this aren't—"

"Please," Rogers said. "Don't be angry, I'll—"

Tanaka's easy smile had faded, white teeth hidden. He looked nervous now. "I'm sorry, Wendy," he said softly. "But we're monitoring. I could tell you were nearly finished, and there's a situation that requires your attention."

Scheer relaxed a bit, and Rogers relaxed, too. Even Tanaka, when he spoke again, spoke more easily.

"Erik Morrison's trying to reach you," he said. "I thought you'd want to know."

Once again, Scheer looked surprised.

DANCING on the Moon was better than Erik would ever have imagined it, and dancing with Wendy Scheer was better than that. The lesser gravity made each step cost a fraction of the effort it would have on Earth, without in any way reducing the essential, elemental pleasure of the act. The weeks of gene therapy and the soreness from exercise seemed small prices, cheerfully paid. Even the long hours he had spent training his body to work properly in the new environment were nearly forgotten now, their memory swept away by the simple pleasure of two bodies moving as one, in three-quarters time.

"Old-fashioned, I know," Wendy Scheer said. Her words were soft, but cut easily through orchestral music, elegant and understated, that seemed to come equally from every angle of the ballroom. "But practical."

"I can imagine," Erik said. The fingers of Wendy's right hand were intertwined with those of his left, and they seemed utterly at home there. Her other hand rested, lighter than anything should be, even under lunar gravity, on his shoulder. She felt warm and alive against him.

Erik led. Step, step, step, slide and step. It had been years since he had danced formally with a woman, but the body remembered. Step, step, step, slide and step. They moved together as smoothly as an ocean's waves. Long steps moved them in a simple waltz, down the long line of dance formed by the other couples who crowded the dance hall floor. Their shoulders remained almost perfectly parallel, with each other and the floor, and Erik forced himself to keep at least one eye focused on the other dancers at all times.

They returned the favor. Every man and every woman could spare at least a moment of each movement to glance in their direction. Men and women alike wore expressions that were envious or approving or both. Easily a dozen times, total strangers had tapped with unwarranted familiarity on his or her shoulder, and those same strangers— most of them men—had asked to cut in. Every time, Wendy had shaken her head, laughed politely, and declined, even before Erik had the chance.

"You're very good," Wendy said. She smiled. White teeth shone from behind red lips, and the world became an even brighter, lighter place. "Light on your feet."

"It's been years," Erik said. He dipped slightly on the

back-step, and she dipped, too, following his lead as effortlessly and precisely as water on rock.

Above them hung the sky of summertime Vienna, pellucid, cloud-flecked blue. Beneath their feet the ballroom floor belied its hard and unyielding nature by appearing precisely like meadow grass. The miraged ballroom was bounded on all sides by trompe l'oeil forest, impossibly lush and idealized. Occasional breaks in the woods seemed to reveal more landscape beyond. Erik knew that they actually hid entranceways, dining areas, audio units, and the like. Some chemical process made the air smell fresh and clean, and a simulated sun riding hidden tracks cast just enough ultraviolet from overhead to make the illusion complete. It was as if they danced in a clearing in a European forest.

"I thought you might miss having a landscape," Wendy said. She had suggested the restaurant when he had called the day before to invite her to dinner. "I did, for a long time, and I'm here because I *want* to be." She paused. "It's not quite the same, of course."

"Very thoughtful," Erik said, meaning it. He thought back to his earliest nights in Villanueva, and the wallpaper images of Alaskan hills and salmon-eating bears. "I did something similar in my quarters."

"No ceiling or floor displays, I'd guess, though," Wendy said. "Not unless they're paying you even better than my sources say."

Again, she smiled.

Erik didn't respond to the implied question. Instead, he said, "Maybe I can access the feeds at home."

"I don't think so," Wendy said.

"They have to be out on the Mesh somewhere," he said.

They had reached the end of the dance line now. The imaged trees of a forest that existed neither here nor anywhere else loomed close. Between them, beyond them, cool shadows seemed to offer the promise of privacy and peace, but Erik knew that the promise was a lie. He paused briefly as he brought his right foot back and to the left, and raised one hand, bringing Wendy's with it. Her other hand came free of him, and she twirled beneath his upraised arm. Then they were moving again, but along a different path. The forest-cloaked wall receded, and its promise receded with it.

"This is all proprietary," Wendy continued. "Zonix sent a stereo crew to Switzerland and Austria for six weeks to get the base footage and spent another six months integrating and refining it. It's not for home use, even with your compensation package."

She was an excellent dancer, much better than he. She moved like an athlete, buoyant and graceful. When he concentrated, he could feel her pulse beneath his fingers, and it was as steady and as regular and as slow as her breath. Dancing with her and in this gravity cost him little effort, but he could tell that it cost her none at all.

"That makes sense," Erik said. "It seems popular enough." Twenty or more couples shared the dance floor with them, and he had been paying enough attention to them that they all seemed faintly familiar now. Beyond that, however, they were strangers. "Tourist crowd?" he asked.

"No," Wendy responded. She had changed her hair since she had last seen him, and it was a black nimbus that seemed to swallow the ersatz sunlight. Her strong features, striking and distinctive, were softened by the darkness that framed them, and her eyes—electric blue now—were bright and aware. He could feel her gaze like a physical force.

At Halo, when she wore tunic and slacks, he had thought her attractive, but not beautiful. Here, now, and even on his guard, he wondered how he could have been so wrong.

"Visitors want to be on the Moon, and they want to know they're here," Wendy said. She was almost as tall as he and could face him squarely as she spoke. "There's low-G free-form and line dancing for tourists. Even with smartshoes, the low gravity makes a difference when you move fast. It's very hard to do anything fast here."

"And waltzing isn't fast," Erik said. Conversation seemed to flow naturally with her, and the right thing to say came easily to his lips.

Wendy nodded. "The waltz is a low-gravity dance," she said.

More notes played as they proved her words true and drifted along through the sea of waltzing couples. The steady, graceful procession had a certain life of its own. The hypnotic rhythm made Erik feel more at home in his body than he could remember since coming to the Moon.

Wendy smiled. "You look happy," she said. "You like this, don't you? I thought you would."

"How do you do it?" he asked, as they reached the end of the line, twirled, and turned again. Wendy hesitated slightly in mid-step, and Erik felt a twinge of regret for interrupting, however briefly, the flow of easy, fluid movement.

"Do what?" she asked.

A stranger's voice sounded in his ear: "May I interrupt?"

Erik ignored the request, not even sparing a shake of his head. Instead, to Wendy, he said, "Make people like you," then paused. Asking the question took conscious effort. "How is it that you make people like you?"

Wendy's first reply was to allow several expressions to ripple across her face in rapid succession—disquiet, concern, resignation, even mild anger. Like images during a Mesh-surfing session, they formed then faded.

"I'm not sure what you mean," she said. She smiled at him, positively beaming. It was as if she had donned a mask.

"I think you do," Erik said. That took effort, too, as a sudden wave of affection and goodwill swept over him. "You may not know the answer, but I think you understand the question." He tried hard to focus beyond her smile and electric eyes and force himself back into some kind of objectivity. "You're too smart and too self-aware not to."

Wendy's shoulders broke rhythm with the rest of the dance. They rose and dropped together in an elegant shrug. "You asked me out to find out why men like me?" she asked. She laughed, a sound like silver bells. "You've had three wives, Erik, and you left someone behind when you came here. You know women. You can do better than that."

He laughed. "You can, too," he said.

She looked up at him, quizzically. For the first time since their lunch together, he had no doubt that her expression was completely sincere.

"That's basic business negotiation," he said. "Change the question rather than answer it. Change the question and try to avoid answering the new one, too. I didn't ask why men like you, Wendy. I asked how you make people like you. People, not just men—and how *you* do it, not why *they* do."

Wendy's sparkling eyes became cool and remote. She wasn't smiling anymore. "I don't know what you mean," she repeated, more emphatically this time.

The remoteness on her face and the irritation in her eyes were both enough to make Erik want to change the topic. But he didn't. "I did some research," he said, pressing on. "I thought at first it might be pheromones, but that didn't make any sense. Too physical. There's no way it would work over the Mesh."

Wendy didn't say anything.

"Then, I considered subliminal cues, like we use in advertisements and behavior mods," Erik said. He said the words clearly and carefully, but softly enough that they would be swallowed up by the ambient noise of music, dancers, and dancing. "But that didn't make sense, either."

One orchestral movement faded, and another welled up to replace it. This one he recognized, at least vaguely. It was Strauss. The dance hall had a better music selection than he would have expected.

He continued, "Those don't work as well as most people think. They wouldn't work anywhere except in processed images, like on the Mesh or wallpaper." He was suddenly once again conscious of the sheer number of dancers who found reasons to gaze in Wendy's direction. "Not in person. Not like it does here."

Wendy didn't say anything.

"And they're expensive," Erik continued. It was easier to continue the conversation if he thought of it as a simple analytical problem. "Halo probably can't afford them, and I think you really do work for Halo. Now, if you worked for Zonix—"

"I *don't*," Wendy said. She almost spat the words, with

irritation that was sincere and obvious enough that Erik almost flinched. "I don't. I wouldn't."

He nodded, studying her, trying again to look past whatever charm or charisma it was that she possessed. It wasn't easy. Wendy looked composed and pleasant, but the set of her features was too rigid to be taken at face value. She was trying to be polite, but not trying to be subtle about it.

"I told you before, I believe in the work I do," Wendy continued. The edge in her voice softened. "Is this why you wanted to see me? Really? The only reason?"

Her entire body language had changed now, so that she seemed tenser and more wary. A moment before, her movements had been effortlessly light and casual; now, grace remained, but was more deliberate. Still nested in his left hand, the fingers of her right hand had tensed and curled. The muscles at her trim waist had clenched, too, and the long steps she took as she danced became more emphatic. She moved like a cat instead of a cloud.

"I don't doubt that," Erik said. He spoke in agreeable tones, and the words, technically true, came more easily than the ones that followed. "I just wonder what that work is. Recruitment? You'd be very good at that, I think."

The words were almost as easy to say as to regret. Wendy Scheer glared at him, and the flashing intelligence that lit her eyes gave way to something more elemental. "I didn't come here for this," she said, with the beginnings of anger. "I don't have to answer your questions." She released him and stepped back.

"No, no, of course not," Erik said, his concentration broken by the widening gap in her composure. Suddenly, all he wanted to do was soothe her and make amends. He reached to take her in his arms again. "Really, I'm sorry, I—"

As if on cue, fingers tapped on his shoulder. "Excuse me," a familiar voice said. "May I?"

Startled, Erik turned to find Enola Hasbro looking up at him, her arms raised to take his. "Hello, Erik." she said cheerfully. "I thought that was you! May I have this dance?"

He looked at her, dumbfounded, his train of thought utterly derailed. The woman raised her arms to him and offered embrace. Moving more on instinct and reflex than anything else, he took them. A split-second later, she had pulled herself close, resting her head against his chest as the music swelled again.

"I'm not the only one who's popular," Wendy said. She smirked as Erik tried to disentangle himself, but Enola Hasbro was proving herself remarkably tenacious. Inexorably, the tide of the dance began to sweep him away from her.

"Wendy!" he said, distressed now. "Wait, I—"

She shook her head. "Go ahead," she said. "I need to catch my breath."

"But—"

"I'm not going anywhere," she said. "Have fun, and I'll meet you in the grottoes." And then she was gone, swallowed up by the surrounding crowd.

Erik cursed softly, but the words trailed off as his mind cleared. His view of the other dancers took on a new clarity and focus, and the perfect forest illusion was suddenly not quite so perfect. Even when she was irritated, the presence of Wendy Scheer had brought with it a certain happy haze. Now, with that gone, the real world was reasserting itself.

"Who's your friend?" Enola asked. "She's cute."

Erik wasn't sure how to answer. "What are the grot-toes?" he asked, instead.

Hasbro nodded to his left. "They're private dining rooms," she said. "Very nice. Through the trees." She jerked her head to one side, pointing at one imaged grove. "Through there." Two steps later, she returned to her own question. "Who is she?" she asked. "Your friend. I'm sure I've met her before."

"I doubt it," Erik said.

"Maybe at Duckworth?" Enola asked.

"No," Erik replied awkwardly. It would have been rude not to respond at all, but he felt uneasy speaking to a near-stranger about someone who was supposed to be his companion for the evening. "She's from Halo."

"Oh," Enola said. She looked slightly surprised, and her eyebrows formed perfect arches. "Maybe that's where I've seen her. In the feeds." She stood on her toes and peered over his shoulder, obviously angling for another glimpse of Wendy. "We saw you with her. She was a very good dancer. I think I could like her."

Hasbro danced well, too, if not as well as Wendy Scheer, and she was very light in Erik's arms. He could not help but be aware of that. He could feel her strain slightly to keep up with him. He felt it but did not care; his mind was still occupied, replaying his conversation with Wendy and trying to remember and second-guess his own reactions.

They all seemed slightly off.

"How about you, Erik?" Enola continued. "I thought you were too busy for a social life. You never return my calls."

"I *am* busy," Erik said. "But I'm sorry if I've been rude."

Hasbro smiled. Her right hand, small and delicate, flowed upward along his arm, shoulder and neck. Her petite fingers toyed with his hair and she giggled. "No," she said. "Not rude."

"We," Erik said, as his mental review of the evening neared its end.

"We?" Hasbro asked.

"You said, 'we saw you,'" Erik continued. "You're here with someone?"

"Just a friend," Hasbro said softly. "I have a lot of friends."

Erik grunted.

"Lucky, too," Hasbro continued. I'm so short, even the dance floor is like a forest. I didn't see you here, but Keith did."

Erik froze, so abruptly that Hasbro almost stumbled and fell against him, hard. Around them, other dancers made sounds and expressions of dismay at the sudden disruption to the orderly dance floor.

"Keith?" he said. "Keith Ramirez?"

Hasbro smiled happily. "You *have* met him!" she said. "He said you didn't know each other!"

"Keith Ramirez is here," Erik demanded. Unmindful now of anything or anyone else, he gripped Hasbro's hand tightly in his and demanded. "Now! Show me where!"

She looked up at him again, less happily now. Her hand strained in his, as she tried to pull away, but he would not let her. "Hey!" Enola Hasbro said. "Let go! That hurts!"

"Where is he?" Erik repeated, but he loosened his grip.

With her free hand, Enola pointed. "Over near the oak grove," she said. Over . . ." Her words trailed off into silence, however brief.

"That's odd," she said. "He's gone."

CHAPTER 16

UNACCOMPANIED now, Wendy Scheer moved along the crowded dance floor in a swift and effortless amble that took her through the remaining dancers without pause or impediment. Slim and graceful, she slipped between the paired dancers as if the dance floor were empty but for her. One after another, men and women glanced in her direction, blinked, and readied themselves to speak. But she moved past them all, before any could actually address her. Negotiating a crowd without permitting herself to become part of it was a skill she had honed through long practice. It was the story of her life. The secret was to avoid eye contact completely without being obvious, never allowing anyone to actually engage with her, while never offering an overt snub or challenge. Another tactic was to keep moving, and moving quickly, without calling any extra attention to herself by stumbling or colliding. That was easy enough.

In a very real sense, she was still dancing, even without a partner. Moving in careful, precise time with the music, she matched the crowd's motion and her own with intuitive grace. Her reflexes and timing, always excellent, had long since been rewritten by her years on the Moon, and she was completely at ease as she threaded her way through the throng. Move too fast, and the others would not have time to get out of her way. Move too slowly, and she would be forced to be rude by ignoring an overture or a nod. The Strauss faded, and something more recent and upbeat took its place, so Wendy adjusted her stride, barely conscious of the music anymore, but still moving in time to it. This dance was unique to her, but one she had practiced every day of her adult life.

Only moments had passed since the Hasbro creature had taken Erik's hand, but Wendy knew that the other woman moved *fast*, too, in a different sense of the term. Even without looking back to check, Wendy felt certain that Enola had already pulled herself close to Erik. Probably, her head was against his chest already. Stepping between two trompe l'oeil trees and into the discreet passageway beyond, Wendy shook her head in mild disgust. She had encountered Hasbro more than once in the Duckworth spaces and had not enjoyed the experience.

Her own gifts were too subtle to allow her to appreciate Hasbro's more blatant ones. Now, however, the other woman's advent had come as a convenient and welcome interruption. Morrison's questions had been entirely too specific for Wendy's tastes.

The corridor's walls continued the forest motif, with the floor covering at Wendy's feet imaged like a worn footpath winding between the trees. The passageway maze serving the dance hall led to more than the promised grottoes; it led more deeply into illusion, as well. Synthetic dusk gathered, then gave way to synthetic night. Soon, simulated stars and an impossible harvest moon lit her progress, and the air was thick with the scent of wood and leaves and forest rot. Night animals seemed to make rustling noises in the shadows, and snatches of murmured conversation—Real? Recorded?—between other patrons found her ears. The reduced lighting and enhanced sensory cues made the forest illusion more convincing. Even Wendy's practiced eyes were almost unable to distinguish which trees were physical installations and which were wallpaper illusions. She knew that some of the tantalizing shadows were real, but only some.

Wendy liked that.

The rest rooms were among the very few areas in this establishment where personal phones would work. Wendy took advantage of that, after she had cleansed her hands and adjusted her makeup. While sub-sink pumps whisked gurgling waters away, she settled into a convenient couch in the lounge area and checked her messages. Listening to her office manager's gentle, summary drone, took some effort, however. Her mind was elsewhere.

Very few in her experience, in her entire life, had ever asked Wendy the kind of questions Erik Morrison had asked. The few who had, had been known quantities— family members or longtime friends, or lovers, or ex-lovers. In every case, she had know the supplicant well enough to steer the conversation in other directions, or to make a judicious answer and know that it would go no further.

That wasn't the case with Morrison.

Despite her research, EnTek's site manager was largely an unknown quantity. She had stumbled badly in their last interview, but she had never imagined that the misstep would lead to the conversation Morrison obviously wanted to have. Rare feelings swept though her, indecision and worry and doubt, all of them alien to her basic nature.

She didn't know what she was going to do, but she knew she was going to have to do it soon.

"RAMIREZ, gone!?" Erik demanded again. Then, with conscious effort, he forced the fingers of his hand to straighten and release hers. He spoke more gently and hoped that she believed him. "I'm sure he's still here, Enola. I can't imagine anyone abandoning a companion as charming as you."

She smiled up at him. "Neither can I," she said, and it was obvious she meant it. "But I don't see him anywhere."

"Maybe he's in the rest room," Erik said. Another possibility came to mind, something that Wendy had mentioned. "Or the grottoes?"

Hasbro rolled her eyes and arched her eyebrows in a quintessential, even archetypal expression of feminine disdain. "Where do you think we just *came* from?" she asked. She pointed, first in one direction, then in another. "*That's* the way to the grottoes, between the oaks. The exits are over *there*," she said, and pointed again. "He wouldn't have gone back to the grottoes without me, and he *couldn't* have without going past us. He didn't. I would have noticed."

"You were occupied," Erik said, politely but pointedly. "You were with me." No longer dancing, they had faced each other in the near-center of the ballroom meadow.

They were blocking traffic, and other dancers were telling them so, with poisoned glances and muttered comments. He ignored them and focused on Enola.

"I would have noticed," Hasbro said, shaking her head. She really was quite lovely, and Erik found himself automatically noting her attributes and filing them away for future reference. She had delicate features and clear, expressive eyes, and skin the color of aged ivory that Erik had seen in museums. She seemed to have done little, if anything, to blunt or emphasize her ethnicity, so that her looks had a certain integrity that he found appealing.

She smiled again as she noticed him studying her. "I keep track of my dates," she said. "I always do. He's gone." Despite her pleasant demeanor, confusion and annoyance colored her words. Obviously, Hasbro was unaccustomed to being abandoned by her companions.

Feeling self-conscious and slightly foolish, Erik raised himself on his toes and craned his head to study the crowd around them. The scent of perspiration was in the air, and the last of Wendy's spell—whatever it was—had faded, so that all he saw now was a milling throng of humanity, precisely the kind of crowd he typically did not enjoy. It was made up entirely of matched pairs, with no unescorted men or women that he could see.

"What were you doing here?" Erik asked Hasbro, settling back into a normal stance.

"What do you *think*?" the petite woman replied, with equal parts hauteur and irritation. Even though she was much shorter than he, she seemed to look down on him for asking the question. "We were dancing. He spotted you and said something, and then I said something, and then—"

"He knew me?" Erik asked.

"Knew who you were, at least," Enola said.

Someone bumped into Erik, nodded an apology, then drifted away. Someone else tapped on Enola's shoulder and said something to her that Erik could not hear. Obviously, the crowd's patience had worn thin. Their unmoving presence in the center of the dance floor was no longer welcome.

"We're being rude," Enola said. She placed her right hand in Erik's left again, and then slid her right along the line of his upper arm and shoulder. "Who needs Keith, anyway?" she asked.

Rude.

Erik shook his head and disengaged himself from her. "No," he said brusquely. "We're not being rude. I am. I'm here with someone, too, Enola."

She made a moue of disgust, the kind of expression that made distaste look charming. "Your friend?" she asked. "She seemed nice, but she's disappeared, too. Maybe she and Keith—"

Erik almost laughed at that. A chance encounter between the elusive Keith Ramirez and Wendy Scheer would no doubt have put an end to his own evening with her, but not in the sense that Enola seemed to think. Instead of laughing, he said, "No. No, I don't think so. She said she'd wait for me in the grottoes."

THE particular dining "grotto" Wendy had selected and reserved was configured along the lines of a small country cabin, such as had been typical decades past. To Erik, however, who had visited more than a few of the modern equivalent, Zonix had erred on many of the details. Glass windows had been imaged along with clay-chinked interior walls, and the faux wood of the table had grain but not texture. The ceiling was acoustical tile, not what he would have expected, but not unheard of, either.

Wendy saw him looking at it. "Miss the sky?" she asked. They were the first words she had spoken since intercepting him in the forest corridor. "I can—"

Erik shook his head. "It's fine," he said. "I'm just surprised."

"It's officially Wednesday," Wendy said. "They configure the place for locals, and locals like to be reminded of Earth."

She had said much the same thing on the dance floor, Erik remembered. "Very rustic," he said. He glanced through the illusionary windows at the equally illusionary woods beyond, and then back at her. "I'd be surprised if most locals had ever set foot in a place like this."

"Maybe not," Wendy agreed. "I've already ordered for us."

The table held plates and several covered dishes. Erik uncovered them, one after another, and found nothing exceptional. Three kinds of cheese, various breads, and what looked like a miniature ham. One caddy held utensils and condiments, and other, bottles.

"Very rustic," he repeated, looking up from his examination.

She shrugged with studied nonchalance. "Most people don't book these rooms just for eating," she said. Then, more seriously, "Are we here only to eat?"

Erik pulled out one chair and gestured. After Wendy had seated herself, he settled into the one opposite her. Some trick of construction made the piece of furniture's pseudo-wood creak slightly as he leaned forward.

"No," he said. "I think we have to talk." His hands,

moving as if on their own, drifted to the serving dishes. The carving knives that had been provided were of professional quality, surgically sharp; they felt good in his hands as he sliced two kinds of cheese and cubed the third. He did not speak as he arrayed the food on his plate and Wendy's, and the only noise in the small room was the clink of steel blade on dishware.

"Music?" Wendy asked, breaking the near-silence.

"If you'd like," Erik said.

One of window images seemed to open. Strains of something vaguely orchestral extended themselves tentatively into the room, muffled and overlaid by forest noises. The music sounded like the work of a pavilion band in the distance, somewhere beyond the trees that were not really there.

"Very nice," Erik said.

"Sondheim," Wendy said. *"Into the Woods."*

He was working on the ham now and was surprised to find that it was real. His surprise must have shown, because Wendy's smile lit the room again.

"Imported," she said. "From Earth. From Virginia."

He nodded appreciatively and sliced the meat quickly, glad for the physical work of the task. When half the miniature ham lay in paper-thin shavings, he added reasonable servings to both their plates. He put hers before her, glanced at Wendy, and gestured at the breads and condiments.

"You enjoy being the host, don't you?" Wendy asked.

Erik looked at her quizzically.

"I placed the reservations, I ordered the food," Wendy said. "You're serving. You like to play the host."

This time, Erik smiled, vaguely flattered that she had noticed, but all too aware that he had to work against the feeling. "I like preparing food," he said. She wasn't doing anything with the condiments, so he took them and ladled small portions of each onto his plate. Corn relish, Japanese mustard, chopped olives in vinegar, red catsup, fig paste. He arranged the dabs of flavor like an old-fashioned painter's palette.

Wendy's approach was simpler. She had pulled a rye biscuit from the bread tray and broken it, and was layering it with cheeses. She set it on a warming plate and thumbed it to "on."

As she waited for the cheese to soften and the bread to warm, she placed a shaving of ham on French bread and ate it in neat, precise bites.

Erik liked watching her eat.

"Besides," he continued. "The evening was my idea."

"And the restaurant was mine," Wendy said agreeably.

"Not quite what I expected," Erik said. He had anticipated something more public. It was strange to realize that only a few days before, with Kowalski and Caspian, he had been concerned with privacy and seclusion in a crowded restaurant. Now, he would have liked very much to have the distracting presence of others.

"How was Enola?" Wendy asked.

"You know her?" Erik asked, surprised.

"I know who she is," Wendy said. She bit into the sandwich she had casually made, then chewed and swallowed. "I think she likes you."

"I think she does, too," Erik said. He remembered how the other woman had felt against him, and how her body had moved with easy, even unwarranted familiarity against is. He remembered the scent of her hair. His body remembered the sensations more clearly than his mind did.

"I think she likes everyone," Wendy said.

"Everyone *does* like you," Erik said and gazed levelly at her. All thought of Enola Hasbro's touch faded, like mist in the morning sun as he considered Wendy Scheer. "We were talking about that, earlier."

Wendy didn't say anything. Instead, her nimble fingers found a soft corn tortilla among the bread selection and layered it with ham, cheese, and chili spread. She rolled and pinned it, then placed it on her warming plate and began preparing another.

Erik could wait, too. The wine caddy held three bottles; he read their labels quickly, selected the one that looked the least objectionable, and opened it. He filled one flute with the red liquid and then held the bottle above a second, poised to pour.

Wendy shook her head. "Just water," she said.

Erik nodded. He filled two glasses with what purported to be springwater and set one before her. He took a single sip of his own wine and then set it aside.

"How do you know Enola?" he asked.

"From visits to Duckworth," Wendy said. She looked slightly startled by the question, but the expression of surprise faded almost immediately. "Nothing social."

"She didn't seem to know who you were," Erik said. Enola Hasbro's words came back to him. "She thinks you're cute." Wendy blushed, surprising and confusing him. She almost always seemed utterly self-possessed, but now, he had surprised her twice, in quick succession.

He didn't like that. He didn't like the vaguely embarrassed expression his words had evoked. For a split-second, he felt the words of an apology take form on his lips, but for only a split-second. Instead, he said, "You're very good at steering the conversation. Very subtle." He was honest as he spoke.

The expression on Wendy's face gave way to a look of polite attention. "Thank you," she said.

Reflexively, Erik reached for his glass of wine. Then he caught himself, and reached for his water and sipped it, instead. Alcohol was a bad accompaniment to conversations with Janos Horvath, and he suspected that the same would hold true of chats with Wendy Scheer. He retraced their earlier conversation in his mind and resumed it.

"I found some data on parapsychology," Erik said. He spoke between bites of cheese and meat, dabbed with various condiments. "Pheromones and subliminal cues don't seem to fit the circumstances, but that might."

"I'm not sure I know what you're talking about," Wendy said. She toyed with a crumb of biscuit.

"Psionics is the scientific word for it, I think," Erik said.

"I know what the words mean, Erik," Wendy said, speaking a bit more forcefully than was typical for her. "Mind reading. Fortune-telling. Mind over matter. If you think I can do any of that—if you think anyone can— you're not the practical man I thought you were."

"Maybe I'm not," Erik said. This time, he permitted himself a sip of wine, but only enough to cleanse his palate.

"Psionics doesn't mean anything," Wendy said. "It's just a catch-all explanation for events researchers can't explain. Even if they aren't really events worth explaining." She smiled yet again, and the light in her eyes became brighter. "People like *me*. Do *I* need an explanation?"

"Maybe not," Erik said doggedly. "But there's more to it than that, and you definitely have an effect on people."

"On you," she said.

"On me," Erik agreed. "And on others. And I'm beginning to wonder if it's limited to people."

Wendy looked at him blankly.

"EnTek processors derive from human tissue," Erik said. "It's not something we publicize, but it's true. The technicians have made a lot of patches, but, at its basic core, the stuff is human tissue."

"I didn't know," Wendy said. "I never even thought about it."

"A lot of people don't have any idea how things work, even things they use every day," Erik continued. He had eaten enough and pushed his plate away. "My assistant tried very hard to get me to try smartshoes, and she doesn't know how they work."

"Controlled magnetics, in the shoe and in the flooring," Wendy said easily. "A processor reads the movements of your foot muscles and—"

"Stop trying to change the subject," Erik said emphatically. The conversation was in danger of slipping out of his control, and it was getting harder to concentrate on the topics of his choosing. "That's not the point. She doesn't know how they work, but she wanted me to wear them."

Once again, Wendy gazed at him without responding. The hints of confusion and worry weren't just on her face now, but were also in her eyes.

"I don't *like* using things when I don't have any idea how they work," Erik said. "I spent years reviewing technical specs on brainware. I'm no expert, but I know their basic functionalities. More than most executives do."

"You're a practical man," Wendy said again. She was gazing steadily in his direction now, but instead of looking at him, she seemed to be looking into him. There was something unnerving about her gaze, cool and analytical and enticing, all at the same time. "But I don't see why you need to tell me about that."

"EnTek provides the processor systems for Villanueva. We use the latest generation systems here," Erik said calmly. "And lately, we've been having some unexplained burps. Or unexplainable ones."

"Now you're changing the subject," Wendy said, and then did the same. "Do you mind if I have some of that wine, after all?" She lifted her glass.

"Of course not," Erik said. He plucked the glass from her fingers and poured. The wine made little splashing noises and scented the air with its bouquet, the memory of sunlight and grapes. She nodded in approval when the glass reached the half-full point, and he passed it to her.

"Thank you," Wendy said. She raised her flute in a mimed toast, and before Erik could stop himself, he had done the same. Both sipped wine, and both set their glasses down in perfect synchronization.

Wendy smiled.

Erik almost cursed. She had broken the rhythm of conversation yet again. Even forearmed with the knowledge of the effect she had on him, he was having a difficult time.

"You're very good," he said.

"You were talking about brainware," Wendy said. "If that's really what you want to talk about."

"I was involved in the earliest days of modern gummi development," Erik continued. He was very conscious that he was using too many words, but at least he was back to talking about the subject of his choice. "Just in sales and oversight, and very early in my career, but I was there." She was very nervous.

Wendy drank some more wine, and Erik was pleased to realize that he didn't do the same. "We use EnTek systems, too," she said. "Almost everyone does. Or clones." She snickered softly. "Not literally, of course. And not the most recent ones, either. Budget cuts."

"In the early days, there were reports of technicians who couldn't work with the new-line gummis," Erik said implacably. "There were crashes and burps and general performance problems with selected test-users. Genetic refinement resolved the problems, but at the time, the joke was, you couldn't work with the systems if they didn't like you." He emphasized the next-to-last word.

"More psionics?" Wendy asked, rolling her eyes slightly. "Look, when you called, you said you wanted to talk about matters of common interest. This isn't."

"I think it is," Erik said. Wendy's evident frustration made him feel as if he were swimming upstream. "I've been doing some more research recently, and yesterday, a thought occurred to me. What would happen if the gummis liked you too much? You confuse me sometimes. Would you confuse them? Would system efficiency increase, or would their throughput degrade?"

"I don't know," Wendy said. "And what you're talking about is too hypothetical to justify a guess."

"I don't think so," Erik said. He shook his head. "Including tonight, I've spent time with you twice, Wendy." He paused. "And both times, I've been so eager to please you that I've had a hard time thinking straight. I don't think its sexual. I think it's something more. Even now, even when I'm aware of the effect, it's hard to work against."

"That's not much of a survey set," Wendy said. Her elegantly painted fingertips were drumming in syncopated rhythm on the tabletop now.

"No, it's not," Erik agreed. "But I know how I can get a larger one."

She looked at him blankly.

"Even the ALC companies don't keep much track of movement within Villanueva, except for our own staffs. But we monitor movements in and out pretty closely." He made himself smile. "What would happen if we mapped your comings and goings against brainware burps in the core gummis?"

Wendy stood. She went to the illusory open window as if to look out of it. Her perfect lower lip folded beneath her flawless teeth, and false moonlight streaming in through the false window did interesting things to her profile. As if in response to her presence, the music changed to something that Erik didn't recognize but welcomed. It gave him something to concentrate on other than Wendy's evident distress.

"I don't know," Wendy said tightly. "Should I care?"

He continued. "If we find a pattern match, I think it would make your position at Halo untenable. You need to be able to work with us, and I don't imagine the ALC would allow you on the premises again." A thought struck him. "And if you had other, more private activities, those would probably have to come to an end, too. And we could probably use pattern matches to backtrack such activities."

She took a deep breath, but didn't say anything.

"And it seems to me that, however you do it, you don't want people to know you do it," Erik said. "If I run the comparisons, it will be a hard secret to keep."

Finally, the poised and confident woman he had known turned to him and said, with glum resignation, "Just between us?"

"Just between us," Erik said.

Her eyes narrowed. "People come here for privacy, Erik. Recorders won't work."

"That's right, they won't," Erik said. He reached into a tunic pocket and drew out a small privacy unit, like the one that Heck Kowalski had brought to their lunch with Rogers Caspian. "I told you—this is just between us."

"I don't know how I do it. *Psionics* is probably as good a term as any." She looked at him steadily. "Most people don't notice it. At least, not that way."

Erik allowed himself some more wine, taking a real sip this time. It wasn't bad. He felt tension ooze out of his body. He had won. "How much control do you have?" he asked.

"Not much," she said. "It's intuitive. Some days, I'm not even sure it's there."

"When did it start?" he asked, honestly curious.

"When I was a teenager," Wendy responded. "I think. It's hard to tell. I was a popular child. People liked pleasing me."

Erik nodded.

Wendy smiled, and her eyes flashed. A new kind of grace entered her body as she turned to face him squarely. Before, she had moved like a cloud or a cat; now, her body language reminded Erik of a snake poised to strike. "So tell me," she said, abruptly, "Why *are* you on the Moon?"

The full force of her personality struck Erik as she spoke. A moment before, he wouldn't have known the answer to her question, but now, startled by her sudden query and swept by a sudden desire to please her, he did. He felt the proper answer present itself, fully formed. It was as if his subconscious had been working on some vast and elaborate puzzle, and as if the last piece had clicked into place.

"Janos Horvath wants me to kill someone," he said with automatic, reflexive candor. "Keith Ramirez, I think."

Wendy smiled, and Erik looked at her, aghast both at the implications of his own words and the fact that he had voiced them.

"You said you didn't know him," she said. "You said that you had no idea what I was talking about, when I asked about him."

"I didn't, then," Erik said. "Things have changed. He seems to know me, though."

She looked at him quizzically, and he quickly summarized his near-encounter with Ramirez on the dance floor.

"If you don't know anything about the situation, then why have lunch with Rogers Caspian?" Wendy continued, as unrelenting as an excavator craft. "What did you talk with *him* about?"

"Why do you think I had—" A brief chill ran over Erik, and he hastily changed the question. "How did you know I had lunch with Rogers Caspian?"

Wendy smiled. "I have my connections," she said. "I have to."

"You seem to know a remarkable amount about my activities and operations," Erik said. "I don't think ALC joint management would be pleased if they were to discover a government operation running a surveillance network here."

"And I don't think the other four ALC companies would be happy to learn that EnTek had stationed an assassin in Villanueva," Wendy responded.

There was some truth to her words, Erik realized.

"Maybe we should work together," he said. "At least to some extent. I think I have something you want."

"What's that?" she asked.

Erik grinned, and watched carefully for her reaction as he said, "Keith Ramirez. If not him, someone who knows where he is."

CHAPTER 17

THURSDAY followed Wednesday on the Moon as surely as it did on Earth. The next local day, when Erik settled into place behind his desk, he was tired and pleasantly sore. The negotiatons with Wendy Scheer had gone late into the night, and he had deliberately taken a labor-intensive route home, to give himself time to think. Wendy had given him a lot to think about, and he had no doubt he had done the same for her.

"Good morning, Erik," Juanita Garcia said. She still didn't seem comfortable with his given name. "I've sorted your correspondence and updated your calendar. The new reports from Production are in, and I'm reviewing them."

"Good. It's going to be a busy day." Erik nodded and glanced at his computer screen. "Tell me, Juanita, who has access to my personal calendar? I'm not entirely clear on the local protocols."

"Just you, Erik," she said quickly. "And me."

"Not Kowalski?" he asked.

She shook her head. She was redheaded today, but the look wasn't very convincing. "He can run queries to the public sections, but not to the personal ones."

"And his calendar works the same way?"

She nodded again.

He looked at her coolly. "Then would you mind telling me how Wendy Scheer knew that I had lunch with Rogers Caspian?" he asked.

Juanita's skin color lightened a few shades. "I—I don't know," she said. "She must have her sources."

"She must. I had dinner with Scheer last night," he continued. "We compared data on some issues. I was surprised to find out how much internal EnTek data Halo had on hand." He smiled tightly. "I think there's a security breach here," he said. "Work with Kowalski to resolve it, will you?"

"Yes, Mr. Morrison," Garcia said softly.

"Good. I want it resolved, and I want to know it's been resolved," Erik said, but the tone of his voice carried another, more ominous message."

"It—it will be," Garcia said, and swallowed. All of her hard-won confidence had fallen away from her. She seemed as timid and as nervous as she had been on his first day on the job.

"And tell Kowalski I want to see him, as soon as possible," Erik said. "He's got some issues to resolve, too."

"LIKE old times, huh?" Doug Stewart said.

"Not so old," Erik replied. "It's been less than a week."

They were seated in the same Fargo's! that had been

the site of their previous meeting, in what was almost the same booth. Erik was drinking brandy with "spring" water, and Stewart had a sizeable tumbler of the blue liquor he preferred clenched tightly in one hand.

Erik sipped brandy, then water, then brandy again, draining the entire shot this time. The drink went down like liquid smoke, hit the walls of his stomach, and exuded pleasant warmth throughout his entire body. It was a sensation he had promised himself for long hours, deliberately refraining from dinner to ensure the purity and impact of the response.

"Do you want to eat?" Doug Stewart asked.

"No food," Erik said. He shook his head. "I just need to unwind. Since getting here, all I've done is eat with people I don't know or like." He glanced at Stewart. "No offense."

"No offense," Stewart agreed, but his eyes said differently. "But I was surprised when you called."

"My schedule had an opening. I had my security chief backtrack your last call," Erik said. "And our last dinner got interrupted. You were going to show me around, and I have questions that only a local can answer."

Stewart nodded. "There's plenty to see," he said easily. He spoke with the earnest good-fellowship of the confirmed drinker.

"All I want right now is drink and talk," Erik said. He was still concentrating on the brandy's welcome warmth and at the smoky taste in his mouth. This was his first drink of the day, and he knew that none that followed would taste as good.

"Well, I can help you with both," Stewart said, with what seemed this time to be total agreement. He gestured at the waitress, who complied by providing fresh drinks and then continued with her rounds. "The food here is nothing special—"

"The food here is awful," Erik said, interrupting. "Prepackaged sludge. I wouldn't miss it."

"Nothing special, but they stock a good bar," Stewart continued. He paused, as Erik's words registered. "Wouldn't miss it?" he asked. "You're leaving? I didn't think that was an option for you."

"I've found a way home, if I decide to take it," Erik said. "And if I don't, I won't be coming here again. That's what you want, too, isn't it?"

He eyed his welcome new brandy, but didn't drink it. Instead, he looked away from it and gazed at Stewart. The other man looked tired and worn. His eyes were rheumy, and a lacy network of burst blood vessels showed through his skin. "You really should see Biome about booze patches," he said. "Or at least buy some facial appliances, like the women use."

Stewart grunted and lowered the level of his own drink another fraction of an inch. He had ordered some bar food for himself, and now he scooped soy-curls into his mouth and ate. Swallowing, he said, "You mentioned that last time."

"And you mentioned Australia," Erik said.

"I remember hearing your name there," Stewart said. "No details, just things. You were some kind of troubleshooter."

"Not to start with," Erik said. Now, he let himself drink again. "But then I solved some problems, mostly by accident." He drank some more. "A fatal accident."

Stewart's drink paused in mid-journey to his lips and returned to the table. Erik could feel the other man's gaze, suspicious and apprehensive, train itself on him.

"Fatal?" Stewart said.

"It was a working vacation," Erik said. "A getaway. Construction of the Sydney Pylon had missed a few milestones. Your friends at Cybrotics were looking for a contract rider and budget increase, and they were using production problems to justify the request. We had to work together on that one—the EnTek processors had to comport with the Cybrotics ones. I was asked to get together with an opposite number, and work things out. I took him deep-sea fishing."

Erik finished the second brandy, as unwanted memories filled his mind. Salt spray and harsh sunlight, and the muted roar of inboard motors, and screams of panic. Even ten years later, what had happened then still wasn't an easy topic for conversation.

"We didn't all come back," he said.

"I—I didn't hear about that," Stewart said.

"It was an accident," Erik said. "I said so, and the courts agreed. But when I came back alone, and when the new Cybrotics systems lead cut his budget request by 30 percent, I found myself with a reputation in certain quarters as a very dangerous man." He glanced at Stewart. "Do I strike you as dangerous, Doug?" he asked.

Again, Stewart made no response.

"As an accident, it would have ended my career. As a *suspicious* accident, it made me a success." He hefted the empty shot glass and considered a third brandy, but decided against it. The man seated opposite him was no Janos Horvath or Wendy Scheer, but dealing with him warranted a certain degree of mental clarity. "I got to go on to new challenges. At least, until Alaska."

"Alaska?" Stewart asked. He had quit drinking, too, but he licked his lips nervously. Erik wondered how long it had been since the other man had been completely sober.

"That was another deal gone bad," Erik said. "We were cleaning up a virus spill in the Clinton Preserve. The bug we use to tailor gummis had gotten loose, and we were working with subcontractors to make good." Again, he looked steadily in Stewart's direction. "One of the on-site managers submitted a revised budget that the Home Office didn't like. I was asked to take the fellow on a hunting trip."

"Oh." Stewart blinked. His own gaze was clearer now, but still worried. "Why are you telling me this?"

"You asked," Erik said easily. "You asked how I ended up on the Moon."

"What happened on the hunting trip?" Stewart sounded like he didn't want to know.

"Nothing. We shot a few of those new-moose and came back. Both of us came back," Erik said, flinching at the painful memory. "The bid rates stayed the same. We lost the Alaska cleanup contract, and I got sent here. I thought that was because I pulled some strings, but now I think there was more to it than that."

"Why are you telling me this?" Stewart asked again.

"Because I want you to know I understand how a chance occurrence can change everything," Erik said. "Right, Keith?"

"I don't have any—" Stewart's words came to an abrupt halt as he finished processing Erik's. He sat bolt upright in the booth and then scrambled to leave it, only to find his path blocked by the newcomer who had settled into place beside him.

"Hello, Ramirez," Heck Kowalski said cheerfully. "Can I buy you a drink?"

"My name's—my name's not Keith," Stewart said, stammering now. His lips were pale, and his eyes darted from side to side. "I'm Doug Stewart. You know that."

"No," Erik said easily. He had the dart pistol in his right hand now, held so that only the barrel protruded, trained in the general direction of his dining companion. "I know that's the name you've been using lately, but you weren't using it when you recognized me in the ballroom last night. You vanished then, just like you vanished the last time we were here, until Wendy Scheer had left."

Stewart nodded. Moving with slow confidence, he raised his hands to his face and peeled the russet sideburns free. "These damn things itch," he said, in a matter-of-fact voice. "They're the only part of being Doug Stewart I mind. What now?"

"Now," Erik said. "We talk about what you found."

EPILOGUE

"HE cached most of it on the surface," Erik said. "In one of the bubble caves. He brought in just enough to prove that he'd found something. The plaque, because it was gold. I think he approached Scheer first, but I'm not sure yet. She gave him some money as a good-faith payment and promised to get him more."

"The files show nothing but terrestrial technology," Janos Horvath responded, via secure channel from Earth. "Antiquated hardware from a century ago. Nothing significant."

"That's what most people thought," Erik agreed. He was sprawled on the sofa in his private apartment, bone-weary after a very long day. The long fingers of his right hand were curved around a brandy snifter, warming the liquid within, potent and auburn, and as yet untouched. "But they were wrong. When enough people realized the real significance, things got pretty hectic for Keith. He got frightened."

"Frightened?" Horvath asked.

"He bolted and ran, and that made more people interested in him. He used the credit from Scheer to go underground for a while, but stayed close enough to the surface that he could follow developments," Erik said. "That's why he approached me at the spaceport. He was hoping to negotiate a deal before anyone else got to me."

"It's just outdated hardware, Erik," Horvath said.

Erik shook his head, knowing that Horvath could not see the gesture. "Read my report, Janos. The hardware Ramirez found left Earth in 1972 and left the solar system in 1983. It has no business being here." He paused. "Something sent it back."

"It could have been a natural phenomenon," Horvath said, but he sounded skeptical.

"If it is, it needs to be investigated." Again, he shook his head, feeling a curious sense of optimism, or even idealism. "No, Janos, one way or another, we're in the deep-space ship business. And it is something we'll have to do in partnership with Halo."

Unmindful now of Horvath's continued comments, he sipped brandy and gazed at the prize he had retrieved from Ramirez/Stewart. It was a gold plaque, with a bas-relief image of a man and a woman and a profiled piece of equipment. It was the same image that Rogers Caspian had so crudely re-created with graphite and paper.

The words on it said, "Pioneer 10."

Coming March 2005 from Ace

Angel-Seeker
by Sharon Shinn
0-441-01260-4
Award-winning author Sharon Shinn returns to Samaria
with this rich, romantic tale that begins where
Archangel left off.

Hex and the City
by Simon R. Green
0-441-01261-2
Lady Luck has hired John Taylor to investigate the origins on
the Nightside—a dark heart of London where it's always
3 a.m. But when he starts to uncover facts about his
long-vanished mother, the Nightside—and all of
existence—could be snuffed out.

Also new in paperback this month:

Rule of Evidence
by John G. Hemry
0-441-01262-0

Monument
by Ian Graham
0-441-01263-9

Available wherever books are sold or at
www.penguin.com